BY REBECCA JAMES

Sweet Damage

Beautiful Malice

SWEET DAMAGE

SWEET DAMAGE

A NOVEL

REBECCA JAMES

BANTAM BOOKS

NEW YORK

Published in the United States by Bantam Books, an imprint of Random House, a division of Random House LLC, a Penguin Random House Company, New York.

BANTAM BOOKS and the HOUSE colophon are registered trademarks of Random House LLC.

Originally published in paperback in Australia by Allen & Unwin in 2013.

LIBRARY OF CONGRESS CATALOGING-IN-PUBLICATION DATA
James, Rebecca
Sweet damage : a novel / Rebecca James.
pages cm
ISBN 978-0-553-80806-3 (hardback)
ISBN 978-0-345-53906-9 (eBook)
1. Cooks—Fiction. 2. Agoraphobia—Patients—Fiction.
3. Sydney (N.S.W.)—Fiction. I. Title.
PR9619.4.J386S94 2014
823'.92—dc23   2014010561

Printed in the United States of America on acid-free paper

www.bantamdell.com

2 4 6 8 9 7 5 3 1

FIRST U.S. EDITION

Book design by Dana Leigh Blanchette
Title-page and part-title images: © iStockphoto.com

FOR CHARLIE

SWEET DAMAGE

I still dream about Fairview.

In my dreams the house is more than it was in life: the building taller and more imposing, the hallways longer and more labyrinthine, the inside colder and darker than the real thing ever was. In my dreams Fairview is a maze of dark passages and shadows, steep staircases that twist and turn in nightmarish knots. I run through the house in a panic, never knowing whether I'm chasing or being chased, trying to escape or wanting to be found. All I know is that a scream echoes loudly through my head—a scream prompted by what I'm about to discover, what I know I'm going to see around the next corner, or the next.

Anna is sometimes in these dreams, lingering, ghostlike and elusive, ahead of or behind me. No matter how much I chase her or call her name, I can never reach her. She'll appear for a moment, smiling, her arm reaching towards me, only to disappear around a bend, or into a shadow, like an illusion or an apparition. A wisp of smoke, dissolving into air.

In my dreams it's as if the house itself has sinister intentions, as if its very foundations contain a malign force that seeps into the floors and walls and contaminates the air within, changing the lives of all who enter.

In real life, though, it wasn't Fairview that was responsible for what happened. It was the people who did the damage.

PART 1

1

"Tim, you're going to have to grow up," Lilla says. "Get a real job."

"I do have a real job," I say. "I go to work. I do stuff. I get paid for it. Seems real enough to me."

"Okay." She sighs. "Maybe real's the wrong word. You need a more sustainable job. One that will at least cover your rent and food. A job that means you can be independent."

"What you're really saying"—I raise my eyebrows at her—"is hurry up and move out."

"Yeah." She shrugs. "Since you mention it, you can't stay here forever. Sleeping on my couch isn't exactly a viable long-term plan. Not with Patrick here." She reaches across the coffee table and grabs her laptop, opens it on her knees. "And if you refuse to get a proper, I mean a more *lucrative,* job, we're just going to have to find you some kind of dirt-cheap alternative."

I close my eyes and hope that she'll get distracted. Stop trying to fix my life. I know I have to sort myself out and I fully intend to. Just not today.

After a moment she elbows me. "Listen to this one. It actually sounds quite good. And it's in Fairlight." She reads aloud: "*Large furnished room in spacious house. Share with one other. One hundred dollars a week.* A hundred bucks, Tim. *Cheap.*"

When I don't reply, she turns, nudges me again. "Are you going to call or what?"

"Must be a dump," I say grumpily. "Mold. Rats. I can imagine it."

"You have no money, Tim," she says. "You'll just have to take what you can get. Dump or not."

She picks up my phone, stabs numbers into it. "Come on." She pushes the phone against my ear so I'm forced to take it. "Just ask. It can't hurt. Stop being such a loser."

Some bloke called Marcus answers and we exchange information. He asks me how old I am, if I'm employed and whether I'm willing to take a trip to Fairlight to see the room and meet my potential housemate, a girl called Anna. I wonder why Anna isn't taking the call herself. He gives me the address and I tell him that I'll head up there later this afternoon.

"Can I just ask one question?" I say before I hang up.

"Of course," says Marcus.

"Why's it so cheap? What's the story?"

Lilla elbows me, makes a face. I ignore her.

"It's a large house," Marcus says in a smooth tone. "Very large. Too big, really, for one girl to live in all alone. You'll understand what I mean when you see it. And Anna's only twenty. It would be helpful to have someone around. That's all I want to say over the phone. If you meet me up at the house, we'll be able to tell you more in person. But rest assured, there's nothing to worry about. The conditions are very reasonable."

Conditions. The word has an ominous ring to it. I wonder why the room hasn't been taken and conclude that the "conditions" can't be as reasonable as Marcus promises. There must be some kind of catch. If something seems too good to be true, it's usually because it is.

Though I'm suspicious of the insanely low price, I decide to go and take a look. Lilla's boyfriend, Patrick, comes home, and the air of hostility that seeps off him is almost as thick as the stench of his aftershave. Suddenly the space feels far too small. Lilla's right. I have to find somewhere else to live. I jog downstairs and out into the burning heat, just in time to catch the next bus to Fairlight.

The house is enormous. Built of sandstone and brick, it stands two stories high and is the biggest and most impressive house in a street full of pretty flash houses. It's the kind of place you can't help but notice as you drive or walk by. The kind of house that makes you wonder about the people who live there. It's surrounded by lush green gardens, big lawns and beautiful trees and is so unexpectedly grand that I wonder if I've made a mistake. It even has a name. *Fairview* is engraved in fancy writing across a sign on the front gate.

I double-check the address. It's definitely the right place, and most definitely not the dump I expected to find.

The front door opens as I'm walking up the path, but it's so bright outside and so dark in the house, I can't immediately see who has opened it. When I reach the top of the steps I find a man waiting in the doorway. He's neatly dressed in a shirt and trousers and he looks me up and down as I approach. I'm scruffy in my shorts and T-shirt, and for a moment I consider apologizing, until I remember that I'm looking for a place to live, not applying for a job.

He puts out his hand. "Marcus Harrow," he says. "You must be Tim?"

He is taller than me by a good head-length. His hair is dark, his face strong.

I hear footsteps approaching from the hallway and a woman appears beside him. Like Marcus, she is tall and dark and dressed in business clothes.

"This is my sister, Fiona," he says. "Fiona, this is Tim."

"We're friends of Anna's," she explains. "She's waiting in the kitchen."

They lead me down a long, wide hallway. It takes a moment for my eyes to adjust to the darkness. The floor is polished timber, the ceiling high and decorated with elaborate plasterwork. We pass numerous rooms, all with their doors shut, and an enormous staircase that leads to the upper story. At the back of the house we come to a big kitchen and dining area. Unlike the gloomy hallway, this room is full of windows and light, with French doors leading out to a courtyard and a garden beyond.

A blond girl is sitting at the kitchen table. She's thin and pale, with an unhappy expression on her face. There's something vulnerable and frail about her that makes me wonder if she's sick.

"Tim," Marcus says. "This is Anna. Anna London."

She stands up, puts out her hand, then immediately withdraws it. She says hello in a very quiet voice and stares down at the table. Marcus said she was twenty. She seems much younger in person.

"Nice to meet you," I say.

"Thanks," she mutters.

"So, Tim," Fiona says. "Marcus said you work in a restaurant?"

"That's right," I say. "Just down in Manly. Not far from here. Ten-minute walk at most."

"And your job is reliable? Secure? You're not likely to be unemployed in the near future?"

"I work for my old man," I say. "I don't think he'd fire me. Wouldn't exactly be good for family relations."

It's meant to be a humorous comment, to lighten the mood, but nobody laughs. Marcus's face remains blank. Anna stares down at her fidgeting hands. Fiona flashes a tight smile. "Very good," she says. "Well, that's probably enough interrogation for now. I suppose we should take you up to see the room."

I follow the three of them back into the darkness of the hall and up the staircase. Fiona leads the way. I walk beside Anna. I try to catch her eye, smile, make some kind of friendly connection, but she stares at her feet the entire way, avoiding my gaze.

"Fairview was built in 1890," Marcus explains as we make our way up. "And so although it's a large and perfectly comfortable house, you might find it lacks a certain modern aesthetic."

Like light, I think.

"It's certainly different from most Australian homes," he continues. "More British in style. Some people don't like it. But I think it has its own charms."

Everything about the house, including the staircase, is grand and generous and carefully made. The place is obviously worth a fortune, but it's also gloomy, and cold. A bit oppressive, even. It's stinking hot outside, the sun so bright the streets seem to shimmer in the glare, and yet in here it's dark and cool and cavelike, another world altogether.

When we reach the second floor, Fiona stops at the first doorway we come to.

"There are a few rooms you could have," she says, "but this is one of the nicest."

She opens the door to what must be the best bedroom I've ever seen. It's large and bright and filled with enough furniture to make it inviting, but not overly crowded. Stepping into it from the gloom of the hall is like stepping from a cave into sunshine. The walls are white, the floors a warm timber. Large windows frame an impressive view of the Harbor. There's a double bed on one side, a wardrobe on the other, and a large timber desk tucked into one corner. An expensive-looking rug sits on the floor.

"There's no en suite," Fiona says. "But there are three bathrooms up here—and one is just across the hall—so you and Anna wouldn't have to share."

I think of the tiny bathroom I've been sharing with Patrick and Lilla for the past few weeks, the squat toilets that were the norm in Indonesia. A bathroom to myself would be a luxury I've never even considered.

The room itself is a thousand times better than I could have imagined. I turn around to take it in, then walk to the window and look out.

"This view," I say, shaking my head. "It must be one of the best in Sydney."

"It certainly is spectacular," Marcus says, stepping up next to me. He stares through the window for a second, then looks at his watch. He straightens up, pulls at the cuffs of his sleeves and moves his feet together in an abrupt, almost military manner. "Right. So that's the room," he says. "Fiona. We should probably get back to the office." He looks at Anna. "I presume we can leave you two here to figure things out?"

"Of course," Anna says, nodding. "You should go."

"Are you sure?" Fiona says. "Are you okay?"

"I'm fine."

Marcus and Fiona say goodbye. As they leave, the sound of their shoes clattering down the staircase is the only sound in the house. Anna doesn't say a word. Nor does she look at me. She stares straight ahead, motionless, trancelike. It's not until the noise of the front door being pulled shut echoes through the passage that she moves. She closes her eyes and puts her hand on her cheek. It's a strange, private gesture, as if she's forgotten that I'm there.

"So," I say. "It's an excellent place."

She opens her eyes. "Thank you."

I wait for her to make some effort at conversation, to ask me a question, or tell me something interesting about herself, but she just stands there, twisting her hands together nervously.

Not only is Fairview like something from another world, but so, I think, is Anna. She barely speaks, and when she does, her manner is so formal it seems unnatural, forced, as if she's speaking from a script. She holds herself in an awkward, slouched-over way, as if she lacks the confidence to stand up properly and face the world, as if she'd rather disappear. Her hands are in constant motion, clasping and unclasping, pulling at her clothes.

I get the distinct feeling that I'll have to take charge of the situation if I want to get anywhere.

The room is so much better than I expected that I'm tempted to say I'll take it, no matter how strange Anna is, or what the conditions are, but I know I should ask some questions. One hundred dollars a week for a room like this is insanely cheap. There must be some kind of catch.

"It's an awesome room," I say. "And I love the house. But when I rang earlier, Marcus told me there were some conditions. His word, not mine. Do you mind if I ask what they are? The conditions?"

She nods and if she seemed uncomfortable before, she is much more so now. She stares down at the floor, twisting her hands together frantically. Her face turns noticeably pink.

"I have . . ." She mutters something so quietly I can't hear it.

"Sorry?"

"I have agoraphobia," she says too loudly.

"Agoraphobia?" I repeat. I'm familiar with the word but have no real idea what it means. "I'm not sure—"

"It's an anxiety disorder," she says. "I have panic attacks."

"Right. Okay. Panic attacks." I smile apologetically. "Sorry. I feel a bit stupid, but I'm still not sure what . . ."

"I can't go out. I panic if I leave the house."

"You can't go out?" I try not to act too startled, but am not entirely successful. *"Ever?"*

"I don't leave the house at all," she says.

"That must be tough."

She blinks, turns away.

"Sorry. I don't really know what to say. I mean, that must be intense. Have you ever—"

"No," she interrupts. "No, I haven't."

"Sorry. I didn't mean to be . . . How long have you had it? How do you get by?"

"I've had it for a while now," she says. "I haven't been out for six months."

A lifetime, I think.

"Marcus and Fiona have been helping," she says. She lifts her chin. "But they can't do that forever."

We're quiet for a minute, both of us staring at the view. I wonder how she can handle seeing all that beauty outside, the sun and the sky, the boats on the Harbor, when she's trapped inside, all day, every day. The idea of looking out at a world that you can't be a part of is unfathomable to me. A kind of torture.

"Okay," I say eventually. "So you need someone to get stuff for you? Groceries? Bread and milk and stuff? Are they the conditions Marcus was talking about?"

"Yes, that's mainly it," she says. "I could shop online for most things, I suppose. But it's not always practical. And Marcus really thinks I should live with someone. In case of, well, an emergency or something like that. Fairview is so big . . ." She trails off.

"So basically you write lists and I get stuff for you?" I say. "Is that how it would work?"

"We could have a system," she says. "Whatever you need to make it easy. I wouldn't be a nuisance."

I lift my shoulders, grin. "I think I'd like the room. If you think I'd be suitable? I mean, I suppose you've got some questions of your own?"

"Not really." She shakes her head. "You can have it if you want. You seem pretty normal, really." For the first time, she flashes a smile. "More normal than I am anyway."

We go downstairs and talk through a few more details. She gives me a key to the front door, shows me where the laundry is, off the courtyard. By the time I leave I'm on a bit of a high. The room is fantastic, and more than affordable, and the house is in one of the best spots in Sydney. Anna is definitely odd, but that doesn't bother me. From what I can tell, she's just timid, a bit nervous—nothing that worries me. Maybe I can even help her, I think. At the very least, I can bring some life into Fairview, open a few doors and windows, let the light in.

2

Anna watches him from the window. As soon as she has closed the front door, she slips into the living room, pulls the curtain back and peeks out.

He walks quickly and with a small bounce in his step—a happy, optimistic walk, the walk of someone who has somewhere to go and nothing to worry about.

She likes the look of him. He isn't outrageously good-looking, but he has an open face, freckled skin and scruffy, windblown hair, which was probably once brown but has been bleached blond by the sun. He has a direct and honest gaze and an easy smile. Things have been smooth for him, she can tell. He is loved, he is confident, he is certain of the order of the world and his place within it. He has never been broken down by life or circumstance, never been betrayed by his own frail mind.

He looks like someone who belongs outside in the wind and the sun and the sea—all the elements that cause her so much fear—the landscape that she has so carefully removed herself from.

She imagines that if she licked his skin he would taste like salt.

3

Even though it's still more than two hours until my shift starts, I walk straight down to the restaurant after meeting Anna. By the time I reach the waterfront I'm feeling positively lucky. Not only is the house close to the beach and the city, it's an easy walk to work, too.

A wiry, fit-looking old guy jogs past me, tilts his chin towards the sparkling water and shakes his head—a gesture that says, *Look at that! Too bloody good!* I smile back, lift my hand to my forehead in a cheerful salute.

The Corso is noisy and crowded, fragrant with the smell of waffle cones from the ice-cream shop and the salty tang of the ocean. Right now the mood is cheerful and up. Later, when I finish work, it will have a different vibe. Booze and drugs will make it seedy—all drunken shouts and fights, broken bottles and sad-faced girls staggering home in heels. But in the early evenings there's always this festive, celebratory feel to the place that I love.

My father's restaurant is directly opposite Manly Beach. Dad's already in the restaurant when I get there. I find him crouched down behind the bar, restocking the fridges.

"Hey," I say, startling him. He grins up at me.

"I found a place to live," I tell him. "Just up the road in Fairlight. It's unbelievable. Has the most awesome view of the Harbor I've ever seen. And it's dirt cheap, too."

"Yeah?" He frowns. "So what's the catch?"

I sink onto a stool, put my elbows on the bar. "Can I have a beer?"

"If you get off your arse and give me a hand I might think about it."

I join him on the other side of the bar, open a case of Victoria Bitter and start sliding the small bottles into the fridge.

"So? Tell me," he says. "How much and what's the deal?"

"Hundred bucks a week—for this beautiful old house near the Harbor. Fairview, it's called. Can you believe that? I'll be living in a house with a name."

"Sounds fancy."

"It is fancy. It's massive, Dad. Has about a thousand rooms. My room has a view you wouldn't believe. Over the water, through the headlands. I'll be able to lie in bed and watch the ferries."

"And?" He lifts his shoulders, urging me to get to the point.

"So, the owner, this girl called Anna, she's got agoraphobia and can't go out. She needs a bit of help. With shopping and stuff. That's it," I say. "No big deal."

Dad's silence speaks volumes.

"What?"

"Gotta say, Timmo," he says. "Seems to me that you're making some weird choices."

I push my fingers through my hair and try to keep the exasperation from my voice. "What do you mean, *weird choices*?"

"I thought you went to Indonesia to get stuff sorted," he says. "I thought you'd come back with some idea of what you wanted."

I went to Indonesia to surf, I think, *not to find myself.*

"But now you're back, you've been bumming around at Lilla's for weeks and now you're going to live in some cheap house and look after a mentally unwell girl . . . all so that you can stay working at the restaurant. So you don't have to go and get a proper job. It's like you're avoiding life. Real life."

Now I can't hide my irritation. "She has panic attacks. It's not that big a deal. And I'm not avoiding life, I just don't know what I want to do yet. I'm just . . . bloody hell, Dad, I'm just—"

"Just what?" he interrupts. "You've got brains. Why don't you use them? Why don't you take advantage of all the good things you've been given? Make some kind of effort to get ahead?"

"Get ahead?" I stare at him. "I don't even know what that means."

"Okay, mate." Dad sighs, goes back to pushing beer bottles into the fridge. "Whatever you say."

I like working at the restaurant. I like working nights and having my days free. I don't want a job that causes me stress, that follows me home like a needy dog and whines at me all night long. But not a day passes without Dad saying something about me making an effort to find a proper career, choosing some kind of definite direction in life.

We work in silence for a while. When I've emptied two cases of VB I stand up, head for the kitchen.

"So when are you moving in?" Dad calls out behind me.

"Tomorrow."

The restaurant opens at five-thirty and by four I've done all the prep I can. I go out front, find Dad sitting at a table doing paperwork.

"You forgot to have that beer," he says. "Do you want to sit down, have one with me now?"

When I was a kid I considered myself guardian of my father's happiness. If he invited me to go fishing, I'd go with him, even though I hated the slimy worms, the stench of the fish, the torment of seeing them drown in air. If he was watching a movie, or a documentary on TV, or the news, I'd sit with him and pretend I was interested, too. I thought he'd miss me if I wasn't close to him—at least that's what I told myself—but then I heard him talking to Mum one night, when he thought I was asleep.

Can't shake him off at the moment, poor little fella. Always stuck to me like a clam. He's a bit of a needy little thing, isn't he? Needs a lot of love. A lot of attention.

His words made me cringe with embarrassment and since then, I'd felt a lot freer to go my own way, do my own thing.

"Nah," I say. "I might just go for a quick surf before service."

Dad lifts his hand in assent, doesn't even look up from his papers.

When I get home the flat is quiet, but Lilla has left a lamp on for me in the lounge. I go straight to the kitchen and open the fridge as quietly as I can, reaching into the back, where I keep my beer.

"Can I have one of those?" Lilla appears in the kitchen. Her hair is messy from bed and she's wearing this black nightie thing, all lacy and revealing. When she stretches her arms up over her head, yawning, the bottom of the skirt lifts indecently high and I have to turn away.

"Only if you get dressed," I say.

She rolls her eyes, but when she joins me in the lounge room a few minutes later she's wearing an enormous old T-shirt that hangs to her knees. She still looks hot. It's still hard to keep my eyes off her. She sits on the couch, legs crossed, beer in hand.

"So, did you get the room?" she asks. "What's it like? A total hole?"

"I got it and it's not a hole," I say. I consider telling her about the house, how impressive it is, but decide not to. It'll be much cooler to surprise her with the real thing. "Why? You didn't think I would?"

She shrugs. "I wasn't sure you'd even try."

"Well, you'll be happy to know I did try. And even happier to know that I got lucky."

Lilla stares down at her beer bottle. "Patrick's not here," she says after a moment.

"He's not?"

"We kind of had a bit of a fight when you left."

"You did?"

"Patrick reckons I act different when you're around," she says. "He reckons I've still got a thing for you."

Against my better judgment, my resolve to accept that Lilla and I are a thing of the past, my heartbeat picks up and a little coil of hope expands in my chest. I try not to feel—let alone show—anything. I try very hard to keep my expression blank.

"We haven't broken up or anything. I still like him, Tim. God. Don't get any ridiculous ideas. I guess he's just picking up on some . . . I don't know . . . old residual feelings. Leftovers or something."

"Leftovers?"

"Something like that."

I stare at her. I drink half my beer in one quick gulp. I should drop it, change the subject, save myself from humiliation. But I don't. Can't. It's as if I've started running down a too-steep hill and just can't stop, no matter how much I want to, no matter how much it's going to hurt when I hit the bottom.

"So?" I say, gripping my beer bottle tightly to hide the shake in my fingers. "The idea of us being together again is ridiculous, is it?"

She gives me a look. I can't tell if it's pity or reproach. "Don't, Tim. Don't even go there."

I drain the rest of my beer.

"Anyway," Lilla says, her voice false and bright. "Getting back to safer topics of conversation, what's the girl like? Your new housemate?"

"Her name's Anna. And she'll be my landlady, not my housemate," I say shortly. I stand up. "And now, if it's okay with you, I need to take a shower."

4

I wake early the next morning, after a lot of tossing and turning and not much actual sleep. I get dressed and pack my stuff—which basically involves rolling up my sleeping bag and shoving my clothes into a backpack, finding my small collection of books and putting my laptop in its case. I leave a brief note for Lilla and walk down to the bus stop.

The day is still cool enough to make it pleasant sitting in the sun and despite the depressing conversation I had with Lilla the night before, I'm feeling purposeful and optimistic. At least now I know where I stand. I just have to remember that, and not get sucked into hoping for more.

When I arrive at Fairview and push the fancy gate open I feel like some kind of imposter. I get around in old shorts, a T-shirt and a pair of cheap rubber flip-flops. I'm pretty sure I don't look like the kind of person who'd live in a house like this.

Anna answers the doorbell almost immediately.

"Man, that was fast." I laugh. "You must have been watching out the window."

I'm joking but she blushes, looks down.

"I was expecting you," she says.

She's dressed in the same shapeless clothes she was wearing yesterday. Her hair is pulled back from her face. I notice again how young she looks, with her timid expression and her hands clasped together.

Getting inside is tricky. Anna stands there, blocking the door, until I have to say, "Excuse me."

She steps aside and reaches out, as if to help me with my bags, but then puts her arm down without taking anything.

"I'm all right," I say.

She follows silently as I walk through the dark hallway. I put my things down at the bottom of the staircase and turn to face her.

"I might just go up and put my stuff away."

"You remember where to go?"

"Yeah. Of course. Thanks."

I leave her hesitating at the bottom of the stairs and head up to my room. It only takes a few minutes to unpack. I put my clothes in the wardrobe, place my books and my laptop on the desk and shove my empty backpack and sleeping bag under the bed. When I'm finished I look around the room in satisfaction. Mine. At least for now. I can hardly believe my luck.

On my way to check out the bathroom I notice Anna at the other end of the hall. When she reaches a small door at the far end she takes a key from her pocket and inserts it into the lock. She must hear me because she stops, pulls the key from the lock and turns around.

"Hey." I lift my hand in a wave.

"Are you okay?" She walks towards me. "Do you have everything you need?"

"Yeah," I say. "Sorry. I didn't mean to disturb you. I thought I might take a look through the house, if that's okay? I haven't really—"

"Oh," she interrupts, putting her hand to her mouth. "I haven't even shown you round properly yet. I'm so sorry. How idiotic. I can't believe I forgot . . . You must think I'm—"

"It seriously doesn't matter. It's totally cool."

I'd prefer to look around on my own. Anna's nervousness, the way she's always so stiff, is a strain. But I don't know how to say so without sounding rude and potentially making everything worse.

"Let's start downstairs," she says. "It's mainly just bedrooms up here."

I follow her down the staircase. She takes each step precisely, carefully, as if she's afraid of falling.

"I would have loved this house when I was a kid," I say. "It would have been the coolest place to play games, especially games where you need a bit of space. Hide-and-seek and stuff like that. Did you grow up here?"

"Yes," she says. "I've lived here all my life." She doesn't stop walking, or turn to look at me, but her voice is friendly enough, so I continue.

"Did you ever get scared? Living in such a big place? When you were a kid?"

"Scared?" She stops now, turns to look at me, her eyebrows raised. "What would I be scared of?"

"The usual stuff. Shadows and monsters?" I shrug. "Ghosts?"

She doesn't reply.

"So what's with the house now? Do you own it?" I ask when we've reached the bottom. As soon as the question is out of my mouth I regret it. I feel like I've just asked her how much money she's got.

But she doesn't seem to mind. She answers in the same neutral tone she's used to answer my other questions.

"Yes. I inherited it from my parents. It's mine."

She must see my curiosity because she tells me before I get a chance to ask. "My parents died in an accident. Three years ago."

"Oh, shit," I say. "That really sucks. Sorry. I didn't realize."

Maybe that explains why she's so strange, I think, *so afraid of the world.*

She takes me through each of the ground-floor rooms. The first is a formal dining room. The walls are a deep burgundy and the room is filled with an enormous dining table, which must seat at least sixteen people. An ornate chandelier hangs from the ceiling. The room has a definite gothic feel.

The next room is the library. Two of its walls are lined floor to ceiling with books. It's filled with reading lamps, coffee tables and old, uncomfortable-looking armchairs. It's a dim and dusty space and smells faintly of mold. It looks as if it hasn't been used for years.

The living room is far more inviting. Unlike the previous two rooms, the curtains are open and light streams in. Several large, soft sofas dominate the room, and from the look of the cushions, they get used regularly. There are rugs scattered on the floor, paintings on the walls. There's also a large, modern TV, and an old stereo in one corner. Other than its size it seems like a normal living room. Comfortable, warm, the kind of place you'd kick back in.

The final room on that side of the passage is filled to the brim with unused furniture. Anna calls it the junk room, and I can see why. Antique furniture, old bikes and haphazard piles of boxes take up every available bit of space.

We cross to the other side of the passage.

"And this is the ballroom," Anna says, opening the final door.

I laugh with surprise. "Jeez," I say, stepping inside. "This is *unreal*." My voice echoes off the walls. Anna flicks a switch and three large chandeliers send light dancing around the room. The walls are white, the high ceilings decorated with intricately patterned plasterwork. The floor is faded, warm timber. There's an open fireplace at one end, framed by an ornate stone mantelpiece. At night, with the chandeliers on and a fire burning, it must be magic.

"Incredible," I say, turning slowly, taking it in. "Have you had a lot of parties in here?"

"Parties? Of course. We used to have them all the time." She barks out a strange, unhappy laugh.

We go upstairs and she shows me through the other bedrooms. They're all just as large as mine but the empty rooms have their curtains drawn, so they seem a lot gloomier. They're all pretty much identical, with timber floors, brass beds, old rugs and long, thick curtains. They'd be nice if someone opened the curtains, if they were lived in, but everything is too still, too lifeless. Our footsteps echo. There's something ghostly and faintly depressing about all the emptiness, the unused space.

"You should get more tenants," I say. "You could run a boarding-house."

I'm joking, but Anna looks horrified, shakes her head violently.

"So which is yours?" I ask.

"This way," she says, and walks to the end of the hallway.

There are three closed doors at this end of the hall. Two doors face each other across the passage, and a third, smaller door sits adjacent. Anna stops at one of the facing doors, but before she can open it, I point to the smaller door, the door she was unlocking when I interrupted her earlier.

"What's in there?" I ask.

"It leads up to the attic," she says. She stares at me for a moment, before adding in an abrupt voice, "I keep it locked."

For some reason I feel as if I've been told off, or warned.

"This is mine," she says, opening one of the other doors.

It's a lot smaller than the other bedrooms, with just a single bed and a small window overlooking the garden. It seems a bizarre choice. Why has she chosen the smallest, pokiest room in the house?

"Nice," I say, not really meaning it. "And that one?" I ask, pointing to the door opposite.

"It's just another bedroom," she says.

"Can I see?"

She hesitates, shrugs, shakes her head—as though she's going through some kind of intense internal dialogue—then she steps forward and opens the door slowly.

This room is different. Unlike all the other neutral colors used upstairs, the walls in here are a soft green. A bright orange paper lantern hangs from the ceiling. A bench seat runs along one wall, empty bookshelves along another. The curtains are a darker shade of green. It's modern, bright, surprising, the colors making it cheerful and inviting.

"Hey. This is cool," I say. "You should have this room."

I think it's a pretty harmless thing to say. Inoffensive. Complimentary even. But Anna glares at me as though I've just said something outrageous. She pulls the door closed so suddenly that I'm forced to step back into the hall.

"Okay, then," she says, making it clear that the tour is over, before adding, strangely, "Thank you."

"Huh, no, thank *you*," I say. "I won't get lost now. Won't accidentally end up in the wrong bedroom at night."

Her face flushes red.

"I meant, you know, one of the empty rooms," I explain. Her self-consciousness is contagious—I can feel my own face turning red. "Anyway, I thought I might go out a bit later. With some mates or something."

I'm explaining myself unnecessarily, only making things worse. Anna nods, her back against her bedroom door, and I can tell she's waiting for me to leave.

"Okay, then. Yep." I smile, lift my hand in a dumb wave and go back down the hall and into my own room. It's a relief to close the door behind me, to have the encounter with Anna over and done with. I wonder if things will get easier between us, if she'll get more relaxed. Maybe it just takes her a while to warm up to people.

I find my phone and text a few mates to find out what's happening. We agree to meet up later for a barbecue at a friend's place in Narrabeen. I shower and get changed. I have a bit of time to kill so I turn on my laptop, check out a couple of surf reports, listen to some music on YouTube. Then I click on to Facebook and do the only thing I ever do on Facebook. The only reason I even joined in the first place. Lilla. I don't think too hard about why, I don't bother reminding myself of my earlier resolutions. I click on to her page, see her recent status update:

Making up is always fun!

So Patrick is back.

A claw of disappointment grabs my throat. I close my laptop and leave.

"See you later, Anna!" I shout as I go.

I'm surprised by how good it feels to be outside, away from the oppressive gloom of the house. But it's not only the house. It's Anna, too. She's shy, or unfriendly, or both, but it's more than that. She reminds me of a bad actor wearing an ill-fitting costume. She's inhabiting her character awkwardly, failing to pull off a convincing performance. It's obvious that she's hiding herself.

5

She hears him call out and she responds with a feeble "Goodbye, Tim. See you later!" but she doubts he even hears her. She listens to his footsteps clattering down the staircase, the sharp bang of the door slamming shut. She can hardly blame him for wanting to get the hell out of here, away from her. She wants to get away from herself, her own spinning mind and pathetic anxieties. If only she could.

She likes him. His presence is already a welcome distraction from the miserable preoccupations that haunt her, her obsession with going over and over the past, wishing she could go back in time.

There's no going back. No matter how much she longs to. The dead can never be brought back to life.

When she's certain Tim has gone she leaves her room and goes up to the attic. She's drawn to it, like a compulsion, an addiction.

As she closes the door behind her and slips the bolt home, making sure there's no possibility of discovery or surprise, she thinks of what Tim asked her earlier—if she'd ever been scared of shadows or ghosts—and smiles bitterly to herself.

If only he knew.

6

When I get back to the house it's almost midnight.

I brush my teeth, wash my face. As I'm drying it I hear a noise that makes me pause. It's high-pitched, some kind of wail. At first I think it must be a cat. I wait for a moment but don't hear it again until I leave the bathroom and step into the hall. It's not a cat, it's a person.

Anna.

I walk to her room and stand outside her door. From here the noise is clear and continuous. She's crying her heart out. I stand there for a moment, listening. I'm tired and reluctant to engage in another awkward encounter but it seems heartless to just walk away from someone in such obvious distress.

"Anna?" I tap lightly on her door. "It's me, Tim. Are you okay?"

There's no answer, nor is there any break in the noise. She just keeps on crying.

"Anna?" I call, louder. "Do you need anything? Can I get you anything?"

She doesn't answer. She doesn't stop crying either. I grab the door handle and start to open it, but change my mind. She must have heard me, she must know I'm here. If she wanted me to come in she'd say so.

"Anna," I say. "I'm going back to my room. I'll be just down the hall. If you need anything or if you want to talk or anything like that, let me know. Seriously. You can wake me up. Whatever. Just, you know, come and get me. If you want." I clear my throat. "I hope you're okay. I'll leave you alone now but I'm happy to help out. Just ask. No worries at all."

I go back to my room and get into bed. If I lie still I can hear her, very faintly. I bury my head under the pillow and fall asleep.

Next morning I wake early and go down to Manly for a surf. I pick up my board from the storeroom at the restaurant on the way. The break is crowded, as I knew it would be, but the waves are excellent and everyone seems pretty chilled out—happy to share, okay with waiting. It's good to be out here. The sun rises higher in the east, making sharp diamonds of light that bob and twist on the surface of the water. Everything's so bright it forces me to squint and smile at the magic of it.

I feel strong out here, as if anything is possible and yet nothing really matters, at the same time. The vast expanse of the ocean, the momentous power of it, gives me a sense of freedom that I never have on land. Out here I don't need Lilla, I don't need anyone. For a brief and beautiful time, nothing matters except me and my board and the waves.

When I finish, I take my board back to the restaurant and put on my dry clothes. I find a plastic tub and swipe some of Dad's coffee to take back up to the house. It's the good stuff. Rich and robust. Packs a punch like good coffee should. I stop at the supermarket to get some food on my way home. I buy fresh eggs and crusty bread, bright red strawberries and plump nectarines. Real maple syrup, real butter. I grab a tub of extra-thick cream and a handful of pistachios. I wonder if I should make breakfast for Anna, too, briefly wonder if she'll be home, before remembering that she doesn't leave the house. She'll definitely be there. She'll always be there. It's a sobering thought. *No wonder she was crying*, I think.

It's almost nine by the time I get back. I take the food straight to the kitchen and unpack. The kitchen's clean, the kettle cold, and there's no sign of Anna, so I assume she's not up yet. I open some of the cabinets and have a good look around. I'm glad to see that the kitchen is filled with excellent cookware: good-quality pots and pans, sharp knives, a cast-iron skillet, a fancy espresso machine. But the actual food supply is another story. The fridge is practically empty except for a carton of milk, a block of cheese and some sad-looking carrots. The pantry is stocked with a sparse supply of crappy food: tins of soup, a catering-sized bottle of tomato sauce, instant noodles. There are no interesting sauces, no spices, not even a clove of garlic or an onion.

As I'm closing the pantry door, something gets stuck beneath it. I bend down to see what it is and find a scrunched-up piece of paper trapped between the door and the floor. I pull it free and unfold it, flattening it against the benchtop. The paper is covered with the name *Ben,* written over and over. The writing gets more and more desperate-looking so that by the bottom of the page the pen has al-most torn through the paper. The handwriting is distinctive, left-sloping, confident. It must be Anna's, and yet it's hard to imagine the brittle, controlled girl I've seen doing anything so passionate.

I have no idea who Ben is—a boyfriend or an ex?—but I'm now convinced my original impression of Anna was right. Her bland, robotic persona is some kind of disguise. A protective armor. The real Anna is hiding.

I fold the paper and toss it back on the floor where I found it—it's not exactly the kind of thing you admit to having seen—and close the pantry door.

As I'm cracking eggs she comes into the kitchen. She's wearing a loose T-shirt nightie thing, spotty and bright, like something a little kid would wear.

"Hey," I say. "I'm making French toast. You hungry? Want some?"

"Okay," she says quietly. "Yes. Thank you."

I beat eggs, heat the pan, while Anna just stands there, as if wait-ing for something. Eventually she speaks. "Can I do anything to help?"

I get her to wash and slice the strawberries and we pass the next few minutes in silence, the sizzle of bread in hot butter the only noise. It should be companionable, comfortable, but I can sense the nervous tension coming off her. "Is everything okay, Anna?" I ask. "I mean, are you—"

"Everything's fine," she says. "I'm sorry. Try to ignore me if you can. I'm just hopeless at the moment."

"You're not hopeless," I say. "Don't say that."

She shrugs.

We eat at the table, sitting opposite each other. I wonder if I should mention the crying I heard last night, but I don't know how to broach it. I decide to bring it up indirectly, give her the opportunity to mention it herself if she wants to.

"I got home about midnight last night," I say. "Thanks for leaving those lights on. I didn't disturb you too much, did I? When I came in? Did you sleep okay?"

"Like a log," she says, her face blank, unreadable. "You didn't disturb me at all. I didn't hear a thing."

She insists on cleaning up after breakfast, so I leave her to it and go up to my room. I spend a while mucking around on the Internet, resisting the temptation to log into Facebook and see what Lilla's up to.

Later, when I'm down in the kitchen about to make myself a sandwich, there's a knock on the door. I hear Anna go down the hall, the door being opened. Voices. Footsteps.

A few minutes later Anna appears in the kitchen with Fiona, who's carrying a bag of groceries, talking animatedly about something. She stops when she notices me, says hello.

"Hey," I say. "Fiona. Nice to see you."

"I've just brought some supplies," she says. She lifts the bag onto the bench. "Milk and bread. Some coffee."

"Sorry," I say, glancing at Anna. "Maybe I should have checked? I already got some of that stuff."

Fiona waves her hand. "Don't worry. I just assumed. I was going past. It's become a habit. Now, you two go and sit down and I'll put these away and then we can have coffee."

Anna and I sit at the table while Fiona unpacks the groceries. She offers instant coffee from a jar, and even though I can't stand the stuff I accept. I want to be friendly.

Fiona must be in her late twenties or her early thirties—she's a fair bit older anyway—and it's as if she has a protective, almost maternal thing going with Anna. She seems more like a mother or an older sister than a friend.

She brings the mugs to the table, offers sugar and milk, then sits at the head, between me and Anna.

She turns to me. "How are you settling in? Enjoying the house?"

"Yeah." I nod. "Everything's good."

"It's not too big for you?" she asks. "You're not getting lost?"

"Not so far," I say.

Fiona starts telling a long and complicated story about some traffic incident she witnessed on the way over. I'm not all that interested in what she's saying, but I'm polite enough to pretend. Anna makes no effort. She sips on her coffee and stares into space, not appearing to register Fiona's words at all.

Anna's bizarre behavior doesn't seem to bother Fiona. She talks on and on, as if the situation is completely normal. It makes me wonder if she's so used to Anna's reticence that she doesn't notice it anymore, or whether she's just learned to ignore it.

When we've finished our coffee Fiona takes our empty mugs to the sink. She says goodbye to Anna, who only smiles vaguely in response.

"Tim, I wonder if you'd mind coming outside for a moment?" Fiona says. "To take a quick look at my car? A dashboard light was flashing on the way over. I'm just wondering if I might need some oil."

"Yeah, sure." I shrug. "Happy to take a look. But I'm not much of a mechanic."

I follow Fiona through the hall and out onto the front porch. She pulls the door shut behind us.

"Look, it's not really the car," she says quietly, glancing back at the house. Her eyebrows—the same thick eyebrows that suit Marcus, but look too masculine for her face—knot tightly together. "I just wanted to let you know that if living with Anna gets too much for you, if you decide you want to move out, Marcus and I will completely understand. It's very important that you don't feel obliged to stay. You're free to move out any time you like. . . . Just remember that."

7

There are only three of us working at the restaurant that night—me in the kitchen, Blake doing the dishes and our best waitress, Jo, on the floor. Of all the people that work for Dad, Jo and Blake are my favorites. Blake's one of those insanely big blokes. A gentle giant. Best thing about him is his perpetual air of levelheaded calm. Serenity is always a good thing in a restaurant kitchen, and Blake's the most serene person I know. The dishes can pile up all over the place and he works steadily on, always managing to smile and keep his cool.

Jo is similarly cheerful, but where Blake is big and steady, she's short and tiny and fast. She has dark hair and bright eyes. On busy nights I swear she keeps the whole place running smoothly with her energy and her uncanny ability to know what's happening at every table.

With the three of us on, service flies by and we have the customers out of there and the place cleaned up by ten.

We sit at the bar. Blake and I drink beer, Jo drinks red wine.

"Good tips tonight?" I ask Jo.

"Twenty-five bucks." She smiles.

"A drink at the Steyne on you, then," Blake says.

"Good idea," Jo says eagerly. "Tim? You up for it?"

"Nah," I say. "Thanks. Might just head home. I'm buggered. Got up early for a surf."

"Nice one," Blake says. "Hey, you still staying out at Collaroy with your ex? Must be a struggle getting home at night?"

"I just moved," I say. "I'm living up the road in Fairlight now. It's a ten-, fifteen-minute walk at most."

"Yeah?" He whistles. "Fairlight, eh? Good spot to live. Did a painting job up there a while back. A beautiful old sandstone house. Enormous place with lush gardens. The lady wanted the dining room red, I remember. We were worried that it'd be too dark, but it turned out pretty nice."

"But that's where I'm living," I cut in.

"Lauderdale Avenue?"

I nod. "Fairview."

"No joke? Yeah, that's the one." He shakes his head. "Man, I loved that house. When I was a kid I used to walk past it all the time. I thought it was a castle, promised myself I'd buy it when I got rich." He laughs, looking down at his stained clothes. "Which doesn't look like it's happening anytime soon. So how'd you end up scoring a place like that?"

"I'm just renting one of the rooms. From a girl called Anna," I say.

"Anna. Yep, that was the daughter's name." He looks thoughtful, remembering. "It was just the three of them rattling around in that big, empty place. Anna used to bring us cold drinks. Real friendly girl, she was." He grins. "Pretty hot, too, if I'm remembering right."

"Not sure we're talking about the same girl," I say. "Anna must be the shyest person I've ever met. She's blond. Thin." I don't mention that she's not exactly friendly or that I'd have a hard time describing her as hot.

"Yeah, she was definitely blond, but shy? No way," Blake says. "Not the girl I'm thinking of. She was charismatic, you know; she had that talent for making people feel special. One of those people everyone likes."

When I get back to the house I notice light and noise coming from the living room. I find Anna curled up on the sofa in her pajamas.

She sits up straight when I enter the room and says an abrupt hello before turning back to the TV. I offer her one of the beers I've brought home from the restaurant but she shakes her head without bothering to look at me. I crack one open for myself, then sit on the sofa opposite her and watch the movie until the first ad break.

"What have you been up to?" I ask, without thinking. There isn't a lot she could do, stuck here in the house all the time.

"Not much," she says, without a hint of irony.

I decide to check out Blake's story. "You won't believe it," I say, "but this guy, Blake, he works in the kitchen with me. Apparently he used to be a painter. And get this, he's pretty sure he painted this house a few years ago. He reckons he knew you and your mum. Do you remember him? Big, tall bloke?"

"Not really," she says, not looking away from the screen.

"Are you sure? Blake was pretty clear. He went on about painting the dining room red, how much he liked you, said you used to bring them cold drinks." I try to laugh but she looks blank, bored even. "You don't remember?"

"No." She turns to face me. Her voice is flat, uninterested, and my enthusiasm for the story suddenly seems stupid and out of place. Anna turns back to the TV and we watch the ads in silence.

I sit there through the rest of the movie and finish my beers. We make polite, neutral small talk in the ad breaks, and all the while, the shadow of the conversation we didn't have lurks like an unwelcome guest in the space between us.

8

Of course she remembers Blake, and the other painters. But talking about the past is something she's not willing to do.

Talking about the past only makes her want to scream.

And if she starts screaming, she's not sure she'll ever stop.

9

I wake with a sudden start. My heart is pounding, as though I've had a nightmare. I closed my curtains when I came up, and now I can barely see a thing. I stare out into the blackness and blink, my eyes wide. I lie there for a minute and concentrate on breathing, waiting for my heart rate to settle down. When I feel calmer I roll onto my side and adjust my pillow.

That's when I see it.

The shape of a person.

Watching me.

There's someone in my room.

"Fuck!" I push the duvet off, fall clumsily to the floor in my haste, my legs tangled in the sheet. By the time I look up again, whoever the hell it was is gone. I get up and go to the doorway, turn on the light. My hands are shaking.

Though I know it's unlikely, stupid even, I open the wardrobe near the door and check inside. There's nothing there but my clothes.

I set off down the stairs, turning on every light as I go.

"Hello?" I shout. "Is someone there?"

My voice seems to boom and echo against the walls, unnaturally loud in the still night, and the resounding silence only makes me more freaked out. The house suddenly seems too big, too empty, too dark. I feel vulnerable and isolated, as if I'm the only person in the world. When I reach the bottom of the stairs I check the front door.

It's locked. I check the dining and living rooms. The ballroom. There's nobody there, no sign of disturbance, nothing.

It suddenly occurs to me to worry about Anna. Maybe the intruder went the other way, towards her room. I run upstairs and pound on her door.

"Anna! You okay?"

I don't wait for a response. I open her door, find the light. She's already sitting up, rubbing at her eyes.

"Tim? What are you doing? What's all that noise?" she says, sounding annoyed. "What's wrong?"

"I saw someone."

"What do you mean?"

"In my room," I say urgently. "In my doorway. Watching me."

She pushes her duvet off and stands up. "Are you sure? Oh, my God. Is the . . . did you check downstairs?"

"The door's locked."

"Both doors?"

"I don't know. Shit. I didn't—I only checked the front."

We go downstairs, Anna wrapping her dressing gown around herself protectively.

"You saw a person?" she asks. "Doing what?"

"I don't know," I say. "It was too dark to see properly. They were just standing there."

The back doors are locked, the kitchen still and quiet. Nothing has been moved or taken.

"I've already checked the other rooms down here," I say. "There was nothing. That's so weird. I mean, how could someone get in without breaking a window or something?"

"They couldn't," she answers.

She no longer looks scared, only tired, a bit impatient. But she doesn't meet my eye properly and it makes me wonder if this is just her normal nerves or if she has something to hide.

Was it Anna watching me? And if so, why? Maybe she wasn't actually watching me, maybe she was just coming to talk, to ask me some question. Maybe she just wanted to make sure I was home. Perhaps I scared her off by shouting out. But why wouldn't she just say so? Why would she lie?

The alternative—an intruder—is even more disturbing. And it doesn't make any sense. Why would anyone break into a house and not bother taking anything?

I don't mention any of this to Anna. It's obvious that she doesn't want to talk; she keeps her head down and her arms wrapped tightly around herself as we turn off the lights and climb the stairs. I say goodnight when I reach my bedroom and she makes some kind of noncommittal noise in response.

My heart is still thumping and I can taste the bitter tang of adrenaline. In my mind I can still see the figure standing in my doorway. I know it wasn't a dream. The memory is too sharp, too clear, and it's not fading the way dreams do. I try to tell myself that I must have been seeing things, that it must have been a combination of beer and fatigue. But I can't shake the ominous feeling, the growing sense that there's something very strange about Anna London and her empty old house.

I go back to bed but spend the next few hours starting at every sudden noise, too jumpy to sleep. I finally doze off sometime after four, but am woken a few hours later by the beep of my phone.

"Shit." I sit up and reach for it, intending to turn it off, when I notice that it's a text message from Lilla.

Get up, lazy. I'm at your place. Open the door. I've only got 20 minutes!

As I'm walking down the stairs I think about what happened last night. The dark figure I saw in my doorway. The whole thing seems distant now. The previously sharp memory is now hazy and smudged by the combination of sleep and the reassuring normality of daylight. And my fear seems like an overreaction.

I open the front door and find Lilla standing on the front porch, hands on hips, dressed in her usual black. She's wearing a miniskirt, showing off her perfect legs. Her short hair is rumpled, her lips are painted red. She shakes her head and launches straight in.

"I can*not* believe it," she says, pushing past me into the hallway. "I thought I must be totally mixed up so I almost knocked at the house next door, but then I saw some old lady coming out, and realized this must really be the one." She stops, looks around in astonishment. "Bloody hell, Tim. You live here? I can*not* believe you didn't tell me. Is this for real?"

Her pushiness, her assumption that I should tell her everything about my life, sometimes makes me laugh. This early in the morning it only irritates me. "I'm here, aren't I?" I say.

She steps up close to me, stands on tiptoe and kisses my cheek. "You need a shave."

She walks down the hallway, running her hand along the wall as she goes, shaking her head.

"Lilla," I say. "Keep it down, will you? Your shoes are bloody noisy. Anna's asleep."

"Whoops. Sorry." She smiles apologetically, pulls her shoes off and holds them in her hand. Then she goes to the dining room, opens the door and peeks inside. "Ooh, look at that. Nice. What a beautiful red."

She walks to the living room and opens that door, too.

"What are you doing? It's seven o'clock in the morning. I need to go back to bed."

"I wanted to see where you were living. And I was running early for work," she says, heading for the room Anna called the junk room. "Wow," she says, stepping inside. "Look at all this gorgeous old furniture. Some of it's just beautiful. Really valuable, too, I bet. Why's it all stacked in here? God, what a waste. Some people obviously have too much money to care."

I stand in the doorway. "Get out of there."

"Why?" she says. "I'm not going to break anything."

I sigh and lean against the door frame. I watch Lilla run her hands along an old timber dresser, open the doors, rummage through the old glassware. She opens the lid of a box and pulls out a handful of old papers and photos, flicking through them one by one.

"Who are these people?"

"I don't know," I say, stepping closer. "They're not mine. Just put them back."

She holds a picture out towards me. A man, a woman and a small blond girl of about eight are standing in a garden in front of a house. It's clearly this house. I recognize the front porch, the stonework, the windows. The girl stands between the two adults, beaming straight at the camera, her two front teeth very prominent. The man, gray-haired and nondescript, smiles, too. The woman, blond like the girl, and beautiful in a cold way, isn't smiling. Her chin is lifted and she stares off to the side. I assume it's Anna and her parents.

Lilla flicks to the next photo. It shows a group of people standing around a table with a cake sitting on it. A girl stands directly behind the cake, looking as if she's just blown the candles out. She's grinning at the camera, her head tipped to one side. There's a strand of hair caught in her mouth.

"Look at her," Lilla says. "What a stunner."

Lilla's right, the girl is stunning. The strange thing is, she looks just like Anna, only there's none of the slouching, twitchy shyness of Anna. In fact, the provocative smile on her face reminds me more of Lilla than Anna. But it is Anna, it must be. I turn the photo over.

17th birthday is written on the back.

"So that's who you're living with?" Lilla says, nudging me. "You didn't mention she looked like that."

Because she doesn't, I think. *At least, not anymore.*

"Let's get out of here," I say. "We shouldn't be looking through her stuff."

I put the photos away and drag Lilla out and across the hall, towards the ballroom.

"Go on," I say, gesturing towards the closed door. "Have a look in there."

She opens the door and takes a startled step back. She looks at me and grins, then rushes inside, spins around, lets out a noisy yelp.

"Shut *up*."

She puts her hand to her mouth. "Sorry. Sorry. But, Tim. This is so. Fucking. Awesome. This house. It's just unbelievable." She frowns. "Why didn't you tell me?" She doesn't wait for an answer. "You know, of course, that you're going to have to organize a party. There's no way you can get away with living here and not having one. It would be criminal." And then she looks at her watch. "Shit. I've got to get going."

She pulls on her shoes, rushes over and gives me another kiss. I follow her to the door and watch her go down the garden path, get into her crappy old Laser and drive away. Lilla's like one of those strong, cool winds that can make you confused and disoriented, but can also wake you up and make you feel alive in a way that nothing else can. She knows the effect she has on me, and she enjoys it. She wouldn't kiss me the way she does, stand so close, dress that way, if she didn't. I always knew she enjoyed creating a stir, being at the center of things. Now I sometimes wonder if she enjoys hurting me.

It's already hot outside. I decide to make the most of it and head out for an early-morning swim.

Fairlight Pool is quiet when I get there. I sit on the edge, dangling my calves in the water, enjoying the warmth of the sun on my back. There's one old man swimming the length of the pool in a slow breaststroke, a woman doing a leisurely sidestroke and another doing a brisk freestyle. She's as fast and as slick and as smooth in the water as anyone I've ever seen. At each end of the pool she does a neat flip and heads back the other way without pausing. I slip into the water and swim parallel to her, trying to match her pace.

For the first three laps I stay ahead of her, but after that I have to slow down, and I swim the rest of my laps in her wake.

"Nice swimming style," I say to her later when I get out of the pool. She's drying off in the sun, her face turned up, soaking in the rays. She looks about fifty, and her body is long and lean, a swimmer's body. She smiles without opening her eyes, or turning my way. "You, too."

I think of Anna as I walk back to the house and feel a renewed sense of pity for her. I couldn't live without the buzz I get from being in the water, the rush I get from being outdoors. I couldn't handle missing out on all this. But she clearly wasn't always this way, and I wonder again how and why she changed from the girl in the photos, the happy girl Blake described, to the person I'm living with now.

10

I don't see much of Anna over the next few days. I pass her in the hall once on my way to work—she says hello, but keeps on going—and another night I find her watching TV in the living room when I get home from work, but I go straight up to my room. She's standoffish and cool, and if she talks to me at all, it's only about something prosaic: an oven element that doesn't work properly, or a window that's jammed shut. Once she gives me a list of things she wants from the shops and I recognize the distinctive left-sloping handwriting from the note I found in the pantry. There's nothing fresh or wholesome on the list. It's all processed or tinned stuff. The shopping list of an old lady.

"Is that it?" I ask. "No fruit or veg? No meat?"

"No," she says coldly. "That's it. Exactly what I've written."

Her unfriendliness doesn't bother me much. The house is big enough that we don't get in each other's way.

So I'm surprised when I go down to the kitchen on Sunday morning and find her slicing apples, humming softly. She's dressed in her usual clothes, but her hair is out of its ponytail, hanging loose around her shoulders and face. She looks more animated than she normally does.

"Hey," I say.

She starts, looks up.

"You're cooking?"

"I'm trying to. I'm not very good, though. I'm having Marcus and

Fiona over for lunch." She smiles hesitantly. "If you're free, you could join us."

I'm surprised, a bit intrigued. "Okay," I say. "If you're sure, then, yeah, I will. I'm not doing anything else. Thanks."

I stand there for a minute, watching her slice apples, thinking about the lack of fresh food in the house.

"Anna," I say eventually. "Do you want me to go down to the shops and get something? There's not really anything here, is there? What are you making?"

She points her knife towards the apples. "I'm making apple pie for dessert. I don't know if it'll work out, but I hope so. And soup for lunch." She puts her knife down and goes to the pantry, pulls out a tin of beef and vegetable soup.

My astonishment must be obvious because she frowns, holds the tin out towards me.

"It's gourmet soup, not just any old thing," she says. "Look, it even has herbs in it."

I take the can from her and pretend to read the label. Gourmet or not, it's still tinned soup. I look up, smile, shake my head.

She snatches the tin from me and puts it down firmly on the benchtop. She folds her arms across her chest and stares at me. Her cheeks are flushed red, like a kid who's been running around outside. And then she laughs, and suddenly I can see that other girl standing before me. The girl from the photos. And Blake doesn't seem so crazy for calling her hot.

"What, then?" she asks. "What am I going to do now? I don't have anything else."

"Isn't that why I moved in here?" I say. "To help you out in situations like this? I can go down to the shops. Get something."

"But I can't actually cook." She looks abashed. "I have no idea what to make or even where to start." She turns back to the sliced apple. "I found this recipe in one of Mum's old books, but it's probably going to be a disaster."

"So why don't you let me do it? I can cook. I'll go down to the shops and get some fish. I know this snapper recipe. It's a cinch. Takes five minutes but tastes awesome. Looks impressive, too. I'll show you how to make it and then you'll have something apart from tinned soup in your cooking repertoire."

"Really?"

"I know how to make a good apple pie, too. I'll get some ginger, it'll give it a lift. And you'll need cream."

I'm walking down the hall towards the front door when she calls out, "Wait!" She rushes towards me, a hundred-dollar note in her hand. "Here, take this. You can't pay for all that stuff. And you should get us something to drink. Some beer or something. Some wine, too, maybe. Whatever you like."

It's a hot walk down to the shops in the sun, and my backpack is heavy and overloaded on the way back. I sweat like a pig and wish I'd brought a bottle of water with me. When I finally arrive back at the house and step inside, I'm glad of the gloom. It might be dark, but at least it's cool.

I load the fridge with beer and supplies, then wash my hands and get to work. I make pastry for the apple pie, add ginger to the apples and put it in the oven. I put together a salad. Anna offers to help and I get her to mix the marinade and spread it over the skin of the fish.

When we've finished we both go to our rooms to get ready. I take a shower, put on a clean T-shirt, my best pair of shorts. I'm back in the kitchen checking on the pie when Anna comes in. She's changed into a red T-shirt and a pair of jeans. There's nothing particularly revealing about her clothes, but I notice her shape for the first time—a body that she's kept completely hidden until now. I must be staring because she hesitates, then positions herself on the other side of the benchtop and clutches her hands together nervously. I feel like a jerk.

"Beer," I say, and I busy myself getting glasses, opening a bottle, hoping that the heat in my face isn't showing on my skin.

We take our beers outside to the small courtyard off the kitchen. I watch Anna take a seat. She lifts her glass and swallows half her beer in one go.

"Is this all right for you?" I say, sitting opposite her. "Out here?"

She hesitates, nods. "I'm usually okay if I'm close to the house. Sometimes I can't . . ." She breaks off, sighs. "I'm fine. I'd say so if I wasn't."

She doesn't look fine. She looks unhappy and on edge. I try to start a conversation, but my attempts fall flat and I resign myself to sitting in uncomfortable silence. Anna finishes her beer while mine's still practically full. I go inside to get the bottle, glad of something to do.

She drinks the next one quickly, too, downing the entire glass in a few hasty gulps, as if it's medicine, and I wonder if she's using the alcohol to calm her nerves. She finishes her second drink before I've even finished my first.

"I think I'll have another." She stands up. "Do you want one?"

"Sure," I say, draining mine. "Why not?"

She brings another bottle out and tops up our glasses, then takes the bottle inside. She seems slightly more relaxed when she returns. She leans back in her chair instead of perching on the edge, and her hands move less frantically. She sips on her third drink slowly. I try again to think of something to say, wishing she wasn't so impossible to talk to, but I'm saved by a flock of galahs that fly in and gather noisily in the trees above us. For a while we're both absorbed, watching the small cockatoos. We don't have to talk.

Eventually, the doorbell rings and Anna jumps up. She puts her hand to her hair, pulls at her T-shirt, straightening and adjusting. "They're here," she says unnecessarily.

Just as they were the first time I met them, Marcus and Fiona are dressed in what I think of as office clothes. Weirdly overdone, I think, for Sunday lunch at a friend's. We get fresh drinks and go back out to the courtyard. Pretty soon it becomes obvious that all the beer Anna has been drinking has kicked in. Her cheeks are pink, her eyes bright and glassy and—most amazingly of all—she talks.

She tells me all about Marcus and Fiona's work. They are both lawyers. She describes how Fiona studied law first, getting top marks at university, eventually being headhunted by a prestigious city law firm. Fiona stays quiet, smiling stiffly at Anna's praise. She tries to change the subject, but Anna ignores her, gushes on. She tells me how Marcus studied law, too, how they eventually had enough combined experience to open a practice together.

"Harrow and Harrow, it's called." Anna beams. "And if you need any legal advice they're definitely the people to see. They come highly recommended."

The change in Anna is so enormous I have to tell myself not to stare. For the second time that day I see a glimpse of the girl Blake described, the girl from the photo: someone pretty, warm, articulate.

"And you already know Tim's a chef," she says, turning towards Marcus and Fiona. "For which I think you two should be particularly grateful. He saved you from a lunch of tinned soup."

"A chef? That must be hard work," Fiona says, looking at me with curiosity.

"Can be a bit grubby," I say. "But I'm only a lowly cook, not a chef."

"What's the difference?" Marcus says. I get the feeling he's trying to be polite, for Anna's sake probably, that he's not really interested.

"A few years studying. But mainly the paycheck," I say. "There's not really a lot to say about it. It's chaotic and it's dirty and it's hot. I'm sure your jobs are a lot more interesting than mine."

"The law is interesting, yes," Fiona says. "Challenging at times. But never boring."

"Well, not often," Marcus adds.

"So how is it being in business together? It's an unusual situation, isn't it?" I say. "I bet there aren't many siblings who could tolerate working together every day."

"It is unusual," Marcus says. "But it works for us."

"Have you got a sister?" Fiona asks. "Or a brother?"

"No," I answer. "Only child."

She glances over at Marcus and widens her eyes, as if to say, *Well, what would he know?*

I find her defensiveness a bit weird, but then all of them seem strange to me, and the three of them together like this have a pretty unique dynamic. They're certainly not like most people I know or would choose to hang out with. My father would call them characters—but not necessarily in a pejorative way. It's just the term he uses when people baffle him. I sip on my beer, smile. "And so how do you guys know Anna?" I ask.

"Oh, we've known each other for ages," Anna says. "Marcus and Fiona did some legal work for my parents and then later for me after they died. We've been close friends for a while now, haven't we?" She puts her hand over Marcus's and squeezes, turns to face Fiona.

"We have," Marcus says.

"We've been through a great deal together," Fiona says. She clears her throat, as if embarrassed even by this very small disclosure.

"And of course we all lived together," Anna says. "Here in the house. Before."

"I didn't know you lived here." I look at Fiona. I'm surprised and genuinely curious. "When was that?"

"We moved out just a few weeks ago," Fiona says.

"No kidding? Why? I mean, why'd you move?"

In an instant, the mood changes from cheerful to somber. There's an extended and uncomfortable silence, weighed down with something dense and unhappy. Anna hunches in on herself, as if she'd like to disappear into the ground.

"Oh. There were reasons," Fiona says. "Things happened. As they do."

Anna nods, stares down at her hands.

"But let's not get into all that," Fiona says, her voice suddenly gruff. "It's a nice day. Why spoil it?"

When lunch is ready Anna insists that we take our plates to the dining room. The table is already set with fancy cutlery and glasses, tablecloth, napkins, flowers in the center. Anna giggles as she suggests where we should sit, and I notice that her speech is slurred slightly, her words tripping over themselves.

When the food is on the table and we've all sat down she gets up again and rushes back to the kitchen. She returns with a bottle of wine.

"I'm driving," Fiona says, putting her hand over her glass.

"Oh, just one more drink," Anna says. "You'll have plenty of time to sober up."

Fiona and Marcus glance at each other.

"We can't stay all afternoon," Marcus says. "Sorry, but we've got to get some work done."

"But it's Sunday," Anna says. "You can't work on Sunday."

"Unfortunate as it is, Anna," Fiona says, "we have obligations to our clients."

I almost laugh at her pompous tone, thinking she must be joking, but when I see Anna's crestfallen face I keep quiet, pick up my knife and fork.

The fish is good—tender and full of flavor—and I devour mine quickly. When I look up I notice that Anna has barely touched her food. She's sitting upright, staring straight ahead. Tears run silently down her face.

"Hey," I say. "Anna? What's up?"

"Oh, everything," she says, lifting her hands, letting them fall onto the table in a hopeless gesture. "Everything. It shouldn't be like this."

Marcus sets his knife and fork down carefully. "Come on," he says to Anna. "Don't cry."

"But I can't stand it," she says, crying so hard now that her shoulders shake. "I miss Ben. I miss him so much I think I might die."

"I know," Marcus says. "I miss him, too."

"I'm going to clean up," Fiona says, standing up. "And then, Marcus, I think we should go. I don't think it's helping, us being here right now." She starts clearing the table, scraping plates, collecting cutlery, making a lot of noise.

I stand up and collect the empty glasses, then escape to the kitchen.

Fiona appears a moment later and together we stack the dishwasher. I fill the sink with water and get started on the pans. Fiona finds a tea towel and dries up. We work silently, while I wonder what's going on. I think the fact that I live with Anna justifies my curiosity, but Fiona's fixed shoulders and tight, pressed lips, her refusal to meet my eye tell me that my questions wouldn't be welcome.

When the kitchen is clean we return to the dining room. Fiona insists that it's time to leave, and the four of us head to the front door.

Anna holds the door open and watches them go. Before they reach their car she runs outside and down the path.

"Please, Marcus," she says, grabbing his hand, forcing him to stop. "Please stay." Her face collapses and she is sobbing again.

"Anna," Fiona says, "calm down. We really do have work to do."

At this Anna only clutches Marcus even more desperately. He stands there, rigid and uncertain, his hands by his sides. He doesn't say anything, doesn't move a muscle, makes no effort to comfort her. Eventually, Anna collapses on the grass and becomes quiet.

Fiona helps Anna get up, persuades her to return inside. "Come on," she says, as they walk past me. "Let's take you up to your room. Get you into bed."

I go into the kitchen, put the kettle on and collect cups, milk, sugar. Marcus follows me in and I keep my back to him as I wait for the kettle to boil.

Soon Fiona joins us.

"Anna's okay now. She's asleep." Fiona ignores the mug of coffee I poured for her and picks up her car keys. "I'll give you my number, Tim. In case you're worried. If you think you need us."

"I might be going out a bit later," I say. I have no definite plans, but I don't want to feel obliged to hang around the house. I shrug. "I mean, I can't really . . ."

"Of course," Fiona says. "You do whatever you need to do. She'll be absolutely fine tonight. She's taken some sleeping pills. She probably won't wake up until morning. But if you could just keep an eye on her for the next few days? Make sure she's okay."

"Tim, how do you think she is?" Marcus says. "Generally? Is there anything you think we should know?"

I hesitate for a minute, afraid of somehow violating Anna's privacy, before deciding that my reticence is stupid. They're old family friends and they obviously care about her. It would be irresponsible not to be straight.

"I've heard her crying at night," I say.

"Crying," Marcus says, nodding. "That's no real surprise."

Fiona smiles, an attempt at being reassuring that only looks forced. "Everything's okay. Really. I know after today you probably feel . . . well, you're probably wondering what you've gotten yourself into. But, honestly, I don't think there's all that much to worry about. Anna's just a bit unhappy right now."

"Is there anything else you wanted to say?" Marcus asks. "You look a bit uncertain, Tim. You can tell us if there's anything worrying you. We're here to help. We don't—"

"Anna's very emotional right now," Fiona interrupts. She sounds strangely unsympathetic, almost scornful. "And her behavior can be a little erratic when she's emotional."

"Right," I say. "Sure. Well, there is this one other thing . . . It's going to sound weird, but I think she might have been in my room the other night. Watching me. I don't know for sure. Anyway, she bolted when I called out. Disappeared. And later she had no idea . . . I mean, the truth is, it was dark as anything and I'd just woken up, so I could have been confused, could have imagined it, but I don't think so. And it felt pretty creepy at the time. Her standing there like that. Freaked me out a bit, to be honest."

"Watching you?" Fiona lifts her eyebrows, glances at Marcus. "Look. Tim. I'm sorry that you . . . Look, here's my number. Call me if you're worried. Or if you think we should come over. Anything."

"Yes. Anything," Marcus says, putting his hand to his chin, rubbing it. "In fact, why don't you give him our email, too, Fiona?" He turns to me. "Sometimes we're in meetings and can't take calls. But one of us is always checking emails."

Part of me balks at the suggestion. At the responsibility it implies. *We hardly even know each other,* I want to protest. But Fiona writes down an email address and I don't object.

As they're leaving I stand in the kitchen and flick the tea towel irritably against the cabinet. I feel as if I've been handed a burden I don't want. It's like being asked to lug a suitcase up a hill without knowing what's inside. I have no real idea what's going on. When I hear the front door open I make a hasty decision and run out to the hall.

"Wait!" I call.

They stop in the doorway.

"I just wanted to ask," I say. "Who is Ben?"

I'm shocked by the look of despair that comes over Marcus's face.

"Ben's dead," he says.

"Ben is none of your business," Fiona adds, her voice brittle. "None of your business at all." And then she turns away, pulling the door shut behind her.

11

She'd known Marcus and Fiona for a while as acquaintances. They'd been to several of her parents' parties over the years, and were mostly noticeable for always going home when everybody else started getting too drunk and wild.

On this particular night Anna had been at a party, but had come home early because she had a headache. As soon as she opened the front door she could hear voices, laughter, the clink of glasses. She planned to slip upstairs, but just as she began tiptoeing down the hallway, her mother's closest friend, Deb, appeared.

"Anna!" She smelt of cigarettes and whisky and her embrace made Anna's skin crawl. Deb was good at pretending to be nice, but in reality she was a snake. A cold-blooded reptile in leopard print. "Come on outside with us and have a drink!"

"I might just go upstairs," Anna said.

"Oh, don't do that," Deb protested, taking Anna's wrist. "Come and say hello. Be sociable."

Anna hesitated, looked towards the staircase with longing.

"Your father's out there," Deb said, her voice loaded with venom. "Enjoying the ladies as usual. Humiliating your poor mother."

Anna often wondered if her father had rejected Deb's advances at some stage. Deb's over-the-top loyalty to Frances had never seemed entirely genuine.

They found Frances in the kitchen pouring champagne. Anna

could tell immediately by the color of her mother's cheeks, the glassy sheen to her eyes, that she'd already had more than a few.

"You're home early," she said, putting her hands on Anna's shoulders and kissing her on both cheeks, the way they did in Europe.

"I thought I might just go up to bed," Anna said.

"Oh, darling, please." Frances sighed. "You can't always go to bed when we've got visitors. Honestly, Anna, you could make a bit of an effort. For your father's sake if not for mine." She picked up a glass of champagne and pressed it into Anna's hand.

Anna went out into the courtyard, where her parents' friends were standing around smoking and drinking and trying to look beautiful. She spotted Marcus and Fiona and went to join them.

Fiona and Marcus made space for her, but conversation didn't flow easily and she was too tired to make any real effort. They stood and smiled awkwardly at each other.

She spotted her father standing next to an attractive woman she didn't recognize. He had his hand on the small of her back and her face was lifted up to his, a coy smile on her lips. Her father couldn't help it if women were attracted to him. He was charming and handsome. Who could blame him for flirting sometimes?

Anna caught his eye and lifted her hand in a wave. He grinned and waved back, made his excuses to the woman, and crossed the courtyard to her side.

Unlike the scratchy and volatile relationship she had with her mother, Anna's relationship with her father was easy and loving. They enjoyed each other's company, made each other happy.

"There you are," he said, bending down to kiss her cheek. "I was wondering if you were going to make an appearance."

She told him about the party she'd been to. The people she'd met. As usual he was interested and engaged. When her mother came to join them, her arms folded across her chest, Anna became immediately self-conscious and what had been an easy conversation became stilted and forced.

The sudden noise of glass shattering made Anna jump.

"Bugger," Marcus said, bending over to pick up the beer bottle he'd dropped on the stone tiles. Anna bent over to help him collect the shards.

"Sorry for frightening you," Marcus said. "You almost jumped a meter high."

"Oh, God, Marcus, you really don't need to apologize," Frances said loudly, getting everyone's attention. "Anna's always been such a nervous girl. She wouldn't even sleep in her own bed until she was twelve. No good for marital relations, I can tell you!" She laughed loudly. "The poor thing used to have terrible nightmares and wander around the house at all hours of the night, half asleep. Once we found her down in the ballroom in the middle of the night. She was crying. Absolutely beside herself. She'd convinced herself that her father had been killed by some kind of monster. It took an hour to wake her properly, set things straight. And he was standing right in front of her!" Frances shook her head and looked around at the group, eyes wide in remembered astonishment. She reached out and ruffled Anna's hair. "I'm afraid Stephen may have overindulged her a bit. Created his own little princess."

"Princess?" Anna echoed, incredulous. "Princess?"

"No?" Frances said. "Not princess. You're right. You're Daddy's precious little flower."

The word *flower* was loaded with years of resentment between her parents, triggered by a small sculpture Stephen had given Anna when she was young. He had made it at one of those business functions—the kind where the team is supposed to bond over some sort of creative activity. It was just a basic flower, bright with red glaze. On the base her father had engraved a message. *For my own little flower! Happy 7th birthday. Love Daddy xx*

Anna had loved it immediately, and had treasured it ever since.

A sudden tide of rage swept aside all the inhibitions that normally kept Anna compliant and agreeable. She stepped closer to her mother. "That's enough," she said, the rage in her voice palpable.

Frances tried to laugh it off, but Anna could see the embarrassment in her eyes—embarrassment and fear—and for a moment she felt drunk with the power of it.

"Why are you such a horrible, jealous person? No wonder Daddy doesn't love you anymore. You can't stand the fact that we get on so well."

"Oh, Anna." Her mother tried to smile. "Obviously that champagne has gone to your head." She put her hand on her chest, and Anna could see the tremble of her fingers. "You always were difficult."

"And you were always a selfish bitch," Anna said, turning on her heel.

She rushed down the hall. She wanted to go up to her room, but there was a couple standing on the landing, kissing, no doubt cheating on their spouses . . . Anna ran back downstairs and out the front door. She paced back and forth in the front garden, her thoughts racing, her fists clenched by her sides. Why did her mother always have to goad her? Push her buttons? Why couldn't she just leave her alone?

It wasn't until she'd calmed down and stepped onto the front porch that Anna realized she'd left her key inside. There was no way she was going to knock. She'd have to wait for someone to leave.

She went back to the garden and sat on the grass beneath a tree. It was getting dark, and nobody would see her there unless they looked carefully.

It wasn't long before she heard voices at the door, and saw Marcus and Fiona leaving.

"That was so weird," Fiona said, after the door had closed and they were walking down the front path.

"Wasn't it?" Marcus said.

"I always thought they were the perfect family," Fiona said. "I had no idea things were so tense."

Anna felt her face burn with shame.

"I felt so sorry for Anna. Imagine your mother telling a story like that. In front of all those people, too."

As they drew closer Anna cleared her throat, letting them know she was there.

Fiona stopped, her hand flying to her mouth. Marcus swore.

Anna stood up. She was glad of the dark because she was certain her face was red.

"Sorry," she said. "I locked myself out."

Marcus recovered first. "Oh, do you want us to—"

"No," she interrupted. "I don't really want to see anyone. Don't worry. I'll go back inside later."

"We can't just leave you out here all alone," Marcus said in his funny formal way.

Anna laughed. "Better off out here than in there anyway. I'll find a way to sneak back eventually."

Fiona stepped towards her. "Why don't you come back with us for a while? We're only in Cremorne."

"Fiona," Marcus said. "I don't think Anna—"

"But why not?" Fiona insisted. "She could end up sitting out here for hours. May as well be comfortable at our house. She doesn't want to go back inside, tail between her legs, and I don't blame her." She turned to Anna. "What do you think?"

It was a surprising and strange invitation—not at all what Anna would have expected. But her headache was gone and the argument with her mother had filled her with restless energy. Even if she did manage to get back inside without being seen, there was no way she'd be able to sleep anytime soon.

"I think it's a very good idea," she said. "Thank you."

They drank whisky and stayed up till early in the morning. It was Anna who did most of the talking. She talked and talked. She told them about her childhood, about her stormy relationship with her mother, stuff she'd never told anyone before.

"I feel sorry for my father," she told them. "Mum is always mad about something. Always making wild accusations. She's insanely jealous."

"Jealous? Of what?"

"Oh, she always thinks he's cheating. But he's not. He wouldn't. Not that anyone would blame him if he did. Putting up with her all this time."

Marcus was quiet, but sympathetic. Fiona asked question after question. Never once did Anna feel she was boring them. Eventually Marcus said goodnight, explaining that he needed to get some sleep.

"You should probably stay over," Fiona said to Anna. "It's too late to go home now."

Fiona lent her a nightie and toothbrush, took her to the spare bedroom and said goodnight. As Anna slipped between the clean sheets she felt as if she'd been liberated from some kind of prison, albeit one largely of her own imagining. Her mother's emotional hold over her had been like a cell with an unlocked door. She'd only had to push the door open and walk through to be free.

If only that sense of freedom had lasted. If only she'd had a chance to enjoy it. But now her prison has closed in on her, it's an even smaller cell, without windows or light, a prison with a tightly locked door that can never be opened, no matter how hard she pushes.

12

Not long after Fiona and Marcus have left, I get a call from Dad.

"Sorry, mate, but do you think you'd be able to come in tonight? Liam can't make it. Fell off his bike and hurt his wrist. I wouldn't ask, but we're fully booked." Normally I hate being asked to work on my day off, but today the idea of going to the restaurant doesn't seem so bad. Better than hanging around the house with Anna. I get ready to go, then knock softly on Anna's bedroom door.

"Hey, Anna," I call through the door. "I'm just heading off to work. Hope you're okay. Call me if you need anything."

I wait but she doesn't respond.

"Okay. See ya," I say.

The restaurant is booked out for an anniversary party. They're not arriving until seven, so when I get there at five I cook an early meal for the staff so we can eat before the rush of customers. I grill up some fish and make a big bowl of salad and another huge one of chips, then we all sit down with glasses of cold lemonade and Coke.

"So, how's it going up at the house?" Blake asks as he shoves chips into his mouth. "Did you ask the girl about the painting? Did she remember me?"

"Anna," I say. "Don't think so. Not sure. She didn't say much."

"What's that?" Dad asks, looking from Blake to me.

I explain about Blake painting the house.

"So you've met Anna, then?" Dad asks Blake.

"Yeah," Blake says. "Nice girl."

"A lot has happened to her since then," I say. "I think she's changed a fair bit. I mean, she's still nice, just a bit quiet these days. Her parents died, for one thing. And someone else close to her died, too. Some bloke called Ben."

"No kidding? Her parents died?" Blake shakes his head. "That's too bad. What was her mother's name again?"

"Dunno," I say.

"And who's Ben?" Dad asks.

"I think he must have been Anna's boyfriend. But I don't know for sure," I explain. "I don't actually know who he is or how he died. I just know he died."

Dad looks at me curiously. "And how do you know that?"

"Because." I frown, trying to think of the best way to explain it. "Anna had some friends over earlier and they told me. I mean, they told me Ben was dead without actually saying who he was. If that makes sense."

"How?" Dad asks.

"How what?"

"How did he die?"

"I told you," I say irritably. "I don't *know*."

"Hey, you guys," Jo says slowly, looking around the table. "Do you remember the story that was in the papers a few years ago? That horrible car crash? A tractor trailer lost control coming down some hill and ran up the back of a car. Totally crushed it."

"Don't remember it," I say.

"This rich couple were killed. And the papers went on and on about their daughter being left all alone. 'Poor little rich girl' they called her. Orphan Annie. It was really sensational coverage. I remember my mum saying it was exploitative," Jo says. "They put photos of her parents in the paper and then these stupid pictures of her looking really sad. Do you think that was your Anna, Tim?"

"Maybe," I say. "Could have been."

"God. The poor thing. Imagine having to put up with that kind of crap."

"And that would help explain things," Blake says. "Why she's changed. Why she's so quiet now."

"It would, wouldn't it?" Jo says, stabbing her fork into a piece of fish. "What a shit situation. Both your parents gone and then your boyfriend dies. She must feel so lonely, so ripped off by life."

"Yeah," I say. "It's all pretty full-on."

I find Anna in the kitchen early the next morning. She's sitting at the table, a mug in front of her. She looks tired, pale, unhappy. She glances up as I walk in and I get the sense she's been waiting for me.

"I'm sorry about yesterday," she says immediately.

I put the kettle on, get myself a mug. "You don't have to apologize," I say.

"Yes, I do. I was an idiot." She puts her hand on her forehead. "I think I had too much beer."

I don't answer until I've made a coffee and sat at the table opposite her.

"First of all," I say, "you didn't behave like an idiot. There's nothing wrong with being sad. And secondly"—I take a breath, smile—"you can blame the beer if you want but it's obvious there's something else going on. There's clearly something wrong."

"Something wrong," she says wearily. "That's an understatement."

"Yep," I say. "I get that." I don't want to be too pushy or ask too many direct questions. Anna's so nervy and on edge—one wrong move and I'm scared she'll flee. I'm pretty sure her sadness is mostly about Ben, but Marcus and Fiona's strange anger yesterday makes me reluctant to ask about him. The whole topic just seems far too volatile. For the time being, at least, bringing up the death of her parents seems like a safer option. "Can I just ask you something?" I say, watching her face carefully. "What happened to your mum and dad? I mean, I know they both died in some kind of accident. But what happened?"

She stares down at the table for a second and I think I've blown it, but when she looks up and speaks, her gaze is direct.

"It was a car accident. A tractor trailer lost control coming down Mona Vale Road one night. Ran them down."

So Jo had been right about the couple in the news. I don't mention what I've heard.

"That sucks," I say. "You must miss them."

She takes so long to reply that I feel sure she's too upset to speak, but eventually she sighs.

"I miss my father," she says. "I miss him every day."

I'm silent.

"I've shocked you," she says.

"Nope. Not really. I guess your mother wasn't perfect, then?"

"Maybe I wasn't the perfect daughter."

"I think there's more obligation on the parents to get things right," I say firmly. "Not to be perfect, necessarily, but at least not to fuck it all up."

"I guess," she says. She stares over my shoulder towards the garden. "We had a big argument shortly before she died. We hadn't talked properly for a week. I said some terrible things. I called her a bitch. And then she was dead."

"Oh," I say. "I'm sure you—"

She continues as if I haven't spoken. "Before she died I wished she'd go away. For ages I'd been thinking about it, wishing for it. I just wanted her out of my life. And then she was gone. Permanently." She blinks, looks down. "You know what they say—be careful what you wish for."

"Yeah, but wishing for things doesn't make them happen. I mean, it's not your fault." I blunder on. "People don't just die because somebody wishes they weren't around. They just don't. You can't blame yourself. You can't—"

"Look," she interrupts. And now she looks at me directly, speaks firmly, and I see a surprising flash of anger. "You seem like a very nice person and I don't want to be rude, but there's something I should say. You're just my housemate, someone to share the place with. Don't assume you can help me. Not in that way."

She puts her cup on the table and pushes her chair back. Before I have a chance to say another word, she stands up and leaves the room.

13

She leaves Tim sitting at the table and rushes upstairs, straight to the attic. Tim is too easy to talk to. It's something in his face: the soft hazel of his eyes, the childlike spatter of freckles across his nose, the hesitant smile he wears when he asks questions. It's impossible to believe that someone with a face like that could hold any malice, or be judgmental, and it's so tempting to blurt everything out to him, tell him every heartbreaking detail, every black thing that's ever happened, and let him ponder and probe the dark places she doesn't dare investigate on her own.

14

I get home from work later that night and find the house in darkness. It's well past midnight and though I'm physically buggered, I'm still mentally pumped from another busy night at work. I need a few beers, an hour in front of the TV, something mindless to watch—and with Anna presumably already in bed it's the perfect opportunity to have the living room to myself. I open the beer I've brought home with me from the restaurant and spread myself out on the couch. I flick lazily through the channels.

I must have dozed off, because suddenly I'm jolted awake by a loud, repetitive banging.

As I sit up the noise stops. Disoriented, I wonder if I really heard it, or if some kind of sharp noise from the TV filtered into my dreams. I turn off the TV, check the time on my phone.

It's almost three A.M.

The pounding starts again. Loud and urgent. The front door.

Shit.

As I stand up, the pounding continues. Deafening. Insistent. A feeling of dread grips me, making my skin go cold. I swallow and shout, "Okay, okay. Hold on a minute!," trying to sound as though I'm not frightened, as though my heart isn't beating frantically and all the blood isn't draining from my face.

I look around the room for some kind of weapon, and settle on a large ceramic bookend. It's heavy enough to do some damage.

"Who's there?" I call through the door. "What do you want?"

There's no answer, only three more knocks, so heavy I feel the floor shudder beneath my feet.

I clutch the bookend tightly in my fist, unlock the door, open it. There's nobody there.

I flick the outside light but it doesn't come on.

"Hello?" I shout. "Who's there? What the hell do you want?"

I don't expect an answer, and I don't get one. I put down the bookend and step out onto the porch, peering into the garden to see if anyone's hiding, but it's far too dark to tell. The massive old trees cast deep shadows, which from here look like dense pits of black. The streetlights don't help at all.

Kids, I conclude. Probably drunk. Making trouble, playing tricks on people. Me and my mates used to think it was fun doing stuff like that.

I peer again into the bushes, but it's hopeless, I can't see a thing. I'd need a strong torch to see any farther than a few meters, and anyway, I'm sure that whoever it was is long gone.

"If you do it again I'll call the police," I call out to nobody, feeling stupid. And then I turn around to go back inside.

The front door is swinging shut.

"Shit." I rush forward, hands reaching out to stop it, but I'm too late. The door slams shut in my face. I twist the handle and push against it. It's locked.

"Fuck." I rummage in my pockets in case I left the key in my pants. I don't find it, but I do notice how shaky and clumsy my hands are. I take a deep breath, tell myself to calm down. The door must have swung shut. A stupid mistake. *My* mistake. No big deal.

I go around the side of the house towards the back, checking windows as I go. It's hard to see in the dark and I trip and stumble and curse under my breath. I can't fucking believe it. I can't believe I've let myself get locked out at three in the morning. I laugh miserably at my own stupidity. I'm so tired I could curl up on the grass and sleep, and I'm considering it as a serious option, perhaps my only option, when I reach the back of the house and see light coming from the kitchen. The French doors are both open, and light spills out onto the courtyard.

"Hello?" I step inside, look around. The kitchen is empty.

I close and lock the doors, pushing against them firmly to ensure they're properly locked.

Did Anna leave them open before she went to bed? Seems unlikely. And I'm sure the lights weren't on before. The house was completely dark when I got home.

Is someone in the house?

I see a shape in the window, a face reflected in the glass. I whip around, a grunt of fear escaping my lips.

Nothing. There's nobody there.

I let out a relieved laugh—it was my own reflection. I'm letting my imagination get out of control. I'm beyond tired, freaking out over nothing.

A bunch of kids knocked on the door and ran away. I locked myself out. Anna left the back doors open. Nothing sinister or strange at all. I just need a decent night's sleep.

I turn the kitchen lights off and head back into the hall.

The front door is wide open.

15

I know I won't be getting any more sleep tonight. I turn the kitchen lights back on and make myself a strong mug of coffee; try to make myself calmer by pretending it's morning.

I take my coffee and go through each downstairs room, one by one. I call out, turn lights on, check behind sofas and curtains. The whole exercise feels a bit stupid and pointless—I don't think anyone is in the house. Not now. But I don't want to go to bed and I need to do something with the adrenaline coursing through my veins.

I go upstairs to my bedroom. It's empty, exactly as I left it when I went to work.

I go through the other bedrooms as well, checking under beds, in cupboards. When I get to the bedroom nearest Anna's, I hear something through the door. A soft, continuous keening noise. It makes the hair on the back of my neck stand on end.

I open the door.

She's crouched on the floor in the corner, her knees pulled up to her chest. Her arms are wrapped around her legs, and her face is buried. She's moaning and crying, muttering something over and over, rocking back and forth.

"Anna?"

I enter quietly, afraid to scare her. I crouch down in front of her and put my hand on her knee.

"Hey."

She stops crying and becomes still for the briefest moment before starting up again. Crying and rocking. Back and forth.

I speak louder. "Anna, are you okay?"

She doesn't respond. Doesn't stop moving. I wait there for a moment, not sure what to do, before deciding I should try to help her up, get her to bed. It's cold in here and she's wearing a very thin-looking pair of pajamas.

"Sorry," I say, hooking my hands beneath her arms. "But I'm going to help you back to your room. I think you're just . . ." I fade off. I don't exactly know what I think. Do I think she's having some kind of breakdown? A bad dream? Do I think she's been running around the house knocking on doors? Locking me out?

I lift her with surprising ease. She's as light as a feather and she doesn't resist. When she's standing she raises her head and looks up at me, blinking, her expression docile.

"Did you hear him?" she asks.

"Hear who?"

"Ben," she says.

I shake my head and put my hand on her back, lead her out of the room, across the hall. When we reach her bed she sighs, climbs in and pulls the blankets up. She turns onto her side and shuts her eyes.

"Okay," I say quietly, not sure if she's even aware of my presence, if she was ever fully awake. "You're okay now. Everything's fine."

I flick the light off and am about to close the door when her voice rings out, sad and small in the darkness.

"He was here. Ben. I heard him. He needed me. I was so happy. I thought he'd come back home. I thought he'd come back to give me a second chance."

16

Though I keep an eye out, I don't see Anna around the house for the rest of the day. I hear footsteps upstairs at lunchtime and I race up, only to see her slip into the attic, closing the door behind her. By the time I'm ready to leave for work I've decided I should find her and check that she's okay, try to suss out what was going on last night.

Her bedroom door is open, the room empty. I knock on the attic door and hear footsteps crossing the floor above me, then clumping down the stairs. The door opens. Anna's eyes are bloodshot, her skin pale. She looks unwell. She also looks openly annoyed.

"Sorry. I'm just leaving for work," I say. I smile. "Are you okay?"

"Absolutely fine," she says abruptly. If she remembers anything about last night, she's not giving it away.

"O-kay," I say. "Um. I . . . about last night. I—"

"Did you want something specific?" she interrupts.

Her expression is so hostile it seems suddenly impossible to bring up what happened.

"Right," I say, now annoyed myself. "Fine. I just thought you might need something from the shops. The fridge is a bit empty. I thought maybe—"

"No," she interrupts. "Thanks. I don't need a thing." She steps back into the attic, as if she can't wait for me to go.

"Cool," I say. "No worries. I'll leave you to it, then."

She nods, then closes the door without saying another word.

17

It was a week after the argument with her mother when Fiona rang to invite her over for lunch.

Marcus cooked, they ate pasta and salad, then afterwards they walked to a nearby cinema to see an afternoon film.

"Hey, how's it going with your mother?" Fiona asked. "Any more dramas?"

"Not really," Anna said. "No dramas. But she's not exactly speaking to me."

"But you're okay?" Fiona linked her arm through Anna's, pulled her closer.

"Yes. I'm fine. I just wish she'd stop being so pathetic." Anna laughed. "I sometimes have these fantasies where she leaves me and my dad."

Fiona frowned.

"You think I'm terrible now, don't you?" Anna said, squeezing Fiona's arm, glancing across at Marcus, who had his eyes on the ground. "You think I'm selfish and ungrateful."

"Not at all," Fiona said. "Sometimes parents can be hopeless. I completely understand."

After the movie, Fiona drove her home. In the car they discussed the film, the characters and plot. Fiona dropped her outside the house and promised to ring her in a few days. Anna waited by the side of the road and watched Fiona's car get smaller and smaller as she drove away.

———

That night she was startled awake by a gentle knock on her bed-room door.

"Anna? Anna?" Her neighbor, Pat, was standing at the foot of her bed.

Anna pushed her covers off, stood up immediately.

"What are you doing here?" She wrapped her arms around her-self, feeling suddenly frightened. "What is it?"

Pat looked terrible. "You'd better come with me, darling," she said, taking Anna's arm. "There's something—"

"Something what?"

"There's been an accident."

When they got downstairs she found the house weirdly busy. Every light was on, and there were two policemen in the kitchen. Anna was surprised when she looked at the wall clock to see that it was only just past midnight.

"What are all these people doing here?" she asked. "Where's Daddy? What's happened? Where's Mum?"

The rest of it was a blur. An officer came and crouched beside her, told her that her parents had been in a car accident earlier that eve-ning. Her mother had died instantly. Her father was in critical condi-tion in hospital. A coma.

On the day of her mother's funeral she howled, surprised by the depth of her grief, the way she longed for her mother.

"I'm so sorry so sorry so sorry," she chanted in her head as the curtains closed over the coffin.

Her father lived for three more weeks and all day long, every day, Anna sat by his bedside in the hospital and willed him to wake up. To live. To stay with her.

"You can't leave me, too," she told him, pressing her face against his still-warm chest. "Don't you dare. I won't let you. I won't."

The day he died she went back to the big, empty house alone. She went straight to her bedroom and picked up the ceramic flower her father had made for her. She curled up in a fetal position on her bed, the flower clutched tightly in her hands, and wept.

18

When I wake the next day it's pouring, and the sky is overcast. It's probably warm outside, humid and sticky, but inside it's cool. I pull on a T-shirt, a pair of jeans and thick socks to keep my feet warm, then head downstairs.

What I find there makes my heart pound.

The kitchen is a mess. Every cupboard door, every drawer, is open. Plates have been thrown on the floor, and shards of crockery are scattered everywhere. Pots and pans and lids litter the entire floor and, judging from the marks on the walls, they were thrown with force. The fridge door is open and jars of food have shattered against the walls and floor, leaving disgusting smears and dangerous slivers of glass everywhere.

This is deliberate. The work of someone in a mad frenzy. Someone very, very disturbed.

I run through the rest of the downstairs rooms, looking for evidence of a break-in, but everything is intact and in its place. The doors are locked tight. I run upstairs to Anna's room and knock loudly on her door.

"Anna? Anna? Are you in there?"

"Tim?"

I open her door. She sits up and pushes her hair back from her face. She looks and sounds annoyed. "What is it?"

"The kitchen," I say, and I don't mean it, but my voice comes out sounding harsh, accusing.

"What about it?"

"Come down and take a look."

She follows behind me. When she sees the mess she takes a step back, puts her hand over her mouth.

"Oh, my God," she says.

"What happened?"

She looks at me, looks back at the mess, shakes her head. She starts to cry. "I don't know. I have no idea."

For a minute I almost believe her. She looks so genuinely startled and afraid, and it's not too hard to imagine that someone else broke in and did this, someone with some kind of ax to grind, or just some random, drug-fucked freak. But there's no sign of forced entry—no broken windows, no jimmied doors.

"I didn't do it," she insists.

"Then who did?" I say quietly, turning away before she can see the doubt in my eyes.

19

The thing is, she can't remember.

Her memories of last night are all a bit of a blur, but she knows she was distraught, desperate with anxiety, frustration, self-loathing.

The day had started badly. She slept in, waking around midday feeling groggy and drained. And she felt distinctly miserable, even worse than usual, on the brink of tears. She went straight up to the attic with a mug of tea, then sat in the big old armchair that used to be her father's and let the tears spill over. She let herself cry until her head ached and her eyes stung.

In the afternoon, after Tim had gone to work, she left the attic and went to the kitchen. She searched the fridge. Milk, cheese, eggs, ham, a half-empty bottle of Coke. There was a loaf of yesterday's bread in the pantry. Tim was good at making sure there was always something in the house. But she didn't want a sandwich, she didn't want eggs. She wanted a big bowl of soup and fresh, crusty bread.

The more she imagined the soup the larger the idea of it became in her head. She not only wanted it, she needed it. It was such a reasonable thing to want, why couldn't she have it?

She found her purse, put her shoes on. She would go to the shops; simply walk outside, turn towards Manly and walk down to the supermarket. No big deal.

She went out the front door, pulling it shut behind her and walked down the path, towards the gate. If she went quickly enough, without thinking, she'd make it. She'd get there. She wouldn't vomit or cry or collapse in a breathless heap on the floor, wouldn't have to be a prisoner to her own fears.

She made it to the gate and started along the footpath towards Manly. She walked quickly at first, head down, determined, concentrating only on the movement of her feet against the footpath, trying to ignore the black knot of fear that was unraveling in her mind. But with each step, her breathing got more strained. Her heart started to pound, her hands to tremble and sweat.

She felt her stomach churn, her bowels twist. Her heart was beating so fast. She looked around her in panic, terrified that she'd be noticed. If someone offered her help right now, or asked if she was okay, she'd be unable to answer. Being seen would only make things worse. She would die of humiliation.

She turned her face to the sky, squeezing her eyes shut to hold back the tears. She could see a weak patch of sunshine through the clouds, through her eyelids; she could see the red of her own blood. It was such a benign afternoon, and there was so obviously nothing to be afraid of out here . . . She tried to breathe: in and out, in and out, in and out. It was no good. She was pathetic, weak, hopeless. She turned around and headed back to the house, almost running the last ten meters to the front door.

Once she got inside she went to the kitchen, found the box of pills she kept in the cabinet above the fridge. She took four Valium with a sip of Coke from the bottle in the fridge. The label said to take one, two at most, but she needed this to work. She closed the fridge door and pressed her back against it, let herself sink to the floor. She wept noisily into her hands.

When she became too uncomfortable and sore, she got up. The Valium had dulled the sharpest edges, but she wanted more. She found some vodka in the pantry cupboard and swigged from the bottle. It burned her throat and made her gasp.

She paced the hall, back and forth, back and forth, then went into the living room and turned on the television, but she couldn't sit still. In the kitchen, she buttered a piece of bread, placing some ham and a slice of cheese on top. After three hasty bites she threw the rest in the bin. Her stomach was knotted, closed up tight, and food was intolerable. She drank some more vodka and went back to wandering the house. As the hours ticked by she started feeling worse, angrier, until she was overcome with an unbearable sense of powerlessness, a conviction of her own irrelevance. She could die and who would really care?

She can't remember much more. She remembers being in the bathroom. Staring at herself in the mirror, weeping.

"I didn't do it," she tells him.

But even as the words are coming from her mouth she can see he doesn't believe her. He turns away, mutters something. His cheeks grow red.

He blushes because he thinks she's lying. He's embarrassed for her. That's the kind of person he is.

20

It doesn't take as long to clean up the mess as I thought. We sweep all the broken plates and glass into a thick bin bag, wipe down the surfaces. Anna brings an armful of towels. We use them to dry the benchtops, the cabinet doors, getting down on our hands and knees to dry the floor.

When we've finished, the kitchen is immaculate and we're both sweating and puffed with exertion.

"We could have some breakfast," I say, collapsing onto a chair, looking at Anna properly for the first time since we started cleaning. "But we don't actually have any food. Or any plates to put it on, for that matter."

"We could have coffee," she says. "I saw some unbroken mugs still in the cupboard."

I make coffee, sit opposite Anna. I'm surprised to see that she's crying.

She tries to hide it. She blinks, looks away, picks up her mug and puts it to her lips.

"Are you okay?"

"I'm just sad," she says eventually. "Very, very sad."

When we've finished our coffee I go up to my room. I'm tired from the events of the past few days, the late nights and disturbed sleep, and I collapse across my bed, close my eyes. I think about Anna smashing up the kitchen. I try to envisage the scene in my mind: a crazed look on her face, eyes wild, throwing things in an insane frenzy. She seems so timid and restrained, so lacking in vital force, that it's hard to imagine her summoning up the required passion for such an act. And that in itself is alarming. Am I living with some kind of psychopath?

Should I be worried?

For the first time, I wonder if I should pack my things and go. Maybe I should have taken more notice when Fiona told me it was okay if I wanted to move out. I should have at least used it as an opportunity to ask a few questions. I should have asked why she felt the need to warn me like that.

Despite my fatigue it's impossible to sleep so I get up, sit at my desk. I click on to the Internet, intending to google agoraphobia to find out whether Anna's strange behavior is some kind of symptom, but find myself logging into Facebook. I torture myself for a minute by looking through Lilla's photos and am startled when a message from her appears in the little chat box at the bottom of the screen.

Hey Tim! Watcha doin' on Facebook? Thought you hated it!

I feel as embarrassed as I would if she'd walked in and busted me. The only dignified response I can think of is to muddy the water with the truth.

Staring at photos of you, of course. What else?

Ha, ha. I knew it. Well, TO EACH HIS OWN. (You big freak.) Hey, anyway, I was thinking. Got some free time tomorrow morning? Catch the ferry into the city with me on my way to work?

Ferry? What happened to your car?

It's in the garage for a few days. Nothing terminal. So, what do
you think? We could have coffee in town and talk about your
birthday party.

What birthday party? I'm not having a party!

Let's talk about it tomorrow. We'll need to catch the 7:30 ferry,
so you need to be at Manly Wharf at 7:15. Don't be late! xoxoxox

I remember my promise to keep in contact with Fiona and Marcus and open my email. I send a note explaining what has happened
over the past few days—Anna crying and confused at night, the
trashed kitchen. I try to keep it brief, my tone as calm and matter-of-
fact as I can. I already feel like a jerk writing to Anna's friends behind her back, I don't want to make things worse by sounding
melodramatic.

Fiona responds within minutes.

Thanks for letting us know, Tim. Do you think we should call a
doctor up to the house?

I'm not sure. I don't feel in a position to answer that question.
You should probably decide. You know more about this than I do.
To be honest I'm starting to feel a bit uncomfortable with this
whole situation—me emailing you behind Anna's back.

Okay. Thanks, Tim. And we understand your hesitation but please
don't worry about contacting us. We only have Anna's best
interests at heart!

21

When her father died, Fiona and Marcus stepped in to help. Fiona organized the funeral and wake—she made the phone calls, drove Anna to appointments, arranged flowers and food. Marcus sorted out the will and finances, made sure Anna had immediate access to her inheritance and to the title on the property.

After the funeral they started coming to the house several times a week. Sometimes Marcus would call in on his way home from work. He'd have a beer or a coffee, tell Anna about his day, make sure she was okay. Fiona would come for morning or afternoon tea and they'd sit in the kitchen and talk. At weekends they'd walk down to Manly and go to a movie.

Her old friends came to visit, too, but suddenly their preoccupations didn't match hers. She didn't want to go to nightclubs, didn't want to watch second-rate bands and get drunk. She started making up reasons why she couldn't go out.

At weekends Fiona and Marcus came to the house together. The two of them would cook for her, they'd spend hours playing board games or watching movies. They'd stay so late they'd often end up sleeping over, taking a room each. Anna would go to bed on those nights feeling safe and content. She'd lie back and listen to the noises they made as they got ready for bed, the rush of water from a tap, the creak of floorboards, the flush of a toilet, and feel comforted and less alone. It was nice having them around. It was good to wake up to the sound of other people, the smell of toast and coffee coming from the kitchen.

In a way it made perfect sense, their developing friendship. They actually had a lot in common. Like Anna, Marcus and Fiona were basically alone in the world. They had no extended family, no relatives.

Anna treasured their relationship, she felt protected and cared for and understood.

One Saturday night she tried to get them to talk about their childhood.

"You know, you guys know all about me, but I know hardly anything about you."

She noticed Marcus glance at Fiona. He cleared his throat. "Perhaps another time," he said.

"Please," she said. "It's okay. Whatever happened, you can tell me."

Fiona's face closed over. She stood up so abruptly that her chair nearly tipped over. Anna could see her hands trembling. Her voice, when it finally came, was artificially bright. "Oh. Look at the time! We really have to go now. Thank you for dinner, Anna."

And there was nothing Anna could say that would persuade her to stay, nothing she could do that would remove the stony look from Fiona's eyes.

The next few days were torturous. Fiona wouldn't answer Anna's calls or respond to her texts. Anna went to their house on the Monday but nobody answered the door. She thought their friendship, which had come to mean the world to her, was over. But Marcus turned up on Wednesday evening with a bottle of whisky. They sat at the kitchen table and drank a shot each in near silence before he started to talk.

"I know people wonder about me and Fiona," he said. "They wonder why we're so close. Most siblings our age don't share a house, or work together the way we do. We had a miserable childhood. I told you once, didn't I?"

Anna nodded. "Yes," she said. "I know your dad wasn't around. That your mum got in trouble with the police a lot."

"We lived with our grandmother," Marcus explained. "Mum just dropped us off for a visit one day and never came back. Fiona was four and I was two. Grandma didn't want us, she made that clear from the beginning. And when you're a kid there's nothing worse than not being wanted. We assumed that she'd eventually abandon us, too." He spoke mechanically. He clearly saw the whole conversation as excruciating, but necessary. She had to resist the urge to tell him not to worry, to leave it all unsaid.

"We were always anxious," he continued. "We worried that we might come home from school one day and find that Grandma had moved out. Or that she might have changed the locks so we couldn't get in. And she played on our fears. Every second thing she said was some kind of complaint about money, how much we cost her, how wicked and selfish we were." He laughed bitterly. "Other kids at school complained about not getting enough toys for Christmas. We spent the whole Christmas break trying to lie low so Grandma wouldn't notice us, because if she did, we'd get an earful about how hard the year had been, how much we'd sucked out of her, how ungrateful we were, stuff like that. We learned never to expect anything, or ask for anything. We learned to keep quiet and keep ourselves to ourselves."

Anna knew how much it was costing Marcus to tell her this. He was a proud and private man, and she was flattered that he trusted her enough to be so frank. He hated drama and he would hate even more to be pitied.

"Fiona used to have these dreams that Mum would come and get us," Marcus went on. "That secretly she wanted us and was saving money, building a house so she could fit us in. I had to remind her that it was Mum who'd left us there. Being reminded of the truth used to make Fiona so angry and upset. She'd make up stories about poisoning Grandma." He smiled, shook his head. "We did have some

Chicago Public Library
Harold Washington Library C
3/4/2015   3:33:30 PM
-Patron Receipt-

ITEMS BORROWED:

1:
Title: Sweet damage : a novel /
Item #: R0442913861
Due Date: 3/25/2015

-Please retain for your records-

LSIM5

fun with those stories, imagining her dead and us living in the house alone. Never going to school, eating chocolate biscuits for dinner every night. The best fun we ever had involved nasty fantasies about Grandma."

"She sounds terrible." Anna suppressed a shudder.

"Anyway, the truth is that when I think about it now I can almost understand why she was so mean all the time. Being lumped with two kids when you're already sixty-three wouldn't exactly be the biggest joy in the world. I've been able to get over my bitterness in a way. Move on a bit."

"And Fiona?" Anna asked. "Does she feel the same?"

"Not quite. She's still very bitter—as you saw on Saturday night. The whole thing upsets her so much. She can't really talk about it. It's understandable, though. You see, it was much easier for me than it was for Fiona. It didn't matter to me that I didn't have nice stuff. The boys didn't really care that I wore my school shorts on the week-end, or if my shoes had holes in them. The girls did notice, though, and they were much crueller. And I had something else that Fiona didn't have. I had her. An older sibling. She looked after me, made me feel safe. Fiona had nobody to do that for her. Home was miser-able, school was a social disaster. She never learned to trust anyone."

"That's so sad," Anna said.

"Yes," Marcus agreed. "Anyway, I wanted to explain things to you. So that you understood what was going on the other night. Fiona's embarrassed about her behavior, and very sorry." He lifted his hand, palm out, when she started to object. "Still, I think it would be much better if you didn't say anything. Don't mention the war, so to speak. She'll be over it soon. We'll just forget it ever happened."

"Of course," she said.

"It must seem odd to you at times, the fact that Fiona and I spend so much time together?"

"No." She shook her head. "I've never really thought about it." And it was true, she'd been too busy enjoying their company to question things.

"You see, Fiona and I have this history in common that nobody else can quite understand. I'm still the only person who really gets her. I'm the only person she can count on to care about her." He frowned deeply. "I don't know how she'd get by without me. Or I without her."

I care, Anna wanted to insist. *I care, too.* But she kept it to herself. She would have plenty of time to prove herself.

22

I don't sleep well that night. I'm in bed before midnight for a change, but every noise, every creak and groan of the house, has me sitting up in bed, heart racing. I'm too wired to sleep, every cell alert and ready to react. I hear a faint, repetitive banging in the hallway and jump out of bed and switch on the light, my fists raised defensively, only to find it's the bathroom blind being blown against the windowsill. At around two A.M. I give up, go downstairs to the living room and watch the second half of a foreign crime movie on SBS. The effort of reading the subtitles makes my eyes ache and I doze off, waking with a start when a gun goes off on-screen.

I go back upstairs and toss and turn restlessly for a couple of hours, only properly falling asleep when the sun has started to rise and I no longer feel intimidated by the dark. I get up reluctantly at twenty to seven when my phone alarm goes off.

Only Lilla could convince me to sacrifice sleep for such an early-morning trip into the city. A pointless ferry ride.

I have a quick coffee in the kitchen standing up, leaning against the bench. I look out at the sky, the clouds moving across it, forming shapes and visions, illusions. I remember the first time I went in a plane as a kid, being so disappointed at the way the clouds seemed to dissolve into nothing as the plane flew through them. Up close they had no substance at all.

It's already hot outside, and I feel immediately enveloped by the humidity, as if somebody has thrown a damp blanket over me. I walk down to Manly, arrive five minutes early and wait for Lilla, who is, typically, late.

I've caught the Manly ferry into the city hundreds of times, but I've never done it in peak hour before and I'm surprised at the crowds of people getting on, the push and crush of bodies, the grim faces, the boring work clothes. The general mood of miserable resignation reminds me why I've never wanted this kind of life.

"I feel like we've teleported to London," I say to Lilla, as we move slowly along with the crowd.

"You haven't even been to London, you dick," she says. "It's just people going to work, Tim. It's what people do. They grow up. Get real jobs."

"Whatever." I shrug. I'm not in the mood for an argument about my choice of occupation. It's okay for Lilla. She's always known she wanted to do something with art. She studied fine arts at uni and though she didn't ever finish her degree it still helped her score a job with an acquisitions firm in the city. It's only a secretarial position at the moment—but Lilla's nothing if not ambitious and I believe her when she tells me she'll climb her way to the top. Lilla's one of those rare, lucky people. She knows what she wants. Not all of us are that certain.

We board the ferry and she drags me up and outside, to the bow. It's less crowded out there. I guess it's too windy for the office types. We go and stand right at the front, holding on to the railing.

"I hope it's rough between the Heads," she says. "I love it when it tips to the side and everyone gets scared."

But the water is calm and the ferry moves smooth and slow. I can feel the sun on my face, my arms, little prickles of heat on my skin. It's going to be a scorcher of a day.

"Aren't you glad you came?" Lilla grins at me.

"It's just a ferry ride," I say, shaking my head. But I am glad. I always enjoy the ferry—the lazy way it moves through the water, the half hour of suspended time with nothing to do but stare out at the view, the small private boats, the other ferries going past on their way back to Manly. Lilla waves at every boat that passes us, both her arms stretched out straight and high, a big happy grin on her face. For someone who likes to pretend she's so cool, she certainly knows how to act like a dopey little kid.

"So, how's it going at the house?" she asks.

"Pretty good," I say. "Apart from all the weird stuff."

"Weird stuff?"

She's interested, as I knew she would be. Her eyes go wide and she drags me over to a seat.

"Tell me *everything*," she says.

I don't tell her everything—partly out of a vague sense of protectiveness towards Anna, partly a bitter reluctance to always let Lilla have what she wants. I share just enough to explain my unease. My confusion.

I don't tell her about Anna's agoraphobia, or her parents, or what little I know about Ben. I only tell her part of the story: the person I saw watching me that night, the mess in the kitchen, the late-night banging on the door.

"So you think it was her? Anna? Watching you while you slept?" She shudders dramatically. "That's so creepy. Weren't you scared?"

"No," I say firmly, and then I shrug. "Well, yes. A bit. It's pretty freaky waking up and seeing someone like that."

"Totally. Bloody hell, Tim, I'd be petrified," she says. "Can't you ask her about it?"

"I did kind of ask about the mess in the kitchen. In an indirect way. She said she didn't do it."

"And you believe her?"

"Not really."

"So do you think she's some kind of fruit loop?"

"I don't know," I say. "I think she's had a hard time. I think she's dealing with a lot of . . . stuff."

"What kind of hard time?"

I shake my head. "Dunno. But I'm not particularly worried. I think she's harmless."

She looks at me cynically for a moment, then grabs my arm, whispers melodramatically, "What if you're wrong? What if she's dangerous?"

"I don't think so. I think she's depressed but I don't think she's dangerous."

I tell her about the night I found Anna crying, the strange dazed look on her face. The way she didn't make any sense.

"Oh, man," she says. "You have to talk to her properly. You can't live with that."

"I will. Later. Maybe."

"Not maybe, Tim. You have to."

Neither of us talks for a moment. Eventually Lilla leans against me, shudders.

"I knew there was something weird about that house. I knew it," she says. "It's probably haunted."

"It's just a house. Bricks and mortar. It's not haunted."

"Well, I wouldn't want to live there. In fact, you couldn't *pay* me to live there." She turns to look at me, eyes wide. "What if Anna goes psycho in the night? Cuts you up and puts you in the fridge?"

I roll my eyes.

"I'm only half joking," she continues. "You could be in danger. I mean, why would she watch you like that? Do you think you should take a knife to bed with you for protection? I'd hate to find out that something bad happened to you."

For some strange reason I feel defensive. Disloyal. Lilla is enjoying this too much. I'm glad now I didn't tell her the full story: Anna's problems would only be juicy gossip to her.

"It's not actually funny," I say, irritated.

"It is actually a little bit funny, but it's scary, too," Lilla says. When I don't respond she puts her arm around my shoulder and my irritation dissolves like honey in hot water. "Never mind. You knew it was too good to be true. If it doesn't work out you can always come and live with me."

"I'm sure Patrick would love that."

"Hmm. Well. Stuff Patrick."

"Things okay between you two?" I ask. I try hard not to look eager, or sound hopeful.

"I don't know. Sometimes it's good. Sometimes I think we're really happy together. But then he can be such a selfish jerk and I wonder if I should just start again. Move out and find a new place." She looks down at her hands. "I even sometimes wonder if you and I should get a place together. We might work well as flatmates."

I don't say a word. I can't, my heart is too busy getting stuck in my throat.

23

I've known Lilla since high school but I didn't get to know her properly until I was twenty. We were loosely in the same social group, and she was often at the parties I went to. We'd say hello, sometimes have a brief conversation, and I definitely always thought she was hot, but not quite my type—too aggressive, too edgy and maybe, if I'm honest, a little bit intimidating.

One night at the tail end of a party Lilla and I were among a group who ended up down at Narrabeen Beach early in the morning. It was one of those days where the beach looked like something out of a postcard: the water tinted an unbelievable shade of Brett Whiteley blue, the sand white, the sun yellow. When we came over the dunes and saw the ocean we all gave this spontaneous gasp in collective awe at the beauty of it, and without saying a word we ran down to the edge, stripped off to our undies and ran straight in.

Lilla and I ended up mucking around. She splashed me, I splashed her back. When I was out deeper she crept up behind me and pushed me under. We stayed in the water for a good half hour, then got out and lay down side by side on the sand, puffed out. I was still half drunk from the night before, and it felt natural and easy to roll over so that I faced her, to put my hand on her bare brown belly, to kiss her.

We escaped from the others and went to a nearby café, where we shared a huge plate of bacon and eggs and sausages. Then we went back to the beach and swam and sunbaked until my skin was red and Lilla's had turned a deeper, darker brown.

Lilla talked. She told me how she wanted to do something creative. She told me secrets about her friends, her past boyfriends. She told me how she had been brought up by a single mother, and how she'd always hated the dingy flat she grew up in, resented her mother's lack of ambition.

"I want something better," she told me. "Much better. No way am I going to spend my life rotting away in some stinking flat in Narrabeen."

Then she asked me all about myself. She asked me what I wanted to do with my life, and was surprised when I said I had no idea. She asked about my friends, my parents. I told her how my dad had started a restaurant, how it was a dream come true for him. I told her I was more interested in being happy than successful.

"But you need to find an ambition," she said, putting her hand on my chest. "The most interesting people are always ambitious."

I didn't answer. Instead, I moved my face closer to hers and kissed her salty lips.

I'd never met a girl who talked so much, who probed so deeply.

I was still living with my parents back then. I knew Mum would be at work until at least seven, and that Dad would be leaving at around three to go to the restaurant. Which left me with a four-hour space of opportunity. At ten to three, I asked Lilla if she wanted to come back to my place and when I asked, the way our eyes locked, I knew she knew what I was really asking, what I really wanted.

She said yes.

I made instant coffee for us both and we took our mugs and a packet of chocolate biscuits to my room. I only had a single bed, but I was relieved to see that at least it looked reasonably clean and in order. We sat on the bed, face-to-face, legs crossed, and drank our coffee. We ate the entire packet of biscuits.

When she'd finished her coffee, Lilla stood up and put her empty mug on my desk. I thought she was going to leave and started desperately trying to think of ways to get her to stay. But instead of leaving, she pulled her T-shirt up and over her head, undid her zip and slid her skirt down over her hips. She took her bra and undies off, too, and I sat there gaping like a fool, too scared to move in case it was all just a dream.

She lay down on my bed, took my hand and guided it to her parted legs, where she was warm and soft.

I was lost.

Afterwards, she wrapped her arms around me, kissed my lips, my cheeks, my eyes. Then she sighed and got up, started pulling her clothes on. I was confused, scared to death I'd done something wrong, committed some kind of unforgivable sex sin. But when she was dressed she bent over and kissed me again.

"Lilla, wait," I said. "I need your number. I mean, can't I call you? Don't you want to . . ." I sat up and reached for her hand. "Please don't go."

"I've got to." She pulled her fingers away, kissed me again, this time very softly. "Let's not ruin a perfect day."

For the next few months I didn't stop thinking about her. The way one side of her mouth went up and the other side down when she smiled, the way her hair hung around her face. The way she tipped her head back and exposed her neck when she laughed—all these things had imprinted themselves on my brain. In the few short hours we'd spent together, the certainty that Lilla was the perfect woman had managed to burrow beneath my skin, swim the length of my veins, and flood through every artery and cell of my body.

It took a year and a half until she was single again, and then another three months of dedicated effort on my part to convince her to go out with me.

We went out for eight months. Eight fiery, electric, fucked-up months. I'd never felt so elated and chewed up and miserable, all at the same time. We fought. We laughed like maniacs. We fucked. It was both the most adult and most ridiculously childish relationship I'd ever had. Once Lilla screamed at me for ten minutes because I ate more than my share of jelly beans. I found her quick anger and her sense of entitlement sexy.

Lilla was renting her own flat. I didn't officially move in—I was still living at Mum and Dad's—but I stayed there almost every night for the entire eight months.

Lilla got to know my parents pretty well because we had dinner at home at least once a week. My dad liked her, I could tell. He laughed at her jokes, teased her when she got too arrogant. Mum was always polite, but she was quieter than usual when Lilla was around and spent a lot of time in the kitchen.

"You don't like her, do you?" I asked Mum on one of the rare nights I stayed at home.

She stopped what she was doing, frowned.

"It's not that," she said. "It's not that I don't like her."

"What is it, then?"

"I don't know. She scares me a bit, I think. Her drive. Her hunger. She seems a bit . . ." She kept her eyes averted, shrugged. "Desperate or something."

"Desperate?" I was getting irritated. I hated it when Mum criticized my friends and yet I knew it was my own fault for asking. Now I needed to know exactly what she meant—just so that I could tell her how wrong she was.

"That's not quite the word. I mean she just seems very driven. Very ambitious. The type of girl who knows what she wants and goes after it."

"And you're always telling me I should be more ambitious," I said. "Double standards or what? Or is this a sexist thing? Okay for boys to be ambitious but not for girls?"

"Don't be stupid, Tim," she said, and then she looked at me directly. "It's not that at all. It's just that sometimes I look at the two of you and I think she's going to eat you alive. She's ruthless. That's the word I was looking for. Ruthless."

I still hadn't even met Lilla's mum. Whenever I suggested it, Lilla made excuses, brushed the idea aside.

"Why bother?" she said. "She's the least interesting person you'll ever meet."

But every few weeks I would bring it up—it just felt too weird to go out with a girl for eight months, to practically live with her, and know nothing about her family—until she eventually agreed to introduce us.

We went to visit Lilla's mother one Sunday afternoon. Her name was Hazel and she looked a lot like Lilla, only with an extra fifty kilos of weight and bad posture and all the vitality drained away. It was bizarre to meet her—like meeting a potential future version of Lilla— a Lilla who'd led a hard, sad life.

Hazel was clearly pleased to have us there. She smiled widely and bustled around getting coffee and a big plate of cupcakes. The flat was surprisingly clean and bright, the coffee good, the cakes delicious. I wondered why Lilla had been so reluctant to introduce us, what she was so ashamed of.

Despite Hazel's warmth, and the obvious effort she was making, Lilla was rude and cold. She brushed Hazel's hand away when she tried to touch her hair, rolled her eyes at everything Hazel said, sat on the couch with a sullen look on her face and flipped through magazines and refused to talk. She sighed repeatedly, noisily, as if she couldn't wait to get out of there.

Lilla's rudeness embarrassed me and to compensate I gave Hazel as much attention as I could. Asked question after question. Listened to story after story.

At one point when Hazel was talking, giving me a detailed description of one of her many medical complaints, Lilla sighed and picked up the remote control. She switched the television on, turning the volume up so loud that Hazel's voice was drowned out.

Hazel looked startled for a moment, but then only nodded as though she expected nothing more. It was as if she had no ability or energy to stick up for herself, as if life had taken her backbone and ground it to jelly. She stood up and went to the kitchen. "I'll get us some more coffee," she said.

When she'd left the room I snatched the remote from Lilla and turned the volume down.

"Stop being such a bitch," I hissed. "What's your problem?"

"My problem? I don't have a problem, Tim," she said, making no effort to keep her voice down. "I just can't stand people who sit around feeling sorry for themselves. I hate all this inertia. I look at my mother and know that's not how I want to be. She's the perfect example of how not to live a life." She looked at me with a sneering expression. "But then you and Mum are quite similar. That's probably why you get along, why you like her. You're both willing to sit around and watch life pass you by."

"What the *fuck*?" Though Lilla could be sharp and abrasive, this was the first time she'd been so deliberately and personally insulting towards me.

She gave me a small, cold smile. "You're both useless. Passive. The pushed rather than the pushing."

I stood up. I was so angry I could feel my hands shaking.

"I'm leaving," I said. "I'm going back to my place. And I'm going for good. You're a bitch, Lilla. A spiteful bitch." I went to the door without looking at her. "Apologize to your mum for me. Tell her something made me feel sick."

I collected my stuff from her flat the next day when I knew she'd be out at work. I left my key on the dining table. I was angry and humiliated and determined to teach her a lesson. I wasn't the passive and weak bloke she thought I was. She couldn't treat me like crap and get away with it.

But my anger didn't last long and after a day or two it became more of an effort to stay away. Lilla called and left messages and I had to make myself ignore them. I surfed all the time to keep myself distracted, to stop myself calling her back. She turned up at the restaurant one night and I got one of the waitresses to tell her I was too busy to talk.

I managed to stay away for almost three weeks but one afternoon while I was out surfing I realized how dumb I was being. I was play-ing the kind of manipulative game I hated. The truth was I missed her. I didn't care if it seemed weak or if it meant I was a passive bas-tard. I just wanted to be with her. We could talk. Sort things out. I took the next wave back to shore and ran all the way to her place.

I knocked on the door. I was dripping wet.

"Oh," was all she said when she saw me. She was clearly sur-prised, but not in a happy way. "What is it, Tim?" She didn't invite me in; instead she stepped out, partially closing the door behind her.

"I missed you," I said.

"Could have fooled me," she said.

"I'm sorry." I reached out and tried to take her hand but she stepped away. I spoke quickly then, desperate to make things better, to remove that distant, indifferent expression from her eyes. "I'm sorry I've been ignoring you. I've been a dickhead, I know. I just want, I just really want to go back to how we were. I still . . . *fuck* . . . I miss you, Lilla. I love you."

It was the first and only time I'd ever said those three words to anyone. It was also one of the only times I've seen Lilla look so un-certain. She blinked, and maybe I'm flattering myself, but I'm pretty sure she was trying not to cry. But then she stepped even farther away, crossing her arms defensively over her chest.

"I've met someone else," she said.

"What?" I nearly laughed.

"And unlike you, Tim, he's got his shit together. He's good for me."

She almost glanced behind her, back into the flat, and that's when I realized that he must be in there. Through the partially open door I noticed her hall table. There was a man's leather satchel sitting on it, with a striped tie draped over the top. The satchel had a fancy red monogram engraved in one corner. It looked like some kind of royal crest and I wondered what kind of wanker would walk around with pretentious crap like that on their bag.

I left then, before I did anything stupid.

24

When we get to Circular Quay, Lilla buys me a coffee. We stroll up towards the Museum of Contemporary Art and sit on the grass beneath the shade of a tree. We don't talk any more about Anna or the house. Lilla tells me about some new sculptor she likes, a woman who uses old wire coat hangers and crepe bandages. I lie down and close my eyes, intending to rest for just a second, and accidentally doze off.

"Hey!" Lilla is leaning over me. "Way to make a girl feel boring!"

I sit up, run my fingers through my hair. "Shit. Sorry. Haven't been getting much sleep."

"So," she says. "Seriously, though, Tim. What are you going to do?"

"About what?" I say, immediately defensive. I assume she's talking about my future employment prospects again.

"About your housemate. The crazy girl."

"Dunno." I shrug lazily and tell her about the lunch with Fiona and Marcus. The emails.

"Although I feel a bit weird about it," I explain. "Like I'm invading Anna's privacy or something. I don't think I'll send any more. Just feels wrong."

"Oh, God, no, Tim," she says. "It's not wrong at all. Imagine if something happened? You can't be responsible for that. Don't be stupid. If they're such good friends of hers, of course they're going to want to make sure she's okay. Of course they are."

"Yeah, but I feel like a creep. I mean, sending emails about her behind her back? There's something off about it. Maybe I should just talk to her. Tell her what I'm doing. Explain that we're just looking out for her."

Lilla shakes her head. "Don't you think they should be the ones to talk to her? If they decide it's the best thing? And if they're lawyers, then they can't exactly be stupid, can they? Let them take responsibility for the situation. For God's sake, Tim, be smart. Protect yourself. Believe me, it's totally not creepy what you're doing, and I have the most excellent creepiness detector. It's totally the right and responsible thing to do."

"Maybe," I say. "I don't know. But, hey, Lilla, how do you even—"

"Shit!" she interrupts, looking at her watch. "I am so bloody late!" She leans over, plants a kiss on my cheek. "You know what, Tim? It makes me feel all glowy and proud inside to see you being so thoughtful about the whole thing. Just keep on sending those emails." She jumps up, stares down at me, grins cheekily. "And don't forget the knife. You might need it."

And as I watch her go I'm overcome by the kiss, busy remembering the feel of her lips on my cheek, and I forget the question I wanted to ask.

I stroll back down to the quay and wait for the next ferry. When I get to Manly I take a walk to the beach, strip to my jocks and run into the water. I bodysurf until I'm too tired to continue, then trudge up the beach and sit on the warm sand until I'm dry.

Back at the house I find Anna in the courtyard. She has her skirt pulled up to her thighs, her bare pale legs stretched out in the sunshine. She straightens up when she sees me, covering her legs.

"Want a Danish?" I ask. "I bought four different flavors: raspberry, custard, strawberry and apricot. In case."

"I—" she starts.

"Of course you do," I interrupt, grinning. "How could you not?"

Despite the fatigue that's weighing me down like a lead suit, I'm in an excellent mood. Though I tell myself it's just the beautiful weather that's making me feel so cheerful, I know deep down that the grin on my face has a lot to do with what Lilla told me about her and Patrick. Things aren't going well between them. Lilla and I might move in together. It's the chance I've been waiting for.

Anna and I eat our pastries in silence. I don't mention the kitchen, or the fact that I'm pretty sure it was her watching me at night. I don't even want to think about, let alone talk about, anything so heavy. And after what Lilla said about Patrick, my being here may only be temporary anyway. There's no need to get overly involved. Besides, though I wonder what exactly is going on with Anna, I know there's probably no single answer. She's grieving. She's unhappy. She's unwell. She's all of the above and more. The thing is, I have nothing to worry about. Anna's harmless. She's someone to pity, not fear.

25

The more she got to know Marcus and Fiona, the more she admired what they'd achieved. Despite their impoverished background and less than ideal childhood, they'd made something of themselves, and it was pure determination, brains and courage that had got them there.

One Friday night, several months after Fiona had stormed out, after things had pretty much returned to normal, Fiona and Marcus turned up at the house with bottles of champagne and baskets full of delicious food: prawns and oysters, caviar, olives, cheese, crusty bread. They were both in particularly good spirits.

"Today we signed a lease on a new building. Harrow and Harrow will officially open in a month's time!" Fiona said as she poured champagne. Anna had never seen Fiona look so radiant. They took the food outside to the courtyard and Marcus and Fiona explained that they were starting a new business, a partnership. They hadn't told Anna of their plans, they'd wanted it to be a surprise.

It must have been the excitement that made them drink that second bottle so quickly. They started on a third, and before long their faces were flushed and they were talking over the top of each other, laughing at stupid things, their voices fuzzy and blurred.

Suddenly Marcus sat up straight, tapped his knife on the side of his glass.

"I need to say something," he said in a mock-serious voice.

"Oh, good." Fiona laughed, and glanced happily over at Anna.

"You two are the most important people in the world to me," Marcus said, lifting his glass. "And I just wanted to say that I love you both."

"And we love you, too," Fiona said, her voice so solemn that Anna almost giggled. "We're a family. The three of us. Forever."

When they'd finished the third bottle, Fiona stood up.

"I'm sorry to be a drag," she said. "But if I drink any more I think I'll be sick."

Anna helped her upstairs and into bed. She was disappointed that the night had ended so early; she was enjoying herself and wanted to stay up, celebrate some more. When she went downstairs she was pleased to see that Marcus felt the same. He'd put a bottle of whisky on the table, two glasses, a container of ice.

"Let's have some of this," he said, lifting the bottle as she entered the room. "I'm too happy to go to bed now."

Marcus was uncharacteristically loose and relaxed. Booze had made his eyes shiny, his smile wide, his conversation easy. He'd loosened his tie and undone the top buttons of his shirt. The front of his hair sat up, as if he'd absentmindedly run his hands through it. They sat at the table, getting steadily drunker, and talked of everything and nothing. At some stage, words stopped making sense, and instead of trying to understand what Marcus was saying, Anna watched his face, noticing for the first time the strong, square line of his jaw, the shadow of stubble on his skin, the deep brown of his eyes. She thought about kissing him, about touching his face, and without even thinking, she reached out and pressed her fingertip to his lips.

Next thing she knew they were clasped together, lips pressed tight. Marcus made a noise in the back of his throat that made her think he must have wanted this for a long time. They went to the living room and stumbled, giggling and clumsy, to the sofa. He was surprisingly strong and decisive, and much less inhibited than she would have imagined. He knew exactly what to do, where and how to touch her. Anna smiled and closed her eyes and held on tight.

26

I spend the next few days working at night, sleeping, then surfing or swimming during the day. Nothing unusual happens at the house and I don't see much of Anna. I don't hear from Lilla, either—no texts or phone calls—and I force myself not to call and harass her about the idea of moving in together. But I think about it endlessly. I create different scenarios in my head: the two of us sharing a flat in Manly, having late-night beers together when I get home from work, getting closer and more open with each other until we both admit we should never have broken up in the first place. Inevitably, my imagined scenarios end up with the two of us in bed. Sometimes it's me who makes the first move, with Lilla opening her arms in welcome, asking why I took so long. Other fantasies have me coming home from work to find Lilla spread provocatively on the sofa, dressed in something outrageously revealing—all for the purpose of seducing me.

I'm having a post-work drink at the bar with Blake and some of the waitresses when I get a text from her.

You still at work?

Yep. Just finished.

Cool.

?

And then she's tapping at the front door, her face pressed up against the glass. Blake lets her in. I introduce her to the others and get her a beer. Everyone else is seated around a table, empty glasses and chip packets in a mess in the center. Lilla perches on a stool, folding one long leg over the other—showing them off. I stand next to her.

"You got here fast," I say.

"We're just over at the Steyne," she says. "Having a drink."

"We?"

She ignores me, lifts her beer, looks around the restaurant.

"It looks good in here. I like the new lights."

"They're not new," I say. "They've been like that for years."

"No kidding?" She smiles. "I guess it's a while since I've been here, then." She takes a swig of her drink then puts it down on the bar, slaps her knee. "Anyway. I didn't come here to talk about the restaurant. I came to talk about that party."

"What party? There is no party."

"Your birthday party," she says loudly, so everyone can hear. "The party you're going to have at that house." I shake my head. "Nah." I don't know why she's talking about parties. I'd rather be making arrangements to move out.

"Oh, come on," she says. "Everyone! Tell Tim he's having a party. Tell him he has to. That as a resident of one of the biggest houses this side of Sydney it's his civic duty."

And then Blake and the others start.

"Why not, Tim?"

"Go on, Tim. Do it. What an excellent idea."

"Yeah!"

"Yeah, well," I say. "I have to check with Anna first. She owns the place."

Lilla smiles, pleased with herself, and slides off the stool. She kisses my cheek and pats my shoulder.

"See you later, Timmy," she says on her way out.

I can't avoid walking past the Steyne on my way home, but I don't have to look in. I can't help myself. I stop walking, press my face to the glass and stare straight in. A bloke sitting close to the window frowns at me and points me out to his friends, who all laugh and make faces. I ignore them and try to see beyond, into the tangle of faces and tables and glasses and flickering light.

I'm just about to give up when I see her. She's standing in the middle of a crowd, talking, animated. I see only girls beside her and for a moment I'm happy, thinking she's just out with a bunch of friends. Next minute he's beside her. Patrick. He puts his arm around her shoulders, presses his face close to her ear, and she turns and kisses him.

I realize too late that I'm standing underneath a light, that I'm just as visible to the people inside as they are to me. Patrick's eyes go wide as he sees me. And when Lilla finishes kissing him he smiles at me deliberately. His expression is cold and smug.

I turn away, start walking towards home. My heart pounds in my chest and I'm burning with angry humiliation as I make my way quickly along the Corso and the length of West Esplanade.

I reach the harborside path and slow down, uncurl my fists.

I'm halfway home when I hear footsteps behind me. I don't turn around to look—I hate looking like I'm anxious, I think it can invite trouble if you let people see your fear—but I move to one side so that whoever is behind me can go past. But the footsteps stop and I assume the person has left the path, gone up to the road or into one of the many houses that line the path.

Suddenly I hear the much louder thump of someone running, getting closer. The noise stops as quickly as it started.

I turn around, but there's nobody behind me.

"Hello?" I call out, and my voice echoes back at me. There are intermittent lights, but some of them are broken and parts of the path are still dark enough to feel sinister at night, if you're in that kind of mood. Normally I like the quiet solitude of this walk, the only noise the distant hum of traffic, the gentle lap, lap, lap of the water, but tonight the quiet seems to sit over everything like a thick blanket, cloying and heavy, suffocating. I want to shake it off, emerge into noise and light and traffic and the security of other people.

I turn back, walking faster now, and move over to the grass so I can hear if anyone comes up behind me. But it soon occurs to me that anyone following could do the same and I wouldn't hear a thing. As I walk my heart pounds and my skin prickles with fear, with the urge to turn around and watch my back.

I don't hear anything for a while, and I start to relax, tell myself I'm just being paranoid. As soon as I step back onto the concrete path the sound starts up again: footsteps behind me. Footsteps almost in sync with mine, but not quite. I stop, and the footsteps stop. I start walking and they start up again. If I wasn't alone, if it wasn't so dark and quiet, I might think it was funny. But I am alone, and it's too dark, too quiet, and the sudden certainty that I'm being followed makes my hair stand on end. A choked grunt of fear slips from my throat.

I swing around. "Who's there?" I call, trying to keep the fear from my voice, to sound amused, even, as if I think this is all a great joke. But the words come out sounding timid and high, and very obviously afraid.

I don't wait for an answer, or to see who appears out of the bushes. I turn around and run as fast as I can.

When I get back to the house I don't bother stopping to say hello to Anna. I go straight up to my room and try to calm down. I pace back and forth and take deep breaths, clenching and unclenching my fists. I sit on the floor and put my head between my legs until my heart rate slows and my panic dissipates.

There's nothing to be afraid of. I'm inside and safe, and whoever was out there was only playing some dumb joke. I'm tired and emotional and not thinking straight. I'm overreacting.

I stand up and turn on my laptop, log into Facebook. Lilla has updated her status with the comment *Lazy, happy daze with lover-boy!* and a whole bunch of new photos. I click through them one by one: Lilla and Patrick mucking around at the beach, Lilla and Patrick drinking in some kind of beer garden or pub, Lilla and Patrick cuddling on the sofa. For all her talk of moving out, she's still close enough to him to spend the day letting him put his hands all over her. In fact, she looks positively thrilled to have his hands all over her. One photo in particular makes my blood boil. Lilla is facing the camera, mouth open, eyes half closed, looking blissed out. She's wearing something very skimpy, a bikini top or a bra. Patrick is behind her, his doglike face buried in her neck. He has his arms around her and, though the bottom of the picture is out of the frame, it's obvious that the palm of his hand is beneath her bra. I have to fight an urge to pick the computer up and fling it out the window.

I go across the hall to shower. I put the water on hard and hot, turn my face up, and wash myself thoroughly. Loads of soap all over my skin, a good handful of shampoo in my hair. I scrub until I know every trace of the restaurant is washed off, and the bathroom is thick with fog. A few tears slip out, and I feel weak and pathetic for letting myself cry, stupid for letting myself get sucked in by Lilla all over again. I have to move on, get over my obsession with her, and it occurs to me as I'm standing there watching the water swirl down the drain that having a party, just as Lilla had suggested, might be a way to help me do just that. It could mark a new stage of my life—publicly, a birthday party, but privately, a kind of moving on.

By the time I've dried myself vigorously and pulled some clean clothes on, I feel a lot better.

It's past midnight but I have a sudden second wind. I go downstairs and get two beers from the fridge. I find Anna in the living room, in her pajamas. She's lying down on the sofa, her eyes barely open, the light of the television flickering across her face. She sits up when she sees me.

She looks wary, as if afraid I'm there for some kind of difficult conversation. I grin, trying to look as cheerful as I can, and hand her a beer. I sit on the couch opposite and lean towards her.

"What would you think about the idea of a party?" I say.

She blinks. "Here?"

"Of course here. Why not? It's the ideal place," I say. "I know it might be impossible or too hard or whatever. With your agoraphobia and everything. So just say so if that's the case. I don't want to make things worse. You probably don't like crowds?"

"No." She shakes her head. "That's not really . . . I mean, I do have a bit of social phobia, but my anxiety is mainly . . . I could manage a party, I think."

"It would just be a casual thing. It's my birthday this weekend. I know it's short notice, but you wouldn't have to do anything. I'd take care of it all. You could just sit back and enjoy yourself."

"A party." She says it slowly, as if testing the idea out.

"Yeah." I grin. "You must know about them? You know, people come over? We put on music? Drink beer? Get drunk and dance? Hopefully have a bit of fun?"

She's quiet for a moment, looking down at her hands. Eventually, she looks up and a slow smile spreads over her face. "I do vaguely remember something like that."

"What do you reckon?"

She nods, takes a sip of her beer, places the bottle carefully on the table.

"Okay," she says. "Why not?"

27

When Tim first suggests having a party, her immediate reaction is dread. The very word conjures up so many conflicting emotions. Her memories of parties at the house are not pleasant: the days of tense, almost hysterical preparation beforehand, the awful, brittle people who would come, the horrible, lonely sense that she'd been born into the wrong family, the wrong world.

Then she thinks of the parties she's enjoyed. Dancing with friends on New Year's Eve. Birthday parties at other people's houses. Bonfires at the beach in summer. All of those parties—the ones she thinks of as fun—were held elsewhere, away from the house, far from her mother.

But now that her mother isn't here to ruin it, why shouldn't she have a party?

Much as she'd like to, she can't hide forever. She has to make some attempt to recover, lead a normal life. And a party in the safety of the house, in her own territory, seems a relatively unthreatening way to be involved, to see people, to remind herself what real life is like. And it would officially be Tim's party, not hers, so if she had to retreat, disappear up to bed, nobody would really notice or care.

She thinks about it as she goes up to her room, brushes her teeth, slips into bed. By the time she's ready to turn off her lamp, the sense of disquiet has changed, and she is more excited than anxious. For the first time in as long as she can remember, she goes to sleep feeling like she might have something to look forward to.

28

Next morning when I go to the kitchen I find Anna sitting at the table, pen in hand, notebook in front of her.

"I'm making a list," she tells me, looking up shyly. "Of things we need to get for your party."

I make coffee and sit beside her. She slides her notebook over and I read down the page.

"We don't need all this stuff, Anna. I was just planning on getting some sausages and beer," I say. "It doesn't have to be a big deal."

And though I've only meant to be helpful, to stop her doing too much, she looks shattered.

"But if you want to . . ." I point at her list. "If you really want to do all that stuff, that's fine. I don't mind. I just didn't want you to do a whole lot of unnecessary work or anything."

"Why?" She looks at me sideways. "Because I'm so busy?" She takes her notebook back, clears her throat. "Could I ask you something, Tim? Would you do me a favor?"

"Sure."

"Would you let me organize this?"

"Well, if you want to . . ."

"And would you let me pay for it?"

"No way."

"Why not?"

I shake my head. "It wouldn't be right. I just—"

"Oh, stop it," she interrupts, and once again I see that spark in her, the fire that she normally keeps hidden. "Of course you can. I want to. I'm not twelve years old. I have money galore, more than I can spend. What am I supposed to do with it, stuck inside here all the time?"

"But things won't be like this forever," I say. "You'll get better. And then you'll need your money."

"But I have plenty. Too much for one person. One little party won't even make a dent. Please, Tim." She shakes her head in an agitated way. "Please don't try to be protective or moral or whatever it is you think you're doing. And don't be embarrassed. I want to do this. It'll be fun. More fun than I've had in a very long time. And I know I said you couldn't help me, but maybe you can. By letting me do this." She's breathless now, her cheeks pink.

What can I say? I don't particularly want a big-deal party. I'd be just as happy with a casual barbecue as I would with some kind of posh catered thing. But how can I refuse? Anna looks so determined, almost desperate.

"All right, then," I say. "Why not?"

"Good," she says. "Thank you. It should be fun."

For all her use of the word *fun*, she doesn't look as though she's having any. Her brow is furrowed, her body tense. She looks anxious and stressed, more like she's organizing a funeral than a party.

29

She asks Tim to write a list of all the people he wants to invite. She plans to design some kind of e-card, email the invitation to his friends.

He sits there for ages, scrolling through the contacts on his phone, thinking, chewing the end of the pen and writing down names and email addresses. He shakes his head, crosses a few names off the list, muttering vague reasons, before sliding the paper across to her.

"That's more than fifty people," she says when she's counted them.

"And what about you?" he asks. "Who are you going to invite?"

"Oh. It's your party, not mine."

"So? Doesn't matter. Invite your friends, too." He gestures at the house. "No way it's going to be too crowded."

It would be easy to lie, to list a whole raft of legitimate-sounding reasons why that wouldn't be a good idea, but she can feel the blush burning her cheeks before she has time to make up a story, compose herself.

"Oh, I don't . . ." she says. "I'll just invite Marcus and Fiona."

"That's it? Just two people?" he says quietly, and she can tell he's feeling sorry for her, wondering how she can be so pathetic, why she doesn't have anyone else in her life.

The first panic attack happened the week after Ben died. Marcus and Fiona were at work and Anna was alone in the house. She had been getting dressed, thinking about how she'd fill her day, missing Ben so much she struggled not to cry, when suddenly she was overcome by an entirely new sensation: a crushing feeling in her chest, a terrible sense of dread.

She had no idea what was happening at first, no idea why she was so conscious of her heart all of a sudden, why her throat had become so tight, why she felt as if wet concrete had been poured into her lungs.

She wondered if she was dying, having a heart attack.

She texted Marcus for help.

Fiona was the one who came, rushing through the front door sooner than Anna would have thought possible, and Anna almost cried with relief at seeing her. Fiona did all the talking once they reached the hospital, explaining everything that had happened, the order of events. Anna listened silently as Fiona told the doctor about her parents' deaths, all about Ben, the whole tragic story.

Panic, the doctor concluded. A mental condition, not a physical one. He told Anna it was a very normal, almost expected response to everything that had happened to her. *Grief can do some strange things,* he told her. There was nothing wrong with her. It was all in her mind.

Unfortunately, discovering it was "only" panic didn't help. The attacks started coming frequently, overwhelming her in the most unexpected and impossible of places—shopping for food, browsing for books at the library. A smothering avalanche of dread would send her rushing for the Ladies'. When she could breathe again, she'd go outside and hail the nearest cab, curling up in the backseat like a lunatic. As soon as she got home she'd go straight to bed and hide under the covers, cry herself to sleep.

With the panic attacks came shame. What kind of person was afraid of the supermarket? What kind of person found it difficult to talk to people, to meet their eyes, in case they saw the truth? What kind of person needed to rush home and hide indoors just so that she could breathe?

The panic and shame grew worse and more intertwined, eventually becoming so bad that all she could do was keep herself hidden, bury herself inside the house and withdraw from everything and everyone.

Ever since her parents died she'd been making excuses to her friends, preferring to spend her time with Marcus and Fiona. The panic only made things worse. She told so many lies and made so many excuses, said no to so many invitations, that people stopped trying. And she found it surprisingly easy to avoid her friends. Most people made a superficial effort, but were ultimately quite happy to be pushed away, happy to be lied to, glad to be relieved of the burden of socializing with her now that she had changed so much.

30

We sit there for the rest of the morning making plans for the party. It's the most relaxed we've ever been together, and apart from the brief uncomfortable moment when I ask if she wants to invite anyone, we pass the time companionably.

I bring my laptop downstairs and while I eat breakfast, Anna uses it to email out the invitations. When she's done that, she looks things up on the Internet. Food, grog, party supplies.

"Balloons," she says. "What color?"

I shrug, smile.

"Silver," she says. "Silver will look great against the white ceiling."

And a bit later: "What do you like to drink? What's your favorite beer?"

"I don't mind, Anna. Seriously. Anything will do."

"I'll order something nice. Something German. They usually do good beer, I think. And French champagne. And some nice food."

Despite my initial reluctance, I start to warm up to the idea of this fancy, more organized kind of party. Good beer, nice food, everything taken care of. Why not? As the morning passes we listen to the ping of emails coming in from friends responding to the invitation. Most of them say they'll be there; one or two apologize and say they can't make it. At each new acceptance Anna writes down the number on her list: 23, 24, 25 . . . 47, 48, 49.

When we get to fifty she smiles. "You're very popular," she says. "Nearly all your friends are coming."

"And look," she says, as an email comes in from Marcus. "All my friends are coming, too."

She starts laughing. I watch for a moment, surprised, but her laughter is contagious and soon the two of us are roaring. We laugh so much that tears come to our eyes and we double over, clutching at our stomachs. We try to stop, to breathe and take control, but each time we make eye contact we only start again.

"Stop it," Anna says eventually, still sniggering. "You're giving me a headache."

"Me, too," I say, taking a deep breath. "Just stop. Breathe. Stop."

"Yes. It won't do at all," Anna says, shaking her head in mock seriousness. "All this happiness. Quick. Let's get back to being miserable."

It's such an unexpected thing for her to say that we look at each other and laugh again.

I barely even notice when an email comes in from Lilla saying she'll be there.

31

She saves the best bit for when Tim has gone to work. A new dress.

She searches for an hour before she finds the right one and orders it. The website guarantees it will be delivered within three days—plenty of time before the party.

Once she's ordered her dress she flicks idly through Tim's bookmarks. They are mainly links to surfing websites—graphic pictures of tiny-looking men on horrifyingly big waves. There are links to a few cooking sites, one to a site on the tsunami. Almost without thinking, she clicks on the last link, which takes her to Tim's Facebook page. Before she has a chance to even look at anything, a message appears at the bottom of the screen.

Back again, Timmy?

It's from a girl called Lilla. Of course Anna doesn't respond. Tim would find out and think she was snooping. Which she is. But, unable to control her curiosity, she clicks through to Lilla's Facebook page and browses through her photos. Lilla is pretty, dark. There are a lot of pictures of her with a well-built blond guy and Anna is surprised by how relieved she is at this visual confirmation that Lilla has a boyfriend. There are hundreds of photos. Photos of Lilla looking wild and outrageous at parties, photos of her wearing skimpy little dresses that show off her tanned, athletic body. Photos of her dancing, riding a bike, hiking in the bush, swimming at the beach, drinking beer in pubs, drinking cocktails in posh bars. There are photos of her in fancy dresses, in tight jeans, in rumpled pajamas. She looks equally confident and sexy in everything. She looks bold, brash, happy, as if she's having the time of her life.

Anna feels a powerful and irrational jealousy—of Lilla's life, her obvious carefree happiness, her 798 Facebook friends—but most of all, of her apparent friendship with Tim.

There's one particular photo that she stares at for a long time. Lilla's standing on the footpath, the facade of a building behind her. She's punching the air with her clenched fist, a huge, victorious smile on her face. There's something about the picture that makes Anna curious, something familiar, something that tugs at her memory.

Still here snooping, Tim?

Another message appears from Lilla, and Anna closes the page, shuts the computer lid and rushes away, feeling ashamed of herself.

And a strange, mildly unpleasant feeling of inadequacy stays with her for hours. It's ridiculous, idiotic. She doesn't even know the girl.

That afternoon she goes to the junk room to find the lights that her mother used to put up for parties. It's early yet—the party's not for a few days—but she wants to set them up so she can show Tim just how spectacular the ballroom will look.

She takes the lights to the ballroom and dusts them off, then spends the rest of the afternoon stringing them up around the walls of the ballroom. She needs a ladder from the backyard and, though she feels anxious walking out there, going into the dark, cobwebby interior of the shed, she manages to avoid a panic attack and makes it back inside, ladder in hand. She works all afternoon and evening. It's a hot, uncomfortable job, climbing up and down the ladder, holding her arms over her head while she hooks the lights up. There are enough lights to make three complete circles of the room. When she's done she closes the door and turns the lights on to get the full effect. She turns the chandeliers on as well, switching them to low, and the combination of chandeliers and fairy lights creates the perfect ambience. Dreamlike, soft, beautiful.

It's past eight and she's hungry. She goes to the kitchen to make herself some dinner. She hasn't had an appetite like this for a long time. She usually sees food as a necessity rather than a pleasure, as fuel that she has to put in her body in order to survive, but tonight she's ravenous.

She toasts three slices of bread and butters them generously. She cuts a mango into pieces and puts it in a bowl with a dash of cream on top. She gets one of the beers that Tim keeps in the fridge and takes it all to the ballroom. She eats sitting on the floor, lights glowing around her, enjoying the atmosphere. For the first time in months she feels a sense of accomplishment; if not exactly happy, she is at least temporarily content. She has a pleasant ache in her arms, and every mouthful of food, every sip of beer, tastes delicious and well-deserved.

Normally she goes to the attic in the evening, but tonight she doesn't want to dwell in the past. Instead, she watches television in the living room. She has another beer while watching a late-night movie, and then another, and another. By the time she hears Tim's key in the door she's feeling tipsy, light-headed.

She rushes to the door and pulls it open.

"Shit," he says, taking a startled step back. He looks almost frightened, but then he smiles and steps inside. "Anna. You scared me."

"Sorry, sorry, it's only me," she says, and she takes his arm, leads him towards the ballroom. "I didn't mean to scare you. I just wanted to show you something."

She closes the ballroom door behind them so that everything is momentarily black. She turns on all the lights.

"Wow," he says, and he turns, taking it in. His wide eyes and delighted grin make it all worth it. "This is awesome, Anna. Awesome."

"And I've ordered balloons and streamers," she says. "They'll be here on Saturday. It'll look even better when I've finished."

Then he does something surprising, wonderful. He puts his hands on her shoulders, leans down and plants a kiss on her lips. "It's beautiful," he says. "Thank you."

She's glad the lighting is dim so he can't see the look on her face, the heat she can feel spreading over her skin.

"Hey," she says, turning away. "Do you want a beer? I've been drinking yours, I hope that's okay . . . But there's still some left. We could have one in here?"

"Okay," he says, laughing, and she rushes from the room, filled with a strange sense of urgency, as if Tim might disappear, as if the delicate thread of happiness she can feel expanding within her might just snap if she doesn't hurry back.

PART 2

32

On the night of the party, she takes her time getting dressed.

She hasn't thought about clothes for a long time. When Ben died she lost all interest. The way she looked, clothes, makeup—all the things that she'd once found so absorbing and believed so important—became immediately irrelevant.

But something about Tim, and the way she's starting to feel when she's with him, has made her care about the way she looks. It's a nice change to worry about something so trivial, to devote her attention to a problem so easily solved.

It's both refreshing and liberating being with someone who didn't know her before, someone who doesn't remember the old Anna London. Tim never looks at her, mouth agape, and wonders what the hell happened to the happy-go-lucky girl he used to know. Eventually she will, of course, have to tell him everything. It's not a secret she can keep forever. But even then, he will only know it as a story, a sad piece of her history, and he will never look at her in the same part-pitying, part-morbidly-curious way her old friends do now.

She showers, shaving her legs and washing her hair. Afterwards, she moisturizes, sprays perfume—two things that used to be automatic but now feel slightly self-indulgent, after going so long without. She puts her new underwear on. It is red and delicate, the bra designed to lift and create cleavage, the matching panties brief.

She pulls the dress over her head and smoothes it over her hips. It's black and figure-hugging, with a pattern of large old-fashioned burgundy roses all over, and a V-shaped neckline. Her shoes are red, too, with wedge heels and thin, elaborate straps that twist around her ankles.

She blow-dries her hair and leaves it loose so that it sits thick on her shoulders, framing her face. She opens the vanity cabinet and scrabbles through her basket of makeup, looking for a lipstick. When she finds the one she wants, in exactly the right shade of red, she pushes her lips out and steps close to the mirror, applying the color carefully.

She looks utterly changed.

She takes a deep breath and smiles at herself in the mirror. She's used to feeling anxious, but this is a completely different kind of nerves. It feels like an eternity, a thousand empty years, since she's had this happy tingle of anticipation in her belly.

33

I dress up for the party—at least, I engage in my version of dressing up, which involves putting on a pair of cargo pants instead of my usual shorts, and a relatively new and intact T-shirt. I wash my hair and try to comb it into something resembling a style, but I look ridiculous and end up shaking it out into its normal mess. I consider asking Anna to help me do something with it, maybe even trim it a bit, but I get the feeling she'd be even more hopeless than me. She pretty much wears a T-shirt and a shapeless skirt or pair of jeans every day. I've never known a girl who puts less effort into her appearance.

Which is why I'm so surprised when she comes downstairs in a dress. A dress that's the very opposite of shapeless.

I must do a double take or make some other obvious gesture of surprise, because she hesitates.

"Do I look okay?" She pulls at her dress, smiles shyly.

"Yes," I say. "You look . . . you look *great*." I lift another bag of ice, making it look like more effort than it is, hoping the heat I can feel in my face appears to be the result of the physical exertion, rather than the embarrassment I'm suddenly feeling.

I don't quite look at her again, but I can tell she's pleased with my answer. She walks over to the ice and champagne, her shoes noisy on the floor, and pulls a bottle free.

"Why don't we open one of these?" she says. "I think we deserve it."

"So do I." I straighten up, managing finally to look at her, to smile.

"You look nice," she says.

"Not as nice as you."

Nice is an enormous understatement but still, I think she understands exactly how impressive she is in that dress, especially with her hair all loose and sexy around her face. She grins, opens the bottle and pours champagne into two plastic glasses.

"Cheers," she says. "And happy birthday."

With the lights on and the balloons up the ballroom looks spectacular, like something out of a magazine. Tables covered with white cloths are arranged around the edges of the room. Glasses are stacked in neat rows. Large white tubs containing ice and drinks sit at the end of each table. We're ready.

People start arriving about twenty minutes later. The first to appear are a group of guys I used to play football with. I haven't seen them for at least a year, but we immediately slip back into our old, familiar ways, teasing and joking. As soon as I open the door they start busting my chops about the house, asking me when I won the lotto. I introduce them to Anna and notice the way they glance sideways at each other. I don't know what they must think, but I enjoy their obvious bafflement, and avoid explaining anything properly, preferring to let them wonder.

Marcus and Fiona are the next to arrive. Anna brings them to the ballroom, where they say hello and wish me a happy birthday in their weird, formal way.

By eight, the house is full of people, and it's crowded and noisy and alive in a way that it hasn't been since I moved in. The ballroom echoes with the sounds of talk and laughter, and I'm high with the energy of it all, the thrill of having so many people I know together in one place. I notice people's faces, the way they look around the ballroom, eyes wide, and I enjoy their reactions to it all.

Lilla arrives late with a scowling Patrick by her side. She strides into the ballroom in her long boots and tiny skirt as if she owns the place. She leaves Patrick leaning against the wall, arms folded aggressively across his puffed-up chest, goes straight to one of the tubs and helps herself to a beer. She smiles when she spots me, lifts her arm in a wave, then comes and stands beside me.

"It's looking pretty swish in here, Mr. Ellison," she says.

"Yep. But I can't take any credit. Anna did it."

She raises her eyebrows. "The mysterious Anna." She covers her mouth and leans close. "Are you sure we're safe?"

I wish I'd never told her about Anna. Lilla's too harsh, too scornful. And I don't want to laugh about Anna. Now that I know her better, I feel a sense of loyalty and protectiveness. And considering all that she's done for me, I feel like an arsehole for ever gossiping in the first place.

"So you brought Patrick," I say, changing the subject. "I don't remember inviting him."

"You didn't," she says. "So I did. He wouldn't like it if I came here on my own. You know that. He doesn't approve of you."

"But we're just friends," I say, sounding more okay with that than I actually feel. "Sounds like Patrick's being a bit unreasonable."

"Maybe he is." She smiles provocatively. "Maybe I like unreasonable men."

We both turn to look and find him glaring over at us. If looks could cause physical harm, I'd be a pulverized and bloody mess.

People keep arriving and there are friends to greet, beers to drink, conversations to have. I enjoy myself for a while, passing from person to person and group to group, catching up, talking about old times. I don't notice Rich and Bee arrive but I hear Richard's loud, distinctive laugh and I find them in the kitchen, hands tightly linked, already surrounded by old school friends.

"Happy birthday!" Rich shouts when he sees me. He lets go of Bee and wraps his arms around me, pulls me close, squeezes too tight. He pulls away and hands me a plastic shopping bag.

"What's this?"

"A present. What do you think?"

I laugh. "Nicely wrapped, mate."

"Yeah, well. Wrapping's not exactly my forte."

Inside the bag is a cake of soap. One side of the soap is pink, the other side brown. The pink side has the word *face* carved into it. The brown side says *arse*.

"Good one." I put the soap back in the bag, punch his arm.

It isn't until I go back to the ballroom to get myself a beer that I notice Anna standing to one side of the room, still talking to Marcus and Fiona. I go straight over, determined to get her mingling, meeting some new people, having fun.

"Hey." I put my hand on her shoulder. "Come and meet some of my friends?"

I've drunk enough to put my arm around her back without even thinking about it. She laughs—a little bit nervously—and doesn't pull away. I can smell her clean, soapy scent, feel the warmth of her against my side.

I introduce her to some of my mates. I can see the surprise, and what I imagine is envy, in their eyes. Anna looks hot, and the house is more than impressive. I'm filled with a sense of pride, as if the house is mine, as if Anna is mine, too. And I strut around like a fool, showing off, imagining that everything is right in my world.

"So," Lilla says, and she glances between us, eyes sharp, taking everything in. She looks at Anna, eyebrows raised. "What an amazing house. You must be the youngest home owner I've ever met. And with the biggest, poshest house I've ever set foot in."

Anna mutters something incomprehensible.

"But maybe that just says something about the people I know." Lilla smiles. "You probably know a lot of rich people."

I flash Lilla a warning look, but she takes no notice.

"I mean, you know, it's probably not that unusual for you," she says. "You grew up with it. It's like . . . I don't know . . . similar types of people tend to hang together." She looks from me to Anna, smirks. "Usually anyway."

I can feel the sudden tension in Anna's back. I should have known to avoid Lilla. I feel like kicking her. Why can't she ever be straightforward and friendly? Why does she have to be so confrontational?

Lilla looks around the ballroom, turning her head in an exaggerated way, as if the room is too big to take in.

"You know, I can't imagine what it must be like with just the two of you living here," she continues. "All those empty rooms. Such a waste, really. And then Tim is out at work, so you must be alone most of the time. One person taking up all this space. It must be quite weird, especially at night. Don't you get scared?"

"No." Anna shakes her head. "Not really. I'm used to it. I've lived here all my life."

"How nice," Lilla says. "To be born into such privilege."

"Oh," Anna says. "I suppose so."

"*I suppose so,*" Lilla repeats, as if testing the words, as if Anna's speaking a language she doesn't understand. Then she smiles, a cold smile that goes nowhere near her eyes, and abruptly turns her back on us, starting up a conversation with someone else. It's an obvious and rude dismissal, I feel like forcing her to turn around and try again, politely this time, just as a parent would with a bratty little kid. But Anna squeezes my side and smiles up at me, letting me know she's okay, so I let it be.

34

When Lilla looks at her, Anna feels as if she's being appraised, challenged and dismissed all at once. She knows that Lilla would probably respect her if she stopped acting like a mouse, showed a bit of guts. She'd only have to do it once—show a flash of anger, snap back at Lilla with a nasty line of her own—and Lilla would leave her be. They'd probably even become friends. But she hasn't got it in her. She can't think of the right words, can't muster enough self-preserving outrage.

Yet Lilla's hostility doesn't upset her. The very fact that Anna is enjoying herself, and not hiding in her room in a blubbering mess, has filled her with an immense sense of satisfaction. She has met people and said hello and looked them in the eye and managed to smile naturally. Tim has his arm around her waist and she isn't squirming away or collapsing to the floor in a heap. She is genuinely having a good time, and the surprise of that, combined with the collective joyful energy in the room, has bolstered her confidence, making her feel almost immune to Lilla's scorn. How can she worry about what a virtual stranger thinks of her when, right now, for the first time in years, she feels like a normal twenty-year-old? A girl who can laugh and smile and have fun. A girl who might even have a future.

35

Anna and I are separated when a bunch of old schoolmates drag me into an argument about the best places to surf on the northern beaches. It's a topic I'd normally find absorbing; instead, I catch myself looking out for Anna, wondering what she's doing, who she's talking to. I tell myself I'm just making sure she's having fun, enjoying herself as much as I am, but when I see a drunk-looking bloke approach her—someone I don't recognize, a friend of a friend, probably—and stand way too close, practically slobbering all over her, I feel strangely pissed off.

Before I can decide whether I should go and rescue her, the doorbell rings. Anna leaves the drunk to his own devices and heads down the hall to answer the door. It turns out to be the caterers. I offer to come and help out, but Anna insists that there's nothing for me to do, and disappears with them into the kitchen. It isn't long before they're bringing out tray after tray of delicious food—sushi, dumplings, gourmet sandwiches—and I'm surprised at both the quality of the food and the sheer amount of it. It must have cost a fortune. I get more than a few nudges from surprised friends, who no doubt expected something more along the lines of a meat pie or a hot dog.

As I'm on my way to thank Anna, Lilla approaches.

"This food is spectacular," she says. A guy in black-and-whites offers us a tray of mini-dumplings, and we take one each, eat them immediately.

"*So* good," Lilla says.

"I know."

"And this champagne is good, too." She lifts her glass. "Not exactly your normal beer-and-chip kind of party, Tim."

"Nope." I feel suddenly embarrassed, even though I have no reason to. Lilla's watching me keenly, and I feel a flash of irritation towards her.

"Got yourself a sugar mummy, huh?" She grins.

"Piss off," I say, and go to walk away, but she puts a restraining hand on my arm.

"Don't be mad. I'm just teasing." She smiles. "Although I do have to admit to being very curious. The other day you told me Anna was a fruit loop, told me all that scary stuff, and now tonight you've got your arm around her, looking very cozy. We're friends, aren't we? Friends should talk to each other about these things."

Friends. There's that word again. My irritation only increases.

"Actually, I didn't say she was a fruit loop. That was your word. I said she's had a lot to deal with."

"Yeah, but the way you saw her watching you? The mess in the kitchen? You can't say that's not strange. A bit bloody freaky."

"Maybe I imagined the person watching me. It's not impossible. It was late and I'd been working. I'd probably even had a few beers. And the kitchen thing? Maybe it is a bit strange. Freaky. Whatever. But we could also be a bit more compassionate and say that it's all understandable. Considering."

"Considering what?"

I shrug. "Life. Considering life. Sometimes it makes you crazy, eh? Anyway, you could try being nice to her. That shit about her money before was just out of order."

"Sorry about that," she says, smiling and looking anything but. "I couldn't help having a little dig. God, Tim, just imagine owning this house at her age. It must be worth millions, and can you . . ."

She doesn't finish her sentence because at that moment Patrick appears. He puts his arm around her possessively.

"Patrick," I say, grinning widely. "Enjoying yourself?"

"Having a great time," he says, flashing an equally insincere smile.

When most of the food's finished and the caterers have gone, we turn the music up. Lilla, naturally, is one of the first to charge into the middle of the room and start dancing. She grabs the nearest person and starts jumping about. Lilla dances the same way she does everything—energetically—and takes up more space than you'd imagine possible.

Anna smiles at me from across the room. I down the last of my beer and grab another bottle, then go over and join her.

"I think we can officially declare the party a success," I say.

We stand there, side by side, in companionable silence, and watch. I'm feeling pretty good about everything, on a bit of a party- and alcohol-induced high, until I see Patrick barging his way into the middle of the dance floor. He lurches onto Lilla like a starved man onto a plate of food. He holds her tight, pressing his groin into hers, and starts his own ugly version of dirty dancing. But he still manages to search me out, meet my eye, give me one of his self-satisfied smirks. The idiot. He doesn't even know how good he's got it. If I had my arms around Lilla I wouldn't bother sneering at him. If I had Lilla, Patrick would be irrelevant.

I grab Anna's hand and pull her out into the hot crush of bodies. I don't ask. I don't think. I'm proving something—whether to Lilla, Patrick or myself, I'm not sure—and it's probably not entirely fair to use Anna for my own dubious purposes. But she doesn't resist or complain, and it doesn't end up mattering because as I dance with Anna, one of her hands held loosely in mine, I forget about Lilla and Patrick. I don't even have to try.

Anna dances with her eyes closed, a small smile on her face. She's not a big, bold, show-offy dancer like Lilla, she doesn't demand an audience, but she moves with a definite rhythm. It's as if all the nerves that normally surround her like a dark cloud have been blown away by the music, by the act of dancing, and she's been transformed into someone brighter, sunnier. There's no sign of the twitchy, awkward girl I've become used to. Right now, she's another girl altogether, and a pretty hot one at that.

I watch her face, conscious of the fact that her fingers are linked in mine, that we're dancing close. I can smell her hair, her perfume. The lights reflect off her cheeks in a way that makes her skin glow. She's so pale and pure-looking. And when she opens her eyes and sees me watching her, she doesn't look away shyly, or become awkward. She fixes her eyes on mine and takes my other hand, and then she smiles in a way that makes me think of the photo I saw in the junk room that day. Sexy and confident. Daring. Her smile briefly reminds me of Lilla—clearly my obsession isn't letting up just yet—and I wonder why I haven't really noticed Anna before. Not this way.

We stay out there for song after song. Sometimes we're pushed close by the others, so that I can feel the soft press of her against me, and it's easy and natural to touch her, to put a hand on her hip, her shoulder, her arm, to hold her hand, and when she reaches her face up to say something to me I feel her breath warm against my ear. I don't watch out for Lilla and Patrick. I don't know where they are or what they're doing. I couldn't care less.

"I'm thirsty," Anna says eventually, and we move to the side of the room, get a beer each.

"Do you want to go outside?" I ask. "It might be cooler out there."

I also think it might be quieter, and that we might get a chance to talk. There's nothing in particular I want to say, but I've never seen Anna so open or relaxed, and it feels like some kind of an opportunity. For exactly what, I'm not sure. To get closer, maybe, to make friends.

But people have already started spreading through the house, pairing off, getting away from the noise and heat of the ballroom.

There's a group of girls smoking in the hall, ashing carelessly on the floor, filling the whole area with the stink of cigarettes.

I'm about to say something, tell them to go outside, but Anna tugs on my hand.

"Don't worry about it," she whispers. "It doesn't matter."

The kitchen is crowded. A bunch of people are playing a drinking game that involves a bloke lying on the kitchen table while a girl stands above him and pours champagne into his open mouth. We stand there for a minute and watch until he chokes, sits up, spluttering champagne everywhere.

I glance at Anna.

"Stop worrying," she says. "It's a party. We can clean it all up tomorrow."

When I see that Fiona and Marcus are outside, I want to turn around and go back in, but they spot us before I get the chance.

"Great party, you two," Marcus says as we approach. "Fiona and I were just saying how good it is to see this place full of people again."

We stand there for a while, drinking and making small talk about the catering and the weather. Fiona doesn't say much, but I notice her watching Anna and me, and I wonder what she's thinking, how much she's seen. I like Marcus and Fiona but there are a lot of people I'd rather spend time with, and I'm about to suggest that we all go back inside when Lilla comes out with a few other people.

"Timmy!" She bounds straight over to me, slinging her arm around my waist. "There you are."

In her black boots and short skirt, Lilla looks particularly striking, and I notice Marcus watching her.

"Aren't you going to introduce me to your friends?" And she looks back at Marcus, her eyes suddenly shining with curiosity.

When I introduce the two of them she takes his hand, doesn't let go straightaway.

"Marcus?" Lilla says. "That's such a nice name. One of my favorites."

"Thank you," he says.

"It's just got such a dignified ring to it." She finally lets go of his hand. "It really suits you."

"Where's Patrick?" I say.

"Oh, he's already gone," she says, waving her hand at me dismissively, turning back to Marcus.

I can't help rolling my eyes at Lilla's flirting, but at least she gets the conversation going. Lilla doesn't do small talk and soon a large group of people have gathered, talking about more engaging things. Sex, surfing, politics, money. Lilla is loud and outrageous and funny, and I notice that Marcus is still watching her. I consider warning him, letting him know she's taken, but decide it's none of my business. He can take care of himself.

Anna sits next to Fiona and the two of them talk quietly, leaning in close. Anna's so vastly different tonight—relaxed and comfortable in her own skin, hands not grasping nervously, eyes not fixed on the floor—that it's hard to reconcile the two different versions. Hard to believe she's really the same person.

Before long, the courtyard is almost as crowded and noisy as the ballroom was, and the conversation breaks off into separate groups. I end up with Rich and a bunch of our old friends from school for a while, all of us laughing our heads off as we compete to tell the most exaggerated account of some of the stupid things we used to get up to.

At one stage Rich does his impersonation of our overly enthusiastic PE teacher, Mr. Beard, which involves a lot of energetic squatting and noisy huffing and puffing. As he springs up from a particularly deep squat, he knocks his shoulder against my elbow, spilling beer down the front of my T-shirt.

"Hey, watch it," I say, pulling the wet fabric away from my skin.

"Sorry, mate." He straightens up, grins.

I hand him my empty glass. "You better get me another one," I say, heading inside for a dry shirt.

Upstairs, I switch the bedroom light on and start towards the wardrobe. I notice movement out of the corner of my eye and turn to look at my bed. It takes a moment for what I'm seeing to register.

Spiders.

36

There are spiders all over my bed. A twitching, scrabbling black mass of them. There are so many that they've almost completely blocked out the normal white of the duvet. A blanket of spiders. Like something from a nightmare.

Fuck!

I take a step back and bring my hand to my mouth, almost gagging with shock and revulsion. They're moving down the bed legs and onto the floor, crawling up the walls. When I look around I see that they're spreading. They're everywhere—climbing on the curtains, the ceiling, the windowsill. Some of them are creeping along the floor near my feet.

"What the fuck!" My skin crawls and I freak out, brushing at my legs and arms frantically.

I bolt from the room, slamming the door shut behind me, and run downstairs. I find Lilla talking to Marcus in the kitchen.

"Spiders!" I say, panting, as I reach them.

"What?" Lilla splutters into her drink. "What did you say?"

"There's a whole bunch of fucking spiders in my room."

"O-kaay," Lilla says slowly, looking at me as if I'm a lunatic. "No need to panic. Just get some fly spray. Or a heavy shoe, or a newspaper or something."

"No," I say, shaking my head. "I mean, there are hundreds. Come upstairs. You need to have a look."

"I'm sure I *don't* need to, actually." She sighs, annoyed, clearly thinking this is some kind of ploy to get her away from Marcus. "I've seen plenty of spiders in my life. But if you're scared of a few little insects, Tim, I suppose I can come and . . ."

"Is everything okay?" Anna appears next to Lilla.

"No. Not really. Just come up to my room," I say to all three of them. "Take a look for yourselves."

"My God," Lilla says when she sees them.

Anna cries out, puts both hands over her mouth.

"Some kind of joke?" Marcus asks.

"I don't know," I say. "If it is, it's not a very funny one." The three of them stand there, looking around. Anna steps slowly backwards, towards the door. Lilla shudders.

"Bloody fucking hell," she says.

"Exactly," I say. "Not really a job for fly spray, is it?" She goes to my desk, stomping deliberately on spiders all the way. She grabs a book, slams it down on a spider on the desk.

"That's not going to work," Marcus says. "You're just going to make a disgusting mess. I've got a better idea. Lilla, come with me."

Lilla follows him from the room and back downstairs. Anna stands just outside the room, in the hallway. She watches the spiders, her eyes wide and darting. She looks from the floor, to the walls, to the ceiling. Her hands twist together in front of her.

"Anna? You okay?"

"I just can't believe . . . Who would . . . ?" Her voice fades and she shakes her head.

"No bloody idea," I say. "No idea at all."

Lilla and Marcus return with two vacuum cleaners. I use one and Marcus the other, while Lilla walks around pointing and ordering. It takes a good twenty minutes to suck the spiders up as they scuttle and run, their quick, panicked movements making us jump and yell. It's a revolting job. We push the vacuum cleaners along the floors, into corners, down the length of the curtains. Marcus stands on the desk to get them off the ceiling. I open the wardrobe doors and search through my clothes.

When the spiders are gone and the bed is clear, I notice something I didn't see before: a large, flat box sitting at the head of the bed. It's one of those cardboard gift boxes. This one is red with a pattern of silver stars on it. The lid sits upside down on the pillow next to the empty box. It's obviously how the spiders were brought in.

"A gift box!" Lilla says, putting the lid and base back together. She pushes it off the bed, to the floor, and kicks it away. "Jesus Christ. Someone's certainly got a totally fucked sense of humor."

Anna waits, watching, from the doorway.

When we can't see any more spiders, and we've checked all four corners of the room and beneath the furniture, we turn the vacuum cleaners off.

"We should change the sheets," Lilla says. "Just to be sure."

"Good idea."

Anna fetches clean sheets and helps Lilla remake the bed. At one point Anna screams, making us all jump. When she realizes it was just the duvet brushing against her arm, she smiles apologetically. Lilla smirks.

"Sorry," Anna says. "Sorry."

"You should be pretty safe now," Lilla says. "Although you might get a few nasty surprises in the coming weeks. When you put your shoes on. And you should definitely, definitely always check your pants."

She grabs Marcus and suggests that they go downstairs and dance off some nervous energy. Marcus doesn't look exactly thrilled with the idea, but he lets Lilla drag him away.

"Better get back to the party," I say to Anna.

She nods silently.

I watch Anna follow Lilla and Marcus down the stairs before I slip back into my room for one last look around. Before I leave I crouch down beside the red box and lift the lid. On the bottom of the box, barely noticeable against the white interior, is a folded piece of paper. I open it up and find a handwritten message inside.

Happy birthday, Tim

It's not the message that makes me drop the piece of paper straight back into the box. It's the words themselves. The distinctive left-leaning slope of them. Anna's writing.

37

When I go downstairs I find Anna in the kitchen. She's leaning against the sink, staring blankly through the window.

"What the hell is this?" I say, shoving the note in her hands. I'm angry but I keep my voice down. I don't want to make a scene. Get everyone involved. "Your idea of a birthday present?"

"What?"

"That's your writing, isn't it?"

She stares down at the paper, nods slowly.

"So, did you write it or not?"

"Well, yes. I did. But I . . ." She breaks off, shakes her head.

I want to insist that she explain herself but her eyes are suddenly wide with fear, and her skin has become deathly pale. She looks too frightened and confused to be confronted right now.

It doesn't make any sense. Why would she look so freaked out if she was the person responsible for putting the spiders there in the first place? And it's almost impossible to believe that she could be faking it, that she could be such a good actress.

"Are you okay?" I ask. "You're white as a ghost."

She lifts her hand to her face. Her fingers are shaking.

"I just can't believe it," she says. "I don't know what's going on." She presses the heel of her hand against her forehead, squeezes her eyes shut. "I've got a terrible headache, Tim. I think I drank too much champagne. I'm sorry. I have no idea what . . ." She opens her eyes, sighs. "How about you? Are you okay?"

I shrug. I don't know what I feel. Confused. Angry. Rattled. Mainly I just want to have a beer and forget about it. Enjoy the rest of the party. Get that feeling of well-being back again.

I'm about to suggest that we get another drink and go back out to the courtyard where we can talk properly, when there's a sharp rap on the front door, followed by the sound of the door opening, more people arriving.

Anna looks at me questioningly.

"Must be the guys from work," I say. "They're the only ones who'd get here this late."

"Oh." She twists her hands together, looks away. "I might go up to bed. I hope that's not rude. I don't think I can . . ." Without saying another word, she turns and leaves the room.

I go into the hall to meet Blake and Jo and the others. Blake has his arm around Jo's shoulders and the two of them look self-consciously pleased with themselves. It would never have occurred to me that they would end up together—Blake towers over Jo, she barely makes it to his chest—but somehow they fit together, suit each other. I wonder when this all happened, and I flash Blake a curious look when Jo's not watching. He gives me a shrug and a slow, happy grin in return.

I show them through the downstairs part of the house. Blake nods in recognition, points out the rooms he painted.

"So where is she?" he asks when we reach the kitchen. "Where's Anna?"

I explain that she's gone to bed with a headache and take them out to the courtyard. When they've all got drinks I slip back upstairs and knock on Anna's door.

"Tim?"

I push the door open and find her sitting up in bed, her legs tucked beneath the blankets. She has her pajamas on. Her face is clean, her skin so washed-out and pale it's almost green. She's clearly not planning on coming back downstairs tonight.

"You disappeared," I say.

"Sorry."

"It's okay. Don't apologize. There's nothing to be sorry for," I say. But I wonder if I'm right. Maybe the truth is she's got a lot to be sorry for.

But there's nothing in her face. No guilt. Nothing I can recognize as malicious or satisfied. We look at each other for a moment. I have no idea what to say and it's clear that Anna doesn't either. It seems impossible even to step into the room. Any of the ease and intimacy I thought we'd established earlier, on the dance floor, has gone. Back to square one. Two strangers.

"Okay, then," I say, stepping back a little. "I'd better just . . ."

"Of course," she says, and sinks back down on her pillow. "You should definitely . . ."

I close her door behind me.

It seems quiet downstairs and it takes me a moment to realize that the sudden empty silence is because the music has stopped. Most people have moved outside. Everyone's more subdued now, talking quietly, a few people dragging on cigarettes, blowing lazy trails of smoke into the air above their heads. Fiona and Marcus approach.

"We've got to get going," Marcus says. He grips my hand tight when we shake, and doesn't immediately let go.

"I sincerely hope your birthday hasn't been ruined by that," he says, in his intense and serious way.

"Nah," I say. "Thanks. Don't worry. It hasn't."

I see them to the door then grab another beer and head outside. Lilla is sitting with the group from the restaurant and a couple of other girls. When she sees me she waves me over. She gets up from her seat and pushes me onto it, then sits on my lap. She wraps an arm around my back, rests her head on my shoulder.

"Hey, birthday boy," she says softly.

"Hey," I say. I keep my hands resolutely off her.

She wriggles in closer, pushes her nose into my neck. "Mmm. You smell good. You smell like Tim."

"Glad I don't smell like Patrick. Or Marcus, for that matter."

She leans back, looks at me. "Don't be mean."

"What are you doing, Lilla?" I say, shaking my head. I can guess why she's on my lap and it has a lot to do with Lilla's ego, and Lilla wanting what she can't have, and not a lot to do with me.

Even so, I let her sit there. I make no move to push her away, no move to protect myself.

She puts her head back on my shoulder and lifts her own shoulders in a shrug. "I don't know what I'm doing. I never know what I'm doing. Do you?"

I have no idea what I'm doing and just to prove it to myself, I put my arms around her, too.

We sit out there for another couple of hours, everyone drinking, talking quietly about nothing much, enjoying the easy company and the cool change that has come with the late-night air. People leave, in groups or in pairs, and it gets quieter until it's just me and Lilla and Jo and Blake and a couple of others. When the last guests eventually get up to go, Lilla and I sit on the porch with them while they wait for a cab. Lilla asks if she can stay the night.

"I won't fit in their cab," she explains. "And anyway, I'm going the other way. It'll cost a million bucks."

I take her upstairs to the bedroom opposite mine.

"I'll just get you some sheets and a blanket," I say.

Lilla wraps her arms around herself, shivers. "It's freezing in here."

"Two blankets, then."

She sits on the bed, bounces, looks around the room.

"I'm not sleeping in here," she says. "No way. Not by myself. It's too scary."

"What's scary about it?"

"Everything," she says. "It's too dark. And listen." She puts her finger to her lips, opens her eyes wide and we're both quiet for a minute, listening to the creak and groan of the house.

"See?" She giggles. "There's no way I'm sleeping by myself in this house."

"Then that's a bit of a problem, isn't it? You can't exactly sleep with Anna."

She gets up and stands beside me, takes my arm and tucks it between her arm and her side. "Of course I can't. Don't be dumb. But I can sleep with you."

"I'm not being dumb." I pull away. "I can't sleep with you, Lilla. *Shit*. Don't do this."

"Do what?" She shakes her head. "It really doesn't have to be a big deal. It's just sleep, Timmy. Nothing more. Anna will never know, if that's what you're worried about. We can even sleep head to toe if it makes you feel better."

Lilla has always had a skill for persuasion and it's late and I'm tired and half drunk and my resolve is weak. I take her to my room.

I turn my back on her as I pull my trousers off, climb into bed in my T-shirt and undies. Lilla's not so modest. She strips to her underwear, undoes her bra and gets in beside me wearing only a very brief pair of panties. I try not to look at the dark circles of her nipples, at the tiny triangle of fabric. But Lilla knows exactly how desirable she is. She lies on her side, her head on her hand, and smiles at me provocatively.

"Happy birthday," she says.

I don't say a word. I don't think about what I'm doing, I just lean forward and kiss her on the mouth. She has her body pressed against mine in an instant and she rolls over, pulling me on top of her, opening her legs wide and lifting her groin up to meet mine, hungry, eager. She pushes my head down towards her chest and I take a nipple in my mouth and feel it rise, harden. She makes a soft groan in the back of her throat, a familiar noise that makes me want to both cry and fuck her at once, and then she pushes me down farther. I'm about to pull her underwear aside, taste her saltiness, when I come to my senses and realize that I'm letting myself get sucked into another one of her traps. Again.

I roll off her. Shift back up the bed so that my head is on my pillow.

"Tim? What the hell?"

I turn away from her and pull my knees up. I feel winded and frantic, like a drowning man who's just been given a snatch of air only to be pulled roughly beneath the water again. I concentrate on breathing, on getting some sense of equilibrium back.

"Sorry," I say, when I can speak again. "That was stupid. We're not doing this. Not now."

"This isn't because of that crazy girl, is it?" she says. "You don't have a thing for her? Tim? Look at me."

"No," I say. "And stop calling her crazy. It's got nothing to do with Anna. I'm just tired of you, Lilla. You and your games." I roll over so I can see her face. "You know what I think? I think you can't stand the thought that I might stop lusting after you for one second. You saw me dancing with Anna and it gave you the shits. And this? Now? It's all just a game. A stupid fucking ego trip. That's what I am to you . . . a convenient ego-boost device."

She giggles softly. "An ego-boost device? That's actually quite good, Tim." She clears her throat, presses the palm of her hand to my chest. "But no, that's not it. You're wrong. It's much nicer than that. It really is. I love you, Tim. I care about you. And, the truth is, I think about you a lot, the times we were together. I miss you. I really do. And if it does have anything to do with that girl it's only because I can't stand to think of you hooking up with someone like that. She's weird, Tim. She gives me the creeps. And those spiders? That horrible present? It was her. It was totally her. I mean, use some common sense. She's the weirdest person you know. Everyone else you know is relatively sane. Who else would do something like that? And you should have seen her face when—"

"Shut up, Lilla," I say. "Just shut up, would you? You have no idea what you're talking about. You don't even know her."

But I can't help wondering if she's right.

38

I can't breathe.

There's a crushing weight over my mouth and nose. A weight that pins my head against the bed, that won't let me move. My mouth is open and full of something soft, something that won't let the air in.

I scream. Or I try to. Without air I can't make a noise.

My head is filled with red. An agonizing, pulsing red. The red of my own blood rushing through my head.

I try to thrash my arms, my legs, but I can't move. Can't do anything. I need oxygen. And I need to use every ounce of energy to get it. To suck air into my lungs.

Everything becomes black. And I feel myself fading, growing weak. Dying.

Then suddenly the weight is gone and I can breathe. Sweet, sweet oxygen. The relief of it is so immense I sit up and gulp it in, gasping and spluttering noisily in the dark.

Slowly my mind comes back into focus, and I take stock. Lilla is asleep and still beside me. I can hear the regular in-and-out of her breath. The room is empty.

Was I dreaming? And if so, why does my jaw hurt? Why do my lips feel bruised? Why does the lingering ache in my chest feel so real?

39

When I wake the next morning I remember the dream before any-thing else. The fear I felt during the night is still there, like a bad taste I can't get rid of. In the light of day it doesn't seem possible that someone would get into the house and hold a pillow over my face—what would be the point? And wouldn't Lilla have woken up if I was being smothered right beside her? I run my hand along the length of my jaw, up and down my neck, checking for soreness. Apart from a throbbing headache from the many beers I drank, I feel nothing un-usual.

"Don't worry," Lilla says, her voice startling in the silence. "We'll tell Anna we slept head to toe. Totally platonic. Just tell her how scared I was." She sighs, stretches her arms over her head, yawns noisily. "If she even asks, that is. Which I doubt. And anyway, you're not exactly married. She won't stay angry for long, if at all."

"I'm not worried about Anna," I say. "Why the hell would I be? And why the hell would she care anyway?"

"You're biting your lip. And your foot is twitching. You always do that when you're worried. And hey, Anna *would* care." She leans over and kisses my cheek, then gets out of bed and starts pulling on her clothes. "And you would care that she cared. I saw you two last night getting all romantic on the dance floor. You must notice the way she looks at you. She watches you all the time. She's totally got a big crush on you. Open your eyes. Stop being so dumb."

"It's not that." I sigh. "It's nothing to do with Anna. It's . . . last night. I had this shitty dream."

"It wasn't a dream, babe." She winks at me, then she makes a more sober face and sits on the bed. "But really. I'm sorry. It was stupid. I had too much champagne. Can we just forget about it?"

"It's not that either," I say, rubbing my jaw. "It's this dream I had . . . I couldn't breathe. As if someone had a pillow over my face. Trying to kill me. I was scared shitless."

Lilla stands up again, starts putting her shoes on.

"I felt as if I was going to pass out, or like my head would explode or something. It actually *hurt*. And I could see all this red. My own blood or something. It was fucking terrifying. Lilla? Are you even listening?"

"Yeah, yeah. Sounds really scary," she says. "But hasn't anyone ever told you how dead boring it is listening to other people's dreams?"

The kitchen and courtyard are a mess. There are empty bottles everywhere, plastic cups crushed on the floor, on the table, on every horizontal surface. Chairs are all over the place, one lying on its side beneath the table. The floor is sticky. I walk through the hall and find more of the same, plus a collection of cigarette butts in one corner. The ballroom is in a similar state, and I hope that at least the mess has been contained to just these areas. I check the living room. There are a couple of empty beer bottles, but no other damage. I get some heavy-duty bin liners and start picking up rubbish.

Lilla follows me around, occasionally picking up a random bottle, and tells me all about her plans for the day.

But I'm distracted and can barely make myself listen. Did Anna really watch me? Does she have a crush on me? And if so, had I made a stupid mistake last night dancing with her? Did I really want to start something with a girl like Anna?

"Lilla," I say eventually, straightening to look at her. "If you're not going to help, why don't you just go home? In fact, don't you think it would be a good idea if you left?"

"A good idea? Why?" She stares at me blankly for a minute before making her eyes all wide, an artificial show of sudden understanding. "Oh, you mean before Anna comes down?"

"Isn't Patrick waiting for you?" I glare at her. "Won't he be wondering where you are?"

"He left me here. He mustn't care that much." She leans towards me. "Don't worry. You can tell Anna I crashed on the couch. She won't suspect a thing." She straightens up. "And anyway, I can't go yet. I need coffee and I need it now, and I'm not going anywhere until I get it."

She turns on her heel and walks towards the kitchen. She stops in the doorway and looks back at me.

"I assume you want one, too?"

Anna comes downstairs just as Lilla is pouring the coffee.

"Want some?" Lilla asks.

"Yes. Thank you," Anna says, looking around the kitchen as if she isn't sure where to put herself or what to do. Lilla, in contrast, seems as comfortable as if she owns the place.

"Take a seat," she says to Anna. "I'll bring it over." Her voice is bossy, patronizing. I shoot her a warning look, but she avoids my eye.

Anna goes agreeably to the table and takes a seat. I think it's actually pretty cool the way she doesn't seem to notice how bitchy Lilla is. Or maybe it's just that she doesn't care enough to react. Either way, despite all her anxieties, she must have some deep inner sense of confidence. Unlike Lilla, she doesn't consistently have her prickles out, doesn't assume the world is looking for a fight.

I observe them silently for a moment: their appearance, their mannerisms; make a mental catalogue of their differences.

This morning, the way they look on the outside, soft and fragile in Anna's case, hard and edgy in Lilla's, is an almost comically exact reflection of their inner selves.

Anna is self-effacing and quiet. Unlike Lilla, she listens to people instead of dominating every conversation. Lilla is irritating, confrontational, spiky, and always has to give her opinion, whether you want to hear it or not. And as I think about this, it suddenly becomes clear to me which type of woman I'd prefer to be with. Anna is content to let others shine; Lilla always has to be the center of attention. Anna minds her own business, does her own thing, doesn't interfere. Lilla sticks her nose into everything, pushes people around, can't help but be critical and sarcastic and mean.

Lilla's need for attention is almost pathological, and in her own way she's probably just as mentally screwed up as Anna. At least Anna has legitimate reasons for her problems. Lilla is just a brat.

And, most important and attractive of all, Anna is available. And from what I can tell, she doesn't tease or play manipulative games. With Anna, what you see is what you get.

Lilla takes the coffee, the mugs, the sugar and the milk to the table, forcing the three of us to sit there together.

"Anyway, what do you do, Anna? Study? Work?" Lilla asks almost as soon as we sit down.

"Oh, well." Anna shakes her head. "Nothing right now."

Lilla lifts her mug to her mouth, gazes at Anna over the rim. "You've just finished a course? Looking for work?"

I have no doubt that Lilla knows exactly what Anna meant by the word *nothing*. Now she's just being nasty.

"No." Anna glances at me, then stares down into her coffee. A hot blush creeps up her neck and across her face, like red wine spilled on a white tablecloth. It's painful to watch, and I wish she'd just tell Lilla that it's none of her business, or lie, make something up: create a fake job, a fake university course, anything to wipe the superior look from Lilla's face. Her voice, when she eventually speaks, is small. "I'm not studying or working. I'm just . . . taking some time to—"

"Anna's had a pretty rough couple of years," I interrupt, glaring at Lilla.

"Oh, no. That's too bad, I'm sorry to hear it," Lilla says, ignoring my glare. Her voice is completely unsympathetic. She smiles, sighs, looks around the room. "But you're lucky to have all this. Lucky to be in a position to *take time*. And it is pure luck, you know. It's not as if you worked for it, or deserved it or anything. It's not as if people who are born poor deserve that either. It's all just an accident of birth. Chance. A toss of the dice. You should be more grateful, Anna—for most of us, when shit happens, we just have to get on with it."

There's a silence before Anna responds. "I am lucky in some ways," she says, looking directly at Lilla now. "But not so lucky in others. Just like everybody else."

Lilla laughs. "Actually, I don't think you can fairly say you're just like everybody else at all. I think you'll find that the playing field is not quite that . . . *equal*. I mean, yeah, we all have shit. That's life. But we don't all have loads of money to help us deal with it, you know? Hard as it might be for you to admit, I'm quite sure money helps smooth out those rough times. In fact, I'm quite sure money means the rough times happen a lot less often."

"Money doesn't stop people dying," Anna says. The blush has gone from her skin and the ice-cold strength in her voice makes me want to cheer.

But Lilla isn't fazed. She only shakes her head. "I hate to be a pedant, but I think you're probably wrong on that count, too. I'm sure money *does* stop people dying. Frequently. Think of all those private doctors. Think of all the extra help private patients get in hospital . . ." She pauses. "Though it obviously didn't help much in your mum and dad's case. Anyway, that's only the secondary stuff, when you're already sick, that's not even counting the primary stuff that stops you getting sick in the first place. The good food. The education. All the extra privilege money brings."

I can't believe what a bitch Lilla is being. I've only seen her act in this deliberately provocative and self-righteous way a couple of times before. Both of those times it was a hilarious performance, delivered to someone who deserved it. But this feels different. Wrong. This is Lilla being a bully, not Lilla taking a bully down.

I stand up, angry, scraping my chair against the floor noisily. I put my hand on the back of Lilla's chair.

"The next bus to the mall is leaving in five minutes," I say. "You'd better get on it because there isn't another one until after lunch."

I'm lying and I know it's obvious, but I don't care. I've had enough of Lilla and her bullshit. I want her to go.

Lilla looks as if she's about to argue the point, but I give her the filthiest glare I can. It clearly has the desired effect, because she blinks and for a moment looks gratifyingly uncertain. She glances into her mug and takes a final sip of coffee, then stands up.

"Okay, then," she says. "I'd better get going. Thanks for the party, Anna. Nice meeting you."

She strides off down the hallway towards the front door without waiting for Anna to respond.

I follow her out. We're on the front porch before I speak.

"What's your problem? Why were you being so bloody rude?"

She hesitates for a moment, staring down at her feet before meeting my eyes. "I don't know," she says. "I just . . . she annoys me." She looks at me carefully, shakes her head. "Don't start anything with her, Tim. She's just so not right for you."

"How the hell would you know?"

"I know you."

"You know me?" I laugh. "So what? Doesn't give you the right to be rude. Doesn't mean you know who's *right* for me. Whatever the hell that's supposed to mean."

"Okay." She scowls. "Fair enough. Maybe I shouldn't have said that. I suppose the truth is I just don't like those types of girls."

"*Those types of girls?*" I say, incredulous. "You're joking, right? You've barely spent five minutes with her. You don't even know her."

"I don't need to spend any more time with her. I can tell exactly what she's like. She's weak, I can see that much. Is that what you really want, Tim? Someone so spoiled they don't even know what it means to work for a living? Someone who contributes nothing to the world? Someone so *useless*?"

I've always known Lilla has a harsh side, but I'm stunned by this. How can she make such a cruel judgment of someone she's only just met? I shake my head.

"You're fucking spiteful sometimes, Lilla. And it's not her lack of a job that bothers you. That's just a convenient excuse, something easy and obvious for you to pick on. You're bloody jealous, that's all. You wish you had what she has. You wish you were more like her."

"Bullshit." She looks appalled. "Jesus, I'd rather shoot myself."

"I know exactly what your problem with Anna is." I count on my fingers as I go. "One, she's nice. Two, she's attractive. Three, she's rich, and four, I like her. And the truth is, she threatens you." I step closer, letting the full depth of my anger show, fueled by the events of the night before, our whole sad history together. I let all these months of pent-up frustration out, and I get no small amount of joy from watching her squirm.

"And just for the record, Lilla, just so you know, Anna hasn't had the easiest time. In fact, she's had a much, much tougher life than you have, and I seriously do not know where you get off calling her spoiled. I mean, what gives you the right to judge her? To judge anyone, for that matter? And what about tolerance, huh? Lilla? And compassion? Remember those words? Your old favorites, remember? Or do those concepts only apply to people exactly like you?"

I don't realize quite how angry I am, or how vicious I must sound, until Lilla puts her hand up and takes a step back. She has tears in her eyes.

"God, Tim. Okay. That's enough." She puts her hand to her mouth and I can tell she's about to cry. I'm startled out of my anger—it takes a lot to make Lilla cry—and I'm about to stop, to apologize even, but she turns away and is gone before I get the chance.

When I turn around to go back inside, I see Anna waiting in the doorway. She must have heard everything.

40

Weak. Spoiled. Useless. At these words, Anna feels an invigorating spark of anger. *You don't know me,* she is tempted to shout. *How dare you? How DARE you?*

But watching Tim's reaction, Anna's rage quickly evaporates. The way he defends her, and the fact that he gets so angry on her behalf, soothes like ice on burnt skin. His defensive words soften the sting of Lilla's cruel ones. She watches him and listens to the passion in his voice and it occurs to her that he genuinely cares. And with that knowledge, she allows the small thread of happiness within her to grow stronger, more certain.

41

Anna and I spend the rest of the morning cleaning. Anna works energetically, and though I watch to see if she's upset by Lilla's remarks, I see very little sign of it. We sustain ourselves on a packet of malt biscuits and frequent cups of coffee, and when we've finished it's past one and the house is clean. We've filled the recycling bin, plus three large boxes, with empty bottles, and there are three huge bags of rubbish tied up in the courtyard.

I make some pasta and divide it onto two plates. I serve it at the kitchen table because it's overcast and cool, and, unusually for a summer's day, not nice enough to eat outside.

Anna eats so slowly I wonder if she doesn't like it.

"Is it okay?" I ask.

"Delicious."

When I've finished I push my plate to the side, watch Anna push her food around without actually eating any.

"So. Last night," I say. "Thanks again. I had an awesome time."

"Oh." She waves my thanks away, glances at me for a second, then stares determinedly down at her plate.

"Anna," I say. "Look. Last night. When we were dancing, I think maybe . . ." I hesitate. Everything about her is telling me to stop. She's hunched over the table. Her hands are shaking. She won't meet my eyes.

"Anna?" I reach out to take her hand but she snatches it away from me so violently I'm stunned.

And then she gets up and does what she always does. She runs away.

42

The way she feels when she's with him scares her.

Tim is solicitous and kind all morning, making her coffee, bringing her biscuits. And cleaning the house together is somehow fun, not at all the boring chore it would usually be. But things are only easy between them while they're busy and preoccupied, while they have something to do. As soon as she sits opposite him at the table she feels her throat grow tight with anxiety. She tells herself to calm down, tries to make her mind blank and empty, but when Tim starts talking about the night before, she knows she can't manage any kind of conversation with him. Her fingers begin to tremble violently, her heart starts to beat too fast. She wants to disappear before he notices the panic. Before he realizes how gutless she is.

Friendship. Love. Romance. Whatever this might potentially become, it's clearly not a possibility for Anna. Love is no longer an option. She can't even bring herself to look at him, let alone talk sensibly to him.

Tim reaches out and touches her hand, and without thinking or understanding why—she's a pure ball of nervous reaction—she snatches it away. She can feel the red-hot flush of shame on her face and neck and she has to turn away.

She flees. Back up to the attic where she can breathe properly, where she can keep her already damaged heart protected and hidden. Safely locked away.

43

When Anna runs off I let her go. I'm too tired and hungover to chase after her. Trying to get close to Anna is impossible, not to mention humiliating.

I go up to my room and crash for a few hours. I wake up in the late afternoon to the sounds of thunder and pouring rain—a full-on storm. I go down to the living room and lie on the sofa, switch between crap TV shows. When I get hungry I ring for pizza. I save a few pieces for Anna in case she appears, but she doesn't, and by eleven I'm ready for bed.

Before I go upstairs I check the windows and doors in every room, making sure everything is secure. I freak myself out a bit as I walk around, jumping at my own reflection, starting at every noise. I wish that I lived in some kind of flat. Somewhere simple and small and cozy. A place with one living area, one bedroom, one bathroom. A place with nowhere to hide. This house has far too many dark shadows, and it creaks and groans as if it's alive. It's impossible to feel secure, to be sure you're not being watched. And as I walk up the stairs to my room I remember the dream I had the night before, the terror and agony of it, and am filled with a renewed sense of trepidation.

I leave the hall light on, my bedroom door open. And despite the nerves that make me strain to hear every noise, I eventually fall asleep.

44

By the time she's reached the attic, anxiety has overcome her and she has to crouch on the floor and breathe her way through a full-blown panic attack. There's nothing she can do once it's started, no way to stop it except bide her time and wait for the overwhelming sense of dread to pass.

When it's over she feels emotionally drained and physically exhausted, as if she's run a marathon. The fear is gone but she's left with a horrible sense of emptiness, an overwhelming loneliness. Nothing will ever change. She has proved it today. Anxiety rules her life—and it won't let her be happy. She's destined to live alone, a madwoman in a mansion, hiding out in an attic, getting more neurotic with each passing year.

The sadness feels like a hole in her belly, an aching void that needs to be filled. She takes a Valium, washes it down with vodka straight from the bottle. She takes the rest of the vodka to her armchair and curls up, pulls a blanket over her legs. She swigs from the bottle, lets her tears fall.

It's probably better like this, she decides eventually. If she knows anything, it's that love is a stupid, risky endeavor. Letting yourself love someone is like ripping your heart from your chest, holding it up in your hands, all bloody and exposed and vulnerable, and hoping nothing or nobody comes along to slap it to the floor and stomp all over it.

45

I don't know what it is that wakes me—some kind of sixth sense, I guess. I sit bolt upright and look around my room. It's dark—the hall light is no longer on. I can feel a damp sweat on my forehead, the pounding of my heart against my ribs.

And then I see it.

The black shape of a person.

Watching me.

It isn't in my doorway this time, but back farther in the hall, closer to the staircase, hidden in the shadows.

For a horrified moment I stare at it as it stares straight back.

This isn't a dream. I'm wide awake.

My first impulse is to hide beneath the covers, to scrabble down and bury my head. To call out for help, like a kid. But I can't do that, so instead I force myself to take a breath and shout.

"Hey! What the hell do you want? What are you doing?"

The figure doesn't move and despite every instinct in my body screaming at me to flee, I get out of bed and approach it. But before I've even made it to my door the figure moves and disappears, blending into the shadows.

"Hey! Stop! Fucking hell! *Stop!*"

I turn my light on and blink beneath the sudden glare. There's nothing. Nobody.

I run down the staircase and when I reach the bottom I flick the hall light on.

What I see makes my blood turn cold.

Painted in something thick and red, in enormous, spiked letters, written over and over again, up and down the length of the hallway.

DEATH LIVES HERE

46

It's not blood, though it looks like it. When I can move again I examine the writing up close, press my finger against it. It's sticky and wet, with a strong chemical smell. Paint. The hallway looks gruesome, the drips and splashes of red reminiscent of an abattoir, the whole scene like something from a horror movie.

Forcing myself not to panic, I walk to the back of the house. The kitchen doors are locked, the room still, quiet and empty. I walk back through the hall and check the front door and the other rooms, though I'm certain I won't find anything. I'm just going through the motions. Moving because I need to.

When I've confirmed that the house is locked and secure, I stop in the hallway and look at the mess surrounding me. I don't know what to do next. Should I call the cops? And say what, exactly? I think my housemate is playing tricks on me? I think she might be slightly mad?

Should I go and find Anna? Confront her? Ask her to explain herself?

The idea is not appealing. It's the middle of the night and I'm exhausted. The last thing I want to do is play detective, put the hard word on poor Anna. But I'm going to have to talk to her eventually. Sort this shit out.

As the rush of adrenaline eases off I realize how much I'm shaking, how fast my heart is pounding. I go to the kitchen and get a beer, drink the entire bottle in large gulps, standing in the light of the fridge.

I trudge back up the stairs; hesitate in the hallway before deciding to check each bedroom, one by one. It's just a token effort—I know I won't find anything.

I stop outside Anna's door and lift my hand, but a sudden idea makes me decide against knocking. I let my hand drop and go to my room. I turn my computer on and this time I do what I intended to do the other day, before I got sidetracked by Lilla. Some research.

I google agoraphobia.

The disorder usually starts with a mild anxiety about a particular place or event, which eventually escalates into a debilitating fear of going anywhere at all . . .

An agoraphobic person learns to fear fear itself, their own overblown reaction to it, their own disordered response to nonthreatening situations . . .

Most of all, an agoraphobic person fears the humiliation they will suffer if they have a panic attack in public . . .

All of which helps me understand Anna's isolation a bit more, and her social nervousness, but none of which explains any of the other weird stuff that has been going on.

I go back to bed when the sun starts to rise.

I wake a couple of hours later. I feel like shit, but I'm desperate to get out of the house and clear my head. I don't bother with breakfast, just make a quick coffee and then head out for a surf.

I try to keep my head down as I walk through the hall, try not to let the words on the wall get to me. But the red is so stark against the white, the letters so large and aggressive, it's impossible to ignore, hard not to stop walking and stare. Even in the daytime it looks horrific.

I surf for an hour then go back to the restaurant and dry off, get dressed. I buy a paper from Humphrey's Newsagency and take it to a café, where I order a big breakfast. It's a relief to be out of the house and away from Anna. It's good to think about other things, catch up on some news, focus on other people's problems instead of my own.

I take my time, eat slowly. By the time I start the walk back up to Fairlight it's almost midday.

I can see that the front door is open from the other side of the road.

Anna is in the hallway. She's still in her pajamas, scrubbing at the walls frantically, sobbing. Red runs in lines down her arms, all over her clothes. It's on her cheeks and in her hair. She's so focused on what she's doing she doesn't notice me come in.

"Anna?"

"Oh, God, Tim," she says, glancing at me for a second before turning back to the wall. Her eyes are bloodshot, her hair is messy. She looks wild. "I have to get this off." She continues scrubbing, moving her arm against the wall in frantic, jerky movements. All her effort is only making things worse. She's spreading paint everywhere.

"Hey." I put my hand on her shoulder. I know she can balk at being touched, but right now she needs my help. "You should stop. We should call someone. Get a professional in to fix this up."

But she doesn't stop. She just moves faster, makes more mess.

"No. No," she says. "I'll do it. I can do it. I don't have anything else to do."

There's a bucket of red-stained water by her side. She bends over, dips her scrubbing brush in the water and then slaps it against the wall, only managing to mix more water into the mess of paint. Red runs in rivers down the wall, onto the floor. She cries louder and pushes the brush around uselessly for a while. Eventually she stops, lets her arms fall to her sides, and leans forward so that her forehead presses against the wall. Her shoulders heave as she sobs.

"Hey." This time I put a hand on each shoulder, turn her carefully around so she's facing me. "Anna. Let's go and—"

"Oh, God, Tim. Please. Help me." She clutches the front of my T-shirt, pulls me against her. It's a natural, normal response to put my arms around her—and at first I'm only trying to provide comfort—but then she lifts her face, kisses me. And I don't resist or pull away. It's nothing like the kind of kiss I would have expected from Anna. It's hungry, passionate, her mouth open and pressed tight against mine, her tongue searching. She tastes strongly of alcohol, and of something sweet, like vanilla. I can feel the soft press of her boobs against my chest, the narrow arch of her back.

Suddenly she stops, pulls away again.

"Oh, shit. I'm sorry," she says. She puts her hand to her mouth, leaves a smear of red paint on her lips. I reach up and wipe it away with my finger.

"Don't be sorry," I say. "I'm not."

She drops the scrubbing brush to the floor, stares at the wall.

"This is pointless, isn't it?"

"You're only making it worse."

"Worse?" She looks at me and smiles. It's one of those surprising, full-on grins that transforms her face. She looks slightly mad with her wild eyes and her messy hair, and red paint all over her, but she also looks kind of hot. "How could things get any fucking worse?"

47

While Anna is upstairs taking a shower I make coffee. She comes back down in clean clothes, her hair wet and tucked behind her ears. She's subdued and she looks very tired, but she doesn't seem nervous. Her hands are still, her manner calm—for once, she looks perfectly comfortable in her own skin.

We take our coffee to the living room and sit side by side on the sofa.

I have a thousand questions, but I don't want to force things. I'm happy to wait.

"You must think I'm absolutely insane," she says.

"Not really. Not insane."

"But maybe I am," she says. "Sometimes I'm really not sure."

"Did you . . . I mean . . . the walls . . . did you—"

"Did I paint them?" She shrugs. "I don't know. But I suppose I must have." She looks at me almost hopefully. "Unless you did it?"

"Nah," I say. "And I'm pretty certain on that point."

I wait for her to continue.

"I can't remember. Sometimes when I feel bad, when the anxiety gets too much . . ." She sighs. "Sometimes I take Valium. Drink vodka. It's not a good combination."

"Ahhh," I say. "So you're a junkie?"

I'm half joking, but she shakes her head vehemently.

"No. No. I'm not that. I don't do it often enough." She hesitates. "At least, I don't think I'm a junkie. Or even an alcoholic. I don't . . .

I only do it . . . well, once or twice a week at the moment." She stops, frowns. "God, maybe I am becoming . . . maybe I should be more careful. I don't need any more problems."

"I was actually kidding," I say. "But, yeah, I mean, if you can't remember stuff it might not be so smart to mix your drugs like that."

I'm about to bring up the person I've seen watching me at night, the spiders on my bed. It seems a good time to find out exactly what she knows. But she leans closer, talks in a rush.

"I wanted to apologize," she says. "For being so hard to live with. I don't mean to be. I don't mean to be rude and abrupt. It's really not in my nature to be awful like that. It's just my anxiety. Sometimes I'm so full of it, so wound up inside, that I can't even look at you. I have this overwhelming fear that people will see inside me and see that I'm afraid, and they'll despise me for it. For being so gutless, such a stupid fool. Such a scaredy-cat."

"But what are you scared of?"

"Nothing. Everything. I'm scared of being scared, I guess. If that makes sense?"

"A bit. It's starting to."

She stands up, puts her hand in her pocket. She pulls a small box out and holds it towards me, smiling shyly.

"I got you this," she says. "And then I couldn't even give it to you. That's how dumb I am."

"What is it?"

"For your birthday."

"You got me a present?"

"I ordered it online. I thought you'd like it. I wrote you a birthday note, too. The one you found the other night at the party? But then I lost it and it didn't matter because by then I'd chickened out of giving it to you. I thought you'd think . . ." She shrugs, puts the box in my hand, sits back down. "Anyway. Here it is. Happy belated birthday."

It's a very small cardboard box. I open it. Tucked neatly inside is a tiny glass cube. There's something inside the glass, but it's so small

I have to hold it up to the light to see properly. I'm amazed when I realize what it is: a minuscule man on a surfboard, legs bent, arms held out for balance. I don't know how it was made—the whole thing seems amazing, impossible—but the surfer and the crest of the little wave beneath him are made up of tiny trapped bubbles of air.

"That is so cool," I say, genuinely thrilled. "He's riding the perfect wave. Forever. Living the dream."

"It reminded me of you."

"It's bloody brilliant." Overcome with gratitude, I surprise myself by kissing her without even thinking about it. I lean over and press my lips against hers.

She doesn't blush or go awkward or turn away. Instead she looks right at me and smiles, and I don't care about the paint on the wall, or the Valium, or the spiders. All I can think is: *beautiful, beautiful Anna.*

48

Tim makes an enormous pot of pasta and they eat in the kitchen. She sucks up her spaghetti unself-consciously and laughs as Tim tells funny stories about the restaurant: impossible customers, cooking disasters, bratty staff members storming out in the middle of a busy night.

When they've finished eating they leave the mess in the kitchen and go into the living room. There's plenty of alcohol left from the party, so they share a bottle of champagne. They both become loose-limbed and talkative, and move closer on the sofa, until their shoulders brush and their thighs press together and their hands touch in a deliberate, lingering way.

The television is on, but neither of them really watches it. They laugh occasionally at stupid ads, or random bits of dialogue from whatever's on, but they spend most of the evening talking. Tim tells her about his parents, about his love of surfing.

And she tells him things, too. None of the huge stuff. She doesn't talk about Ben. But she tells him enough. He asks about her anxiety and, surprisingly, she finds it easy to be honest. She tries to explain the crippling fear that keeps her in the house. The dread of humiliation, the belief, when she's having a panic attack, that she might even die.

And it's not as painful or as embarrassing as she would have imagined. Tim's sympathetic without being patronizing, and telling him the truth about at least that one aspect of her life, laying all her insecurities out so candidly, is liberating. She feels lighter when she's done, as if she's shed an unnecessary layer of heavy winter clothing.

But when he asks what she does in the attic she finds it impossible to answer him. She doesn't want to lie, but nor can she tell him the truth. Not yet. She bites her lip, turns away.

"It's okay." He takes her hand. "Forget I asked."

And so they talk of lighter things, music and sport, their favorite movies. They have more in common than she would have guessed. For a while she forgets everything—her history, her sadness, her anxiety—and simply lets herself believe that this can be real, that she can be happy again, that she can be the sort of person who laughs easily, who kisses boys. The sort of girl who can fall in love.

49

At two A.M. we go upstairs. We hold hands and walk slowly, reluctant to go our separate ways. We stop outside my bedroom door.

"You could come in," I say. "It would be nice to have some company. I'll wear my shorts. Your virtue will be safe, I promise I won't—"

"Shut *up*," she says, laughing.

"So?"

"Okay." She nods, bites her lip, looks mildly nervous for the first time that night. "I'll just go and put my nightie on."

While she's gone I brush my teeth and change into a pair of tracksuit bottoms and a T-shirt. I turn the main light off and my bedside lamp on, then get beneath the duvet. I lie on my side and wait. When she returns I lift the duvet for her. She slides in beside me, right up close, and turns so that her back presses against me. I switch the bedside light off, put my arm around her.

"You okay?" I ask.

"Yes," she says, and she takes my hand, squeezes. "I'm more than okay."

"Me, too," I say.

I close my eyes. And for the first time in what feels like weeks, I don't worry about weird noises or intruders, I don't jump at every noise and shadow, and pretty soon I'm sound asleep.

50

When I wake the next morning she's gone. I roll onto my back and sigh, assuming that when I see her next she'll be anxious and cold, we'll be back to square one. But she appears a minute later with two steaming mugs of coffee.

"Hey." I sit up. "Good morning."

"Hey yourself." She smiles. She hands me both mugs then climbs up onto the bed and sits cross-legged on top of the duvet.

"So," she says, taking her mug back. "I have to say something."

"Okay."

"God, this is hard." She takes a deep breath. "Well, first of all, last night was great, don't get me wrong. It was so nice spending that time with you, and getting to know you. And sleeping with you." She smiles shyly. "But I feel I have to say, well, that I don't want you to feel obliged to me in any way. I mean . . ." She pauses and breathes again, her cheeks now burning red. "I like you. I like you a lot. But I know that—especially to someone like you, Tim—the whole agoraphobia thing must seem really full-on. Something you probably wouldn't want to get involved with. And I understand that. I understand completely."

She puts her hand on my knee over the sheet, and runs her thumb around and around while she speaks, in a way that I find very distracting. "Just, please, don't think that you have to feel sorry for me. If you don't want to . . . if you don't like me that way, I can deal with it. Trust me. I've dealt with a lot worse in my life."

I could back off at this point. I could apologize and tell her that

I've reconsidered. She's giving me the perfect chance. And a few weeks ago I would have done exactly that. I would have run a thousand miles from a girl like Anna and such a messy situation. Instead, I decide to let this happen.

Primarily, I guess, I'm in lust. I want to have sex with her. And now she has her hand on my knee and even though I don't think she means it that way, the movement of her fingertips feels incredibly sexy.

Also, the fact that Anna has just been so courageous makes me feel that I should be equally brave. She's taking a risk, so why shouldn't I? And what is there to lose anyway? What's the worst that can happen?

And then there's Lilla. I'm sick of myself and how pathetic I am around her: the way I always make myself available whenever she wants me, the way I always end up feeling bruised and angry afterwards. I don't fully understand the hold Lilla has over me, but I know that it's destructive, damaging. A new relationship could be the perfect antidote—the cure to my obsession.

"My dad told me I should always have an open mind, be willing to try anything," I say.

"He did?"

"More or less. Yeah."

"He probably didn't have me in mind when he said that."

"Who knows what he had in mind," I say. "I get to interpret it any way I like. I'm not worried about your agoraphobia. I don't care. I know you'll get better."

Anna smiles then, and it's such an enormous and unabashedly happy smile that it makes me laugh. I grab her hand, rub my thumb over the soft skin of her palm.

I have loads of questions. The spiders on my bed, the destroyed kitchen—did she do those things and if so, why? But I don't want to overwhelm her, or come across as critical. I don't want to ruin what feels like the fragile beginning of trust. So I decide to ask about Ben. I get the impression that he might be at the heart of things, that understanding what happened to him will explain a lot of the crazy stuff that has been happening.

"Can I ask you a question? About Ben?"

Her smile fades. She doesn't say anything, but she doesn't move away or tell me to shut up either. Eventually she nods.

"What happened to him?"

Her eyes fill with tears. She sits up straighter, and tries to pull her hand away from mine, but I don't let go. She starts to cry. A stream of tears runs down her cheeks, her neck, into the neckband of her T-shirt, so that it is soon stained dark. She cries without making a noise. She doesn't try to wipe her tears away, or hide them. Instead she stares straight ahead, at some point directly over my shoulder, and lets them fall. It's as if, just by mentioning his name, I've smashed down a dam wall. There are so many tears.

I'm alarmed at first, sure I've done the wrong thing. I've never seen someone cry like this before and I don't know how to stop it or how to help her. But eventually it occurs to me that it's okay. It's not my job to stop it, not even my job to try to make her feel better. The best I can do is just stay here with her. Let her cry.

I don't know how long we sit there like that. I do know that she cries for ages, that my back starts to ache from sitting in one position for so long, and the palms of our hands grow sweaty together. At some point I lean forward and use a corner of the sheet to dry her cheeks, the top of her lip. I don't let go of her hand, and she doesn't move or react. She just keeps on crying.

Just when I'm desperate to move, and about to ask if she needs a glass of water or another coffee, she takes a deep, shaky breath.

"He died just over six months ago now," she says.

"You must have loved him a lot."

"Of course I loved him. Of course I did."

"He was your boyfriend." It's a statement, not a question. I'm sure I've got that part, at least, figured out.

"Oh, God, Tim, no. He wasn't my boyfriend." She looks upset by my mistake and I make a quick mental readjustment. Not her boyfriend. So who the hell was he?

"He wasn't my boyfriend," she says. "He was my son."

51

She hasn't allowed herself to properly remember Ben since he died. The sequence of events that led to her pregnancy, his birth, the horrifying day he died, is too painful to recollect. All she knows is that the moment she knew he was gone—his little body cold and pale and lifeless as a piece of stone—all the light disappeared from the sky. The world became black—her very soul abandoned her.

She feels now as if the past months of solitude and silence have left her roughly stitched up, a vulnerable layer of new skin covering the boundless black inside. But remembering is agony. Remembering is like pulling on the scar, tearing the stitches apart, exposing the gaping black hole where her heart used to be.

52

"What? He was your *son?*" I feel as though my head has been filled with something heavy and dense. Her words have gone into my ears, but can't get through to my brain. What she's saying makes no sense.

"Yes."

We're both silent for a minute while I try to take it in.

"You had a son and he died?"

"Yes."

And though I knew something bad had happened to her, this is so horrible, so far beyond any of the possibilities I could have imagined, that I'm rendered speechless. I shiver, feeling suddenly cold, as if someone has dragged an ice cube down my spine. I suppress a powerful urge to stand up and pace the room, to swear and kick the walls, to let off some of the nervous energy that has flooded my body. I force myself to breathe, to be still, to stay put.

I watch a tear slide over her cheek, down her neck.

"I just, I can't . . ." I shake my head. "You were a mother?"

"I *am* a mother," she says. "I still very much think of myself as Ben's mother, whether he's here or not."

"Anna. Bloody hell. That's . . . I don't know what to say."

"There's nothing you can say. Don't say anything."

We sit there without talking while she cries some more. I don't say a word. What can I say? This is so far out of my experience. I've never even been close to anyone who died, and from everything I've ever heard, losing a child is the worst thing that could happen to a person. It's unthinkable, an offense to the natural order of the universe.

As I watch Anna cry, I'm struck by how dignified and beautiful she is. She has endured the worst possible thing a person can go through. And all the time I've been living with her she has dealt with this grief, keeping it to herself, trying to cope alone with something so tragic and huge. Before, I thought she was weak; I ignorantly assumed that a stronger person would have been able to overcome the anxiety that kept her trapped. Now I think she's courageous.

"I didn't mean to get pregnant," she says, wiping her face with her sleeve. "It was such a terrible shock when I found out. And Mum and Dad were dead and I had no other family left."

She sniffs again and takes a big, shaky breath. And then she tells me.

53

She was eighteen, only months out of school. Far too young to be a mother.

The positive pregnancy test felt like a joke at first—too insane to be real. She giggled in a strange, hysterical way when she saw the two lines. Then she burst into tears. When she'd dried her eyes and cleaned up her face, she went straight back to the chemist to buy another test.

She didn't see a doctor. She didn't tell Marcus. Or Fiona. She stopped drinking alcohol and cut down on coffee. It wasn't hard. She felt queasy and couldn't tolerate the thought of such extreme flavors anyway. Marcus and Fiona didn't suspect anything—she would accept a glass of wine and simply forget to drink it, and they'd just laugh at her and tell her she was vague. She explained her tiredness, her sudden need for early nights, by saying she had some kind of persistent bug.

She didn't make a decision to keep it. She simply did nothing. By the time she went to the doctor she was sixteen weeks pregnant.

"You can still have an abortion," the doctor explained. "It's just a little more complicated. You may need to stay in hospital."

"But I don't know what to do." Anna put her hand on her stomach. "I haven't decided."

The doctor smiled kindly and put her hand on Anna's shoulder. "Actually, I think you have."

The following week she felt the baby move for the first time. The tiniest flutter, like the wings of a moth brushing against her insides.

The week after that, she told Marcus and Fiona.

"My God," Marcus said.

"How many months?" demanded Fiona, her eyes going straight to Anna's belly.

"Four. Nearly eighteen weeks."

"Oh. So, you're—"

"Yes. I'm going to keep it," Anna explained. "I've decided. It's due in June."

Marcus didn't say a word. He cleared his throat and sat down, then got straight up again and went to the window, stared out.

Fiona glanced at him irritably, sighed, and turned back to Anna.

"That's—well, it's all just quite unbelievable," she said, frowning. "Frankly, I think it's a bit irresponsible. You're just . . . well, you're just too young."

She went on, telling Anna how difficult it would be, how hard and life-changing babies were. Anna let her rant. She knew it came from concern, rather than judgment or unkindness. She tried to catch Marcus's eye while Fiona talked. She wanted to let him know—through a smile, an expression—that he didn't need to worry. Fiona would never need to know. Though he had never explicitly told her so, she knew that Marcus feared Fiona's disapproval. And somehow Anna understood that this baby being Marcus's was something that Fiona would disapprove of, very much.

For her own sake as well she wanted to keep the truth hidden. She valued her relationship with Fiona and Marcus too much to jeopardize it. She would happily keep a secret if it avoided upsetting the status quo.

Anna and Marcus had never discussed the night they'd spent together, never made a single reference to it. They weren't more physically intimate afterwards, or closer, or more casual. It was as if it had never happened at all. Anna wasn't offended. She knew it was just the way he was, and that his reticence had nothing to do with her. He was just far too self-contained to want or need that kind of relationship. And that was fine by her. She liked things the way they were between the three of them, and a more intimate relationship with Marcus would only change things unnecessarily. The baby didn't need to change anything. The baby was his, yes, but that didn't matter. Nobody had to know. It could be their secret. They would never have to discuss it, or even properly acknowledge it. It would just be.

"And the father?" Fiona asked eventually. "Where is he? What does he think?"

"Oh." Anna waved her hand dismissively, made sure she didn't look at Marcus. She willed herself not to blush. "He's nobody. He doesn't want to be involved. He's not really the type. I don't mean to sound flippant or anything, but it's just not important."

Fiona sighed again and Anna thought she was going to argue, insist on knowing who the father was and forcing him to take responsibility. But instead she came and stood behind Anna's chair, put a hand on Anna's shoulder.

"I know you must be afraid," she said. "But we're here. We're here with you. You're not alone."

Fiona and Marcus moved in and the next few months were some of the happiest of Anna's life. With people in the house, it was transformed. Marcus and Fiona helped her paint her bedroom—a soft green, a beautiful, calming color—and together they hung fresh curtains and filled the room with new things for the baby. A white crib, beautiful bed linen, an upholstered chair, things for the baby to chew on and squeeze.

And as the months went by Anna grew bigger, slower. She spent a lot of time dozing, content to do nothing but wait. Wait for Marcus and Fiona to come home from work and keep her company, wait for the weekends, when they would play Scrabble, take long, slow walks in the sun. Wait for the baby to come.

Anna and Marcus never discussed the baby's paternity. But Anna knew that he knew. When the baby started kicking, she suggested that he try to feel it. He refused at first, becoming shy and uncomfortable, but one day he succumbed, put his hand on the taut skin of her stomach and waited. Anna watched his eyes become wide and round. His obvious amazement made her laugh. In the later months, when the baby was much more active, kicking visibly through her skin, he'd willingly put his hand on her belly when invited. And he would look at Anna as if she was amazing, the first woman in the world to grow a baby. Beneath his gaze Anna felt clever, unique, irrationally proud of herself.

Labor started in the middle of the day. Anna had always assumed it would happen at night, while she was in bed. But it started while she was shopping at the mall. She was buying baby clothes. The first pain was in her back, and though it was sharp enough to make her stop and take a breath, she assumed she'd pulled a muscle, or twisted herself the wrong way. She was thirty-eight weeks and didn't expect the baby to come early. She didn't expect to feel it in her back.

The pains kept coming. They had agreed that she'd ring Fiona when labor started, but Anna found herself wanting Marcus. She called his mobile.

"Marcus?" she said when he answered. "I think it's started. I think I'm in labor."

"Where are you?" he said. "I'm leaving now. I'll come and get you."

He drove her to the hospital. On the way she became convinced that it was a false start, that she'd be sent home again, but after they'd parked and were on their way to admissions, she was seized with such overwhelming pain that she had to stop and lean on Marcus. It seemed to last for such a long time and hurt so much, she assumed she must be well advanced, that she would have a quick labor. But she was only in the early stages, and the pain continued for hours, getting worse and worse as the night went on.

"I can't have a baby when I'm in this much pain," she cried, during a brief lull between contractions. "It's stupid. It hurts too much. There must be something wrong."

But the midwives, with their calm, mellow voices, their annoyingly smug faces, assured her that everything was going perfectly.

"I can't do it!" she screamed in the early hours of the morning, just as the nurses changed shift. "I've had enough. I'm going home!"

An hour later Ben slithered out between her legs and cried gustily. She reached for him and the pain miraculously stopped. All of a sudden she loved the midwives, she loved Marcus and Fiona, she loved the entire world. Most of all, she loved her new baby son.

54

As she talks about Ben's birth and his short life, her entire manner changes. She seems softer, more open, and her eyes glow with an almost palpable sense of pride and happiness. It's good to see—however temporary it is—her face so clear and free of shadows. For a moment it's as if she has forgotten. But when she comes to the next bit of her story, Ben's death, her bearing changes dramatically. She hunches over and her face draws down. Her hands twist in her lap. And the only thing left in her eyes is pain.

55

The day Ben drowned was a clear, sunny day, and though it was winter, it was warm enough to open the windows, let some fresh air into the house. Ben was eight weeks old—and for Anna those eight weeks had been miraculous. She hadn't realized that love could be so expansive, so consuming. Had never realized how willing she'd be to surrender every minute of every day and every night to take care of another human being.

She seemed to waste hours and hours each day just gazing at him, staring at the wonder of his little body, his hands and feet, his eyes, his breathtaking smile.

And while on the one hand she felt busier than she ever had, and more productive, and far more needed, she also felt somehow looser and more free than she had before. She felt liberated from worrying about normal things like time, or studying, or cleaning the house. She existed purely for Ben. She slept when he did. Woke up when he needed her. She carried him everywhere, spent hours sitting in one spot either nursing him or patting him to sleep over her shoulder. She wandered around the house in big T-shirts and long skirts, her hair piled high on the top of her head in a loose bun. She felt bounteous and beautiful, voluptuous, womanly. She felt strong and capable and serene.

On this particular morning Ben was fractious and irritable. She'd been up since four and when Marcus came into the kitchen she was relieved to see him.

"Let's take him out," Marcus said, pushing open the French doors, letting the warmth of the day in. He was in one of his rare cheerful moods. He was usually so serious and reserved—and when he was in a mood like this it was hard not to respond, hard not to feel infected.

Anna laughed. "Okay. Yes. What a brilliant idea."

He crouched down beside Anna so that his face was level with Ben's. He used the voice he reserved specially for the baby. "Would you like to go out, young man? Enjoy the day? See some of this beautiful country you've been fortunate enough to be born into?"

Fiona came down to the kitchen a while later and as she helped herself to a bowl of muesli Marcus asked her what she'd like to do.

"Why don't we take the ferry over to the botanical gardens?" she suggested. "Have a picnic."

"A picnic's a brilliant idea," Anna said. "But let's not go anywhere on the ferry. What if Ben starts crying? We'll be stuck."

"We could walk down to Fairlight Pool?"

"We always do that. Let's go somewhere else," Anna said. "Some-where we can drive to. Just in case."

"I know a place," Marcus said. "Haven't been there for years. But there's plenty of shade. You can walk, Fiona, and Ben and Anna and I can relax on the grass."

Fiona made sandwiches while Anna went upstairs to pack a bag. She was ludicrously excited—she'd barely been out of the house since Ben had been born. She ran around her room shoving things in her bag: sunscreen and sunglasses, nappies and creams. A big hat for her, a little one for Ben.

Marcus drove, and when they got there they carried the pram down the stairs to the picnic area and spread blankets beneath a tree. They ate sandwiches and grapes, drank cupfuls of cold orange cordial. Fiona read a book; Marcus lay on his back, hands behind his head, and dozed. Anna fed Ben, then lay on the grass beside him and showed him things—blades of grass, smooth stones, green leaves. After a while Fiona put her book down and said she was going for a walk.

There was a large, noisy family having a barbecue nearby. There seemed to be a lot of kids, aged somewhere between two and fifteen, all of them either shouting or laughing. Once the noise would have bothered Anna but since becoming a mother herself she appreciated children, understood how important they were. She watched the mother tend to one of the smaller children before sending him off with a pat on his bum. The woman looked tired but happy. Anna smiled at the noise and imagined that she might one day have a large family. She imagined she would enjoy the energy and chaos of all those people.

At one stage a ball landed heavily on their blanket, rolling close to Ben's head. A kid followed immediately behind, all breathless and red-faced, and grabbed the ball and ran off again, without apologizing. He stomped over their blanket, upsetting their cups of cordial in his haste and Anna felt a sharp flash of anger at his obliviousness, his lack of care, and then she laughed inwardly at how easily her new sense of tolerance turned to irritation.

After a while Ben became tetchy and Anna knew he was tired and needed sleep. She fed him again and put him in his pram. But he wouldn't settle. He clenched his fists and whined, his face scrunching up like an old man's.

"I think I'll just take him for a walk," she said to Marcus.

"Uh-huh," he said, without opening his eyes.

Anna was surprised how difficult it was to push the pram through the overgrown grass. It was an expensive pram, but meant for city walking and smooth surfaces, not rough, uneven earth. She found it hard going, the too-small wheels kept getting clogged with grass, blocked by stones. She had to stop frequently, which made Ben cry. She thought he would be happy once she could get some speed up, but when she reached the smooth concrete of the ramp his cries only got louder, more frantic. She searched the bottom basket of the pram for his pacifier but couldn't find it. Ben started crying louder.

"Sorry, little man," she said. "So sorry. I just need to find your pacifier."

It would take far too long to push the pram back through the grass so she left it on the concrete and dashed back to the picnic area. She searched briefly around their blankets, and in the baskets and bags of food, but with no luck.

"I'm just going back to the car," she called out to Marcus. "Watch Ben for a second?"

He didn't answer her, or open his eyes, but he lifted his hand in acknowledgment.

She grabbed the car keys and dashed up the stairs to the parking lot. When she found the pacifier tucked into Ben's car seat she sighed with relief. She locked the car and started strolling back down to the picnic area.

It only took a second or two to register the blank space where the pram had been. She didn't panic at first; she didn't think anything at all. She merely turned her head to look around, assuming that Marcus had moved him—that he'd taken him for a walk or back to the picnic area. She wasn't worried.

It wasn't until she looked towards the bottom of the ramp and saw the familiar black curve of the pram handles arcing out of the water, like two strange exotic birds, that she broke into a run.

56

Her story explains everything: her sadness, her anxiety, her isolation.

"Anna. My God. He drowned? That's . . ." I shake my head. "The poor little boy. Poor you."

I don't say the obvious thing. I don't say, *I hope you don't blame yourself, Anna,* because saying that would be like opening the door to an avalanche of pain. Saying that would be acknowledging something too ugly: the horrible certainty that she must feel terrible, responsible. That she must be racked with guilt.

It was an accident, a freak accident, one of those fucked-up things that happen in life, but still, I know she must hate herself.

"Can I tell you something?" she asks, looking down at her lap. "Something I've never told anyone?"

"Of course."

"I've always thought . . . I've always wondered if something else happened that day."

"What do you mean?"

"The ramp. It barely had a slope. In fact I didn't even notice that it sloped towards the water until later, until afterwards. And I'd left it sideways to the slope, facing towards the picnic area, that's the way I was walking. And I just stopped. I didn't turn the pram around to face the water or anything." She sighs, pushes her hair back. "And I know I locked the brake, Tim. I know I did. I was always so careful about things like that. I really was. I was so scared that something might happen to him. And I could remember pushing the lock down. For days afterwards I could really clearly remember the feel of the plastic bar on my foot, the clicking noise it made when it was locked in place."

I watch her face carefully, wait.

"I never mentioned it, not to anyone, there didn't seem any point . . . but there were these other people there that day. This big family with a whole bunch of really wild kids. And I always wondered if one of those kids had . . . just by accident, or just some kind of silly game or something . . . maybe just bumped it. Unlocked it. Turned it the other way or something. Maybe they saw it rolling into the water and freaked out. Ran away. You know what kids are like."

"You should have said something, Anna," I say. "You should have told someone."

"I couldn't. I couldn't go around blaming anyone else, could I? Ultimately it was my fault. Even if someone did unlock the pram or bump into it or even push it. I left him there. I was his mother. I was responsible for him."

"And what about Marcus? He was just as responsible. You asked him to watch."

"He was half asleep. I should have checked that he heard me, that he really understood. I shouldn't have been so complacent. And what would it help anyway if I found someone else to blame? Ben's dead. He isn't coming back. Whether it was my fault or not. Ben is gone."

57

He doesn't turn away or look uncomfortable. His gaze remains direct and open.

He believes her.

And despite her words, her assurance that what people think could make no possible difference, the knowledge that Tim believes her fills her with a beautiful warmth, a satisfying and intense relief. The tension that normally keeps her so trapped and tight and afraid falls away so that she feels soft and buttery, immensely comforted. And her heart expands with happiness in a way that feels perfect and new.

58

"Come with me. I want to show you something," she says, getting up, holding her hand out towards me, and I know by the expression on her face that she means to take me to the attic.

There's a crib in one corner. Next to it a big armchair. The crib is made up with sheets, a soft baby blanket. A colorful mobile hangs over it, yellow ducks and red balls. There's a chest of drawers next to the crib with a collection of framed photos sitting on top of it. Anna holding her baby. Close-ups of Ben's face.

She walks to the crib, reaches up to the mobile and twists the key. The ducks go round, a soft lullaby rings out in the air.

"I just come up here. Sit right here next to his crib." She steps back and lowers herself into the armchair. Fresh tears fall from her eyes and she takes a shaky breath. "I just pretend. That's all. I pretend I'm waiting for him to wake up. I pretend none of this ever happened. That he never died. And sometimes I even believe it. For a second or two. Sometimes I get this wonderful content feeling, like I'm just a normal mother waiting for her baby to wake up. I almost feel happy. And those moments make it worthwhile." She lifts the blanket to her face, presses it to her nose, closes her eyes. "I used to be able to smell him on this. For ages. I think the smell has gone now. But still. It reminds me of him."

"You've spent a lot of time up here?" I ask. "Since he died?"

She nods. "I was on my own most of the time anyway, especially once Fiona and Marcus left. May as well be up here."

"Why did they even move out? I would've thought you'd need them. I would've thought they'd want to help. Be around for you."

She's quiet for a moment, folds the blanket in half on her lap. She keeps her eyes down, smoothes the fabric with her hand. "I'm sure they wanted to help. In fact I *know* they wanted to help. I just don't think Fiona could cope. I was pretty messy when Ben died. Pretty bad. Imagine the emotion of today times ten. And then think of living with that day after day after day."

"Pretty intense," I say.

"And then imagine if you're Fiona, someone who hates even normal displays of emotion. Marcus tried to explain it to me. He said that they had such a messy, unpredictable childhood that now, as an adult, she needs to be in control of things. Of her environment, of every single thing in her life. Well, you can't control grief. You can't even really help the person who's grieving." She laughs sadly. "I think the fact that it just went on and on and on, scared her. Made her feel useless."

"Okay," I say. "I suppose that makes some kind of sense. But . . . one thing . . . while I'm asking questions . . ." I hesitate.

She lifts her head. "Go on."

"The green room?" I ask. "Was that yours before? Was that where you and Ben slept?"

"Yes," she says. "Fiona and Marcus and I did it up before he was born."

"And you shifted into the smaller room after he died?"

"I couldn't stand it in there afterwards. Couldn't sleep. I took my father's old office," she says. "All the other rooms just seemed too big. Too empty."

"Did you ever consider moving?" I ask gently. "Selling up? Getting something smaller?"

She shakes her head. "No. I couldn't. This was Ben's home. This is where he lived. I could never leave."

We're both quiet for a moment and I wonder where things will go from here. What do you do with a person so broken and sad? I feel tongue-tied and inadequate. What she's been through is so huge, so profound, I feel like we come from two fundamentally different worlds. We share a language, a culture, but now that seems like surface stuff. Inside, she's different, foreign, and that scares the hell out of me. I knew exactly what I wanted from her earlier—sex—but now that seems inappropriate and impossible, crude even.

She must sense my thoughts, my confusion, because she stands up and takes my hand, stares straight at me, her expression frank and intense.

"Tim," she says. "Can you do me a favor?"

"Of course. What?"

"You don't have to . . ." She sighs. "You're looking at me differently. And I don't want you to. It's not necessary. Or helpful. I'm sad. Okay. My baby died—I will always, always be sad. But that's not all of me. I'm still a girl and yesterday I remembered that. It was the best I've felt since Ben died. And I know what I've just told you must feel really heavy and serious, but if you could just forget about it for a while? I just want to feel good again. I want to kiss you. I want to get that feeling back again. Last night I felt more alive than I have in forever . . . and right now I just want you to stop looking at me as if I'm an invalid, and start looking at me the way you were last night—as if you like me, as if you think I'm hot." She takes a deep breath and smiles. Her cheeks are red, her eyes wet. She looks more beautiful than ever.

"I do like you," I say. "And you are hot."

"So kiss me, then," she says. And I do.

59

They go back to Tim's room. They move slowly, carefully, both of them self-conscious at first, both trying to seem more confident than they feel. They undress each other, then get beneath the duvet, and once they're both enveloped in the cozy warmth their self-consciousness disappears and they move close, press together, kiss. They take their time, they take hours. They touch and kiss each other all over. Mostly she keeps her eyes closed so she can focus on sensations: the feel of Tim's fingers on her belly, his lips on her neck, the salty smell of his skin, the scratch of his stubble; but when she does open her eyes, she finds Tim smiling at her, his green-hazel eyes wrinkled up at the corners, an expression of surprised delight on his face.

And for a while she's happy, taken up in the moment, remembering what it's like to give and receive pleasure, what it's like to feel alive.

60

The next morning I wake late. Anna's still asleep, curled on her side, facing me. Her expression is peaceful, her lips are turned up, almost as if she's smiling, and I get a buzz from that, from the fact that I've made her happy. I get out of bed as quietly as I can and go downstairs to make coffee.

I go through the familiar process on autopilot, my mind drifting back upstairs, to yesterday. I'm certainly no virgin, and I don't think I'm particularly inexperienced for my age, but being in bed with Anna was a revelation. I've never spent so much time, gone so slowly, taken so much care. I've never before felt so conscious of the other person. I've never fully realized just what a beautiful, transformative thing sex can be.

When I eventually take the mugs back upstairs Anna's sitting up, the sheet pulled high and tucked under her arms. She smiles, lifts the duvet for me.

It's strange, but Anna, naked like this, more exposed and vulnerable than she's ever been, is more comfortable, more at ease, than I've ever seen her.

Anna and I stay in bed all morning and half the afternoon. A couple of painters arrive to fix the mess in the hallway and I get up to let them in but I go straight back to bed and leave them to it. I only get up because I have to take a shower, go to work. I get to the restaurant at four, at least an hour later than I should, considering I'm on my own in the kitchen and have a lot of prep to do. But I'm on a sex high, full of energy, and I get everything done in record time. I think about Anna as I work, what we did together that morning, the night before, what we'll probably do again tonight, and every time I think of her, I get a buzzy, happy feeling in my gut.

I notice Dad watching me from the kitchen doorway. I realize I've been humming and I have a big dopey grin plastered on my face.

"You're in a good mood," he says.

"Brilliant surf before work," I say. There's no real reason to lie, but whatever's happening between me and Anna is still too new. I don't want to talk about it, spoil it by exposing it.

"Yeah?" He looks surprised. "Where was that?"

It's only then I remember that the wind had been onshore when I'd walked to work, and the entire northern beaches would have been crap.

"Dee Why," I say. "Turned out better than it looked. There was an okay break in front of the clubhouse."

"No kidding," he says. "Who'd you go out there with?"

"Just some mates," I say, turning away, uncomfortable with the lie.

Later, in the middle of service, when the kitchen is hot and my hands are full, I hear a text come in. I only look in case it's from Anna.

Tim—Sorry!

Lilla. I push the phone away, ignore it, get back to work. Another text arrives a few minutes later.

Been thinking about it nonstop. I was totally and completely out of line. I feel terrible and I'm really, really sorry. Lilla xx

I'm still busy, hands full, so I don't text her back immediately. When I finally get a chance to pick up my phone, another message appears.

Don't torture me. I really am genuinely sorry. I was being a dick. Can we let it go? Be friends?

Not torturing, I text back. *At work. Flat out.*

Am I forgiven?
This time.
xoxo. Love you. Thank you. And SORRY.

After service I clean up faster and more efficiently than usual, and am ready to leave by half-past ten. Just as I'm turning the kitchen lights out, my phone buzzes again. Another message from Lilla.

You still at work? Come and meet me for a drink at the Steyne? I'm here already. I'll buy you a beer.

It occurs to me that this is the first time I've ever felt inclined to say no to Lilla. She's lost her hold over me. It's just gone. And suddenly, despite everything she's said and done, I feel sorry for her.

What's up? I write back.

Several things. Can we just talk? Won't take too long. Promise.

I find Lilla in a corner booth, cradling a beer in her hands. There's another full glass on the table.

"That one's for you," she says.

I slide into the booth opposite her.

"What's happened?"

She sighs.

"Actually, don't tell me," I say. "Let me guess. You've broken up with Patrick?"

She nods. Her bottom lip quivers and her eyes grow glassy, but she doesn't cry. Lilla doesn't cry easily.

"He's a cheating arsehole," she says.

I try not to look too cynical, too smug, too anything.

"I knew something was going on," she says. "He was acting all strange when I got home yesterday. Something was weird. I just had a feeling, a sixth sense. Anyway, I left my phone in his van with the record function on. He goes out there all the time. Makes these mystery phone calls. He says it's business but that's just bullshit. Anyway, I totally busted him." She slaps her hand down on the table. "The bastard. I recorded him talking to someone. He told her he couldn't wait to get her naked."

"You recorded him? Without him knowing? Wow, Lilla, the trust. It's remarkable."

She rolls her eyes. "So I recorded him. He cheated. I don't exactly think I'm the bad guy in this particular situation." She digs around in her bag, pulls out her phone and starts fiddling around with it. "You want to hear it?"

"No, no, thanks." I don't bother pointing out the hypocrisy of her outrage. No point kicking a dog when it's down. "That sucks," I say. "But you're better off without him."

"Whatever," she says. "I didn't exactly expect sympathy from you. Not after the other day."

I don't say anything. I'm not about to make it easy for her.

"Speaking of which, I was wrong and I'm sorry," she says. "I was being a bitch."

"You were," I say. "A complete bitch. Why?"

"I'm not sure." She stares at her beer, takes a sip, puts her glass down. "I was thinking about it all last night. God, I had a shit night, Tim. Had the most enormous fight with Patrick, so I had to stay at Mum's flat. And then I couldn't sleep because all this crap was going round and round in my head."

"Yeah?"

"The thing is, though, I wasn't actually all that upset over Patrick. I mean, I knew we were going to break up eventually. It was inevitable. I was more upset about the fight you and I had. I felt like crap afterwards, thinking about some of the things you said to me. In fact, I think I just did the whole recording thing so I could bust Patrick and get my mind off my own behavior. Make someone else feel like the bad guy for once." She takes another sip of her drink, and when she looks up she really has got tears in her eyes. She smiles weakly. "You did me a favor. Made me think a bit. And I owe you an apology. A big one."

I shake my head, ready to tell her to forget it, but she puts her hand over mine.

"No. Just listen. I need to say some stuff." She leans forward. "I couldn't get to sleep last night. I was feeling sorry for myself at first, feeling homeless and friendless and hard done by. I kept thinking how unfair everything was, how mean you were, what a shit Patrick was. And then for some reason, I don't even know why, I remembered what the principal at school told me that time I got suspended for playing a trick on Kelly Putland."

"No idea what you're talking about," I say. "Don't remember the girl or the trick."

"Doesn't matter. The point is what the principal said. She basically told me I'd get exactly what I deserved if I didn't wake up to myself and start treating people right. She said I was selfish, self-obsessed. She said I needed to learn some empathy. God, Tim, it was really horrible, really hard to listen to. *So* confronting and awful. Anyway, I stayed up all night and thought everything through—honestly, you know? I thought about how I treated Patrick, how I never properly committed to him, how I was always looking out in case there was someone or something better. I always do that. I always think the grass is greener somewhere else. Anyway, then I thought a lot about my reaction to Anna, and my fight with you, until eventually I had this, well, this epiphany, I guess, and I realized that I was being completely unfair to Anna. I lay there and I tried to imagine what it must be like to be her, you know? I tried to make myself have some empathy for her . . ." She lifts her hands. "And eventually I realized how lucky I actually am. To have my sanity. To be mentally healthy. The thing is, Tim, Anna's such a hopeless case I just couldn't imagine what it must be like to be her. And that in itself says a lot, don't you think?"

I roll my eyes. "Don't beat yourself up too much, Lilla. And, don't worry, Anna's nowhere near as hopeless as you seem to think. In fact she's—"

"Okay. Whatever," she interrupts. "That doesn't actually matter. The point is, I want to apologize. You were right. I was being intolerant and bitchy and I'm sorry."

"No worries." I shrug. "Thanks."

"And there's something else, too. Something you and I need to resolve."

"What?"

"It's about the other stuff you said. In bed. The night of the party." She puts her hand on mine, squeezes. "You were right. I've been stringing you along. Using you as an ego boost, just like you said. I know how you feel about me and I suppose I wanted you to keep feeling that way. It's nice having you there, just in case, you know? Like a big security blanket. But it's not fair. I know that now. The truth is I just wanted you to want me, even if I didn't want you back. It's a crappy way to behave. Especially when I know I just want to be friends. I don't want anything else. You need to know that." She takes a breath. "I'm sorry, Tim. Really sorry."

Her admission, which would have stung like hell a few short days ago, slides over me without leaving a scratch, and I'm surprised by the complete lack of hurt, by my own indifference. "It's all good," I say. "Apology accepted. No harm done."

She looks surprised. "That's it?"

"What do you mean, *that's it*? What were you expecting?"

"I don't know. A bit more than that. You were pretty angry with me the other day. And I probably deserve your anger. I certainly deserve something."

I shrug, lift my glass, drink my beer. Despite her supposed new insight, her insistence that she wants to change, she looks distinctly unimpressed by my lack of reaction. I'm sure she'd prefer it if I broke down in tears, begged her to come back to me. She doesn't like me being indifferent, so eager to leave her.

"So," I say. I'm impatient to get going now—I want to get back to Anna. "Is there something else? You said there were several things you wanted to talk about."

"There is one more thing." She lets go of my hand, sits up straighter, clears her throat. "I need a favor."

"Yeah?"

"Can I stay at your place for a while?"

That makes me laugh. Sometimes I can't help but admire Lilla's nerve. "Anna's place, you mean?"

"Anna's place, then. Can I? Just for a week or two?"

"I thought you said it was a hole."

"I didn't say that. Maybe I said it was weird or spooky. I probably said it was cold. I'm quite sure I never used the word *hole*."

I watch her face, take a slow drink of my beer.

"Look, I've got nowhere else to go, all right? I can't stay at the flat with Patrick. Not now. And if I stay any longer at Mum's you'll be visiting me at East Wing before long. I'll go mental. I'm ready to strangle her and I've only been there one night." She leans forward. "Come on, Tim, you owe me. I let you stay with me and Patrick when you got back from Indonesia. And that wasn't exactly the ideal situation. I just need somewhere to stay until I can sort myself out. A few weeks, tops. I know I'm going to have to apologize to Anna. And I will. And I am really sorry. I'm prepared to do a fair bit of groveling."

"I don't think so," I say.

"Why not? Really. I'm genuinely sorry. Surely Anna will—"

"No," I interrupt. "What I mean is you won't have to grovel. I doubt that Anna has even thought about it since you left. We've been a bit preoccupied."

She looks at me carefully. "So? You're really together, then?"

"I guess."

"What do you mean, you *guess*? Either you are or you're not!"

"I suppose we are, then," I say.

"You said Anna was having a hard time," Lilla probes. "So what happened?"

I shake my head. "Not gonna say. It's none of your business. If you really want to know about Anna you'll have to ask her yourself."

Lilla begs me to tell her, promising to be discreet and sensitive, but I keep my mouth shut. While we finish our beers I direct the conversation on to other things—work, the weather, neutral stuff like that. She tries to convince me to stay and have another drink but I tell her I have to go. I say goodbye and promise to ask Anna tonight and get back to her straightaway.

Anna is startled by Lilla's request—not surprisingly—but I tell her what Lilla said and how sorry she is, and Anna is quiet for only a second before she gives me her answer. I text Lilla, letting her know she has a place to stay, and then I toss my phone aside and give my full attention to Anna, who is warm and soft and willing beside me.

61

Lilla turns up the next morning. I'm just returning from the shops when she arrives in her shitbox of a car. She drives too fast up the driveway and parks right up near the house, crunching on her hand brake so that the tires skid. As if that isn't enough of an arrival, she follows up by tooting her horn twice and jumping out of the car.

"I'm here!" she shouts, waving.

"No kidding," I say. I leave my backpack on the front porch and go over to her car, which is stuffed full with boxes and bags.

"Holy shit, Lilla. What have you brought?"

"Clothes. Music." She shrugs. "Just the essentials. Not that much."

I reach into the backseat, grab a garbage bag full of clothes. Lilla takes another one and we walk into the house.

"So where's Anna?" she asks. "Is she out?"

For a moment I think she's joking, or being deliberately mean, then I remember that she doesn't actually know about Anna's agoraphobia. I wonder if I should at least have told her about that—it might have spared us all some future awkwardness. But Anna appears at the end of the hallway and walks towards us, and it's impossible to mention it.

"Hi, Lilla." Anna smiles. "Do you need a hand?"

Lilla lets her bag of clothes fall to the floor. Before she speaks, she glances at me, looking sheepish, embarrassed. I almost feel sorry for her.

"Thanks so much for letting me stay," she says. "Really. It's fantastic. I just . . . well . . . I don't know what I would have done otherwise."

Anna waves her hand dismissively. "It's nothing. Don't worry about it."

Lilla looks down, pushes the toe of her shoe into her bag of clothes. "I was rude the other day and I'm really sorry. It was stupid. I don't even know why I behaved like that. You must think I'm awful, a real idiot." She looks up, smiles tentatively. "But I'm not. At least, I'm going to try hard not to be from now on. You'll see. And if I do behave like a dickhead again I give you full permission to tell me so, or just kick me out. Whatever you prefer."

Anna laughs. Lilla treads untidily over her bag of clothes and gives her a hug.

Lilla insists on seeing each room before she chooses one—and naturally she barges her way into Anna and Ben's old room.

"This is gorgeous," she says. "I'll have this one." Anna is silent, bites her lip, looks down at her feet.

"Maybe not, Lilla," I say. "Maybe you—"

"It's okay," Anna says. "It's fine, Tim. She can have it."

Lilla either doesn't notice Anna's aversion to the idea or doesn't care. She claps her hands together. "Great," she says. "I just love this shade of green. So calming and fresh. I just love it!"

We help Lilla get her stuff upstairs. Anna manages to help without actually going outside, and without making that fact obvious. By the time we've emptied her car the room is covered with bags and boxes, clothes spilling out everywhere.

"Thanks so much, you two," Lilla says, looking around. "You guys should go and have fun—I can pack everything away. I've actually taken a bit of time off work so I can move and get some other stuff done, but I promise I'm not going to be a nuisance. I'm going to get this done in a flash, then I'm going out. Shopping for some new clothes. Retail therapy. You'll see." She looks at Anna. "I'm totally not going to get in your way. You won't even know I'm here."

62

Tim has to work early that day to prepare for a busy night and he leaves the house before lunch. Anna sits in the attic for a while but eventually gets hungry and goes downstairs. She stops at Lilla's room and knocks on the door. Lilla's room is tidy, her things packed away, her bed made. There are already a few books stacked in the built-in shelves, a retro vase, a large framed photo of Lilla looking glamorous. There has been nothing on those shelves since Anna removed Ben's things and stored them in boxes: his books and rattles, his stuffed panda, a yellow giraffe that Fiona had bought him. The toys he was never old enough to appreciate. Seeing Lilla's things where Ben's used to be hurts like a blow, stops her dead in her tracks.

"Hey, Anna." Lilla is staring at her. "What are you doing? What are you looking at?"

"Nothing." Anna shakes her head, forces herself to breathe, to smile. "I'm on my way to the kitchen. Do you want something to eat? An omelette?"

"Sure," Lilla says. "Sounds great."

Lilla sits at the kitchen table and watches while Anna cooks the eggs. Anna's still not a versatile or creative cook, but Tim has shown her how to make a few things, one of those being a decent omelette, and she's become good at making them light and fluffy, just the way Tim does.

"This is good," Lilla says when she's taken a few mouthfuls. "You can cook."

"No," Anna says. "Not really. Tim's just shown me a few things."

"So? You and Tim?" Lilla lifts her eyebrows suggestively. "How's that going?"

"Fine."

"Do you think," Lilla says, waving her fork in the air, "that it could be serious between you two? I hope so, for Tim's sake. He's the kind of bloke who really needs a girlfriend. You know what I mean? The kind of bloke who's a bit lost when he's on his own."

Anna can't believe what she's hearing. And though she's no longer angry, or even hurt—she's been far too happy to really give it much thought—she heard every word Lilla said to Tim the other day, remembers perfectly well the way Lilla described her.

She doesn't respond, but that doesn't seem to bother Lilla. She leans back, runs her hands through her hair.

"You know, of course, that Tim and I used to go out? Before Patrick? We broke up because we had this big fight about my mum. He just doesn't understand what it's like to grow up disadvantaged. He has such a tight family. The whole nuclear thing, you know? And he has no idea what it's like to be poor, otherwise he wouldn't be wasting his time in that bloody kitchen. Although, God, I really shouldn't be saying this to you. You obviously don't know what it's like to be disadvantaged either." She gestures at the room, then smiles apologetically. "Sorry. Don't mean to be rude. It's just that rich people like you are just completely oblivious to what it's like for others. I know you can't help it. It's inevitable. Just comes with the territory."

Anna concentrates on her omelette.

"Anyway, what I was going to say before I sidetracked myself is that Tim's such a nice guy—even though he's totally hopeless in so many ways—he's also really loyal and honest and stuff. An excellent boyfriend, really. You just have to convince him to fix a few things, you know, take his mum and dad's advice and try a bit harder. Wear some nicer clothes, get a better job, stuff like that."

Anna makes an effort not to get offended at Lilla's comments about rich people. She has learned that Lilla is always blunt and insensitive, an expert at dumb remarks, and it would be a waste of energy to take offense. But the comment about Tim's parents sticks in her throat. She has never met them and it's slightly painful to realize that Lilla knows a lot more of Tim's history, his past.

"So." Lilla drums her fingers on the table, not at all perturbed by Anna's silence. "Are things okay for you right now? Tim mentioned the other day that you were going through a hard time. I mean, you personally, not you two together." She leans forward, tilts her head to the side sympathetically. "I know I don't deserve your trust. I mean, God, you must think I'm a complete bitch, but I am actually a pretty good listener. People tell me that all the time. I know it's probably hard to believe but I can be a good shoulder to cry on. If you need someone, that is. If you want to talk?"

Anna shakes her head, forces a smile. "I'm fine. But thank you. That's a nice offer."

Lilla stares at Anna thoughtfully. "You're quite a private person, aren't you? I envy people like you, people who can keep their feelings and stuff to themselves. I'm all over the place. A complete open book. Gush gush gush, blah blah blah. I can't stop myself." She flashes a wry smile. "As you've no doubt noticed. You'll probably know my whole life story by the end of the day. Feel free to tell me to shut up if I annoy you. I won't notice, otherwise."

Anna doesn't say a word. She doesn't feel particularly annoyed by Lilla; instead she feels wary, on guard. She knows the type of girl Lilla is: curious and engaging but also smart and manipulative, the kind of person who wants to be involved in everything, to have an impact on everyone she comes in contact with, to always be thought of as special. She's the kind of girl who wants to know your secrets— not necessarily because she wants to help, but just because she can't stand being left out. And so she sidesteps her way around Lilla's questions, avoids revealing anything personal.

Lilla's curiosity makes her feel defensive, as though she needs to be vigilant, cautious, as if the questions themselves have the potential to peel back her skin, layer by layer, until she's left exposed and raw and vulnerable.

63

"There's someone here to see you." Dad leans into the kitchen. I'm just wiping the benches clean. I've done most of my prep and I've still got a good half hour before service starts.

"Who is it?"

"Michael? Mark? Didn't catch his name properly."

I'm surprised to find Marcus standing on the other side of the bar. It's not a happy surprise. I'm not in the mood for making stiff small talk, and at the sight of him I feel an unexpected but definite rush of hostility. I'm annoyed that he's here, but I'm even more annoyed that he ever had a thing with Anna. Anna told me that it was only one night, that it was never anything serious. But they had a baby together and no matter how insignificant and brief their relationship was, they will always share the momentous reality of Ben. But I'm being a jealous turd and it's pathetic and I have no real right to feel that way.

I force myself to smile and lift my hand in greeting. "Hey."

"I just had a meeting with a client up the road. Noticed your restaurant and thought I should drop in and have a look." He stands there, stiff and upright, and looks around the room. "Nice place."

"Take a seat. Relax."

He pulls out a stool and sits down, puts his satchel on the counter.

"Can I buy a beer?"

"We're not licensed to sell booze unless you order food as well. So, no, you can't buy one. But I can give you one."

I grab a Boags from the fridge, take the cap off, put the bottle and a clean glass on the bar.

"You sure?" he says. "Thanks. I owe you one."

We don't have a lot in common, and it's a struggle to think of what to say, so I ask him who he had to meet in Manly. He tells me a convoluted story about some rich arsehole involved in some kind of property dispute. I try to follow the story, try to appear interested, but I find my thoughts drifting. I think we're both glad when he finishes his drink.

"I should probably get going," he says, standing up.

"Yeah," I say. "Thanks for dropping in."

It's then that I notice his satchel. It's made of a soft brown leather, expensive-looking, with a large red logo engraved in one corner.

"Is that a designer bag?" I ask him.

Marcus looks down at the case, then lifts his head and smiles. "No, you can get leather bags like this anywhere. But I guess you could say the engraving's designer. Fiona had it done for me."

"Right. A one-off. Cool."

"That it is," Marcus says.

I stand there for a moment and watch him go, my heart racing, my head full of confusing thoughts.

64

After lunch she goes back up to the attic. She sits in the armchair for over two hours but finds herself growing unusually restless. Bored even. Usually she can sit there for hours and hours. Normally she can easily waste most of the day in the presence of the crib, Ben's blanket and photos, in the simple act of being numb. But being with Tim has changed things, filled her with a restless energy, all her senses heightened, as if she's been charged with electricity. She finds herself fidgeting, remembering the smell and taste of Tim, reliving their time together, wondering what the time is and how soon he will be home. She gives up after a while and gets up, locks the attic door behind her.

She's so startled to run into Lilla in the downstairs hallway that she screams loudly, takes a step backwards. She'd been so distracted thinking of Tim that she'd momentarily forgotten there was another person in the house. Forgotten that Lilla had even moved in.

"Oh, Jesus," Lilla says. "Sorry."

Anna puts her hand to her chest, breathes out.

"I scared you to death," Lilla says, laughing.

Anna nods.

"I didn't mean to. Sorry." Lilla looks at Anna curiously. "But then you're easily scared. I bet it doesn't take much."

"I don't know," Anna says defensively. "I think most people would scream if they ran into someone in a dark hallway."

Lilla looks doubtful. "So? Where have you been?"

"Upstairs. In the attic."

"The attic? Really? Again? Weren't you up there before?"

Anna nods. "I thought you were going out?" she asks, suddenly remembering what Lilla had said earlier.

"I was going to but then I got this great idea." Lilla grabs her arms, smiles excitedly. "And I wanted to do it quickly while you weren't around. I wanted to surprise you. I mean, I knew you must be around here somewhere, doing your thing—whatever that is—but I thought if I hurried I could get it done before you emerged back into the light."

Anna watches Lilla's face, trying to gauge things, to understand whether there's some kind of cruel double meaning behind Lilla's words.

But Lilla's smile is wide and inscrutable.

"Come on," she says. "Come and take a look." She leads Anna down the hall towards the living room. When they get there she pushes the door open with a flourish. "Ta-da!"

The room is barely recognizable. The sofas have been moved, the entire room rearranged. Coffee tables that Anna recognizes from the junk room sit at the end of the sofas. Large potted plants give the room a sense of lushness. The pictures have been changed, the ornaments replaced. An enormous green rug in the middle of the floor ties the whole thing together. The room looks transformed. Beautiful. Both more modern and more spacious.

"The sofas work much better facing this way, don't they? I could see that they would as soon as I saw this room. And I brought these potted plants in from the courtyard." Lilla walks around the room, beaming. "And all the other stuff? The coffee tables? This gorgeous rug? I found them all in that junk room. Which shouldn't be called a junk room at all, by the way, it's more like a treasure room. Anyway, I took the old stuff and put it in there. And I rolled up the old maroon rug. It was far too dusty and old-fashioned. Did nothing for the space."

Anna stares, trying to take it in. She can't believe that Lilla has done so much so quickly.

"Where's the flower?" Anna asks, suddenly noticing that it's missing. She runs over to the sideboard. "The ceramic flower that normally sits here. Where is it?"

"Oh, I put it in the junk room," Lilla says dismissively. "Just so tacky. I wrapped it in newspaper in case it was a treasure or something." She sighs happily, collapses back on the sofa. "Looks fantastic, doesn't it? I bet you had no idea it could even look this good. I'm buggered now, though. I did it in a mad rush so I could surprise you. I just couldn't help myself. I knew it was all wrong the way it was." She looks around, a satisfied smile on her face. "So? What do you think? It looks a lot better, doesn't it? Much more inviting. Bigger, too."

It does look better, but Anna can't bring herself to feel pleased about it, or to be grateful for Lilla's effort. She can barely bring herself to smile. She can feel the scowl on her face, her tightened lips.

"I hope you don't mind," Lilla says. "Oh, God, you do mind, don't you?" She sits up straight, looks imploringly at Anna. "Don't be upset, Anna. Don't look like that. It's just that I could see immediately how to improve it. It was all so sad and neglected. And I know you're not up to this kind of stuff right now. I know you're depressed. I know you're having a hard time. I just thought the room would look a lot better this way and I thought it would make you happy. But I've upset you, haven't I? You don't like it? You prefer it the other way?"

Anna goes to the door, wanting only to get away, be alone.

"It's very nice," she says stiffly. "Don't worry about it."

And then she turns and leaves the room.

65

Later that night, when I've finished work, I return from having a shower to find Anna sitting on the edge of my bed. She's chewing her fingernails, looking thoughtful. She watches me as I go to my wardrobe, drop my towel, get dressed.

"What's up?"

"Lilla," she says. "Did you know she rearranged the living room?"

"That was Lilla?" I say. "I noticed that. Didn't know who . . . It looks all right, though, doesn't it?"

"Don't you think it's a bit rude? Doing that in someone else's house? The day you move in?"

"I guess so." I shrug, pull my boxers on. "But that's Lilla."

"It's annoying. So intrusive. She acted like I should be grateful, but I just wanted to tell her to put it all back the way it was."

"You should have, then. If that's what you want. It's your house, Anna. Tell her to change it back tomorrow. Or I will if you want."

"No. Don't worry." She shakes her head. "It doesn't really matter. It probably is actually better this way. It looks more spacious or something. I've never really thought about it. I kept it the way my parents always had it. But that's not really the point. Whether it looks better or not is irrelevant. It's just Lilla's arrogance that annoyed me. She didn't even ask first. It made me feel really strange. I had no idea what to say."

"Don't let it bug you," I say. "That's just Lilla. She can't help herself. She has to fix everything, change the world, even the things that don't need fixing."

When we're lying in bed she asks, "Does Lilla know about my agoraphobia?"

"No."

"You haven't told her anything?"

"Nope. But I will. If you want me to."

"Oh, no, don't tell her. Not unless you have to. I don't want to make a big thing of it. She'll work it out if she stays long enough, and if she doesn't, then it doesn't matter, does it? It's so . . . I don't know. It's just so *uncool*. It's embarrassing. *Agoraphobia*. It's even got an ugly name. And Lilla's so full of life . . . she'll just think I'm completely nuts. And anyway, it's not the real me. At least, I hope it's not." She looks at me then, bites her lip. "Although I wonder sometimes. You must see me like that. You must think I'm this weak, timid person, too scared to go out. You've never seen me any other way." And then, before I have the chance to say anything, she takes my hand and squeezes. Her voice is determined. "I'm going to get better, though. I'm going to force myself. I promise you, Tim. Before the year is up, I'm going to be better."

I watch her face and marvel at how beautiful she is when she's not feeling self-conscious. The last few weeks, as we've become friends, and then lovers, it's as if she's transformed before my eyes, shed a rough and uncomfortable skin to reveal something smooth and natural underneath. She seems like a different person from the girl I first met, that awkward, unfriendly girl who could barely talk to me, or look me in the eye.

"I couldn't think of anything more awesome," I say, pulling her close. And for the first time, I wonder if I might be starting to love her.

66

The next day, when Tim has gone to work, she goes up to the attic again. For a while she considers not going up at all, as a way of making some kind of point to Lilla, proving that she has other ways of keeping herself occupied. But then she feels ashamed of herself for caring what Lilla thinks. She refuses to alter things for her, to bow beneath the pressure of Lilla's scorn.

She doesn't sit in the armchair as usual but spends the time cleaning. She carefully dusts the photo frames, picking each one up, tenderly polishing the glass over Ben's face until it is smudge-free. She dusts the chest of drawers, the windowsills and crib sides. She remakes Ben's crib with fresh sheets. She cleans until the room is perfect and fresh. Fit for a prince.

As if it matters. As if anybody cares.

When the room is immaculate she goes downstairs, locking the attic door behind her. She turns around and is startled to find Lilla watching her from the other end of the hall.

"Anna, hey," Lilla says as she approaches. "Up there again? What on earth do you do up there?"

Anna considers lying for a moment, making something up, but nothing feasible comes to mind, and she can feel her face turning red even at the thought of it. Lilla's so whip-smart she'd know the second Anna lied.

"Nothing much," she says abruptly, hoping Lilla will drop it. "Just sitting."

"Sitting?" Lilla's eyes go wide. "Wow. You really do have a life of leisure."

Anna tries to change the subject. "I'm just going downstairs to get something to eat. Do you want something?"

"Not really. I just ate." Lilla stares behind Anna, towards the attic door. "Can I go up? Have a look? You must have the most fantastic view up there."

"I'd rather not."

"Oh, come on, Anna," Lilla pleads. "Don't be so secretive. The longer you keep me out of there the more curious I'll get. You must know that." She stamps her foot, then smiles as if trying to disguise her impatience. "You must know I can't stand being left out of things."

Anna sighs. Lilla is unbelievably persistent. Annoyingly so. But then maybe telling Lilla about Ben would be a good thing. Knowing the truth might help Lilla understand Anna a little more. It's not that Anna wants sympathy, and she definitely doesn't want Lilla's pity, but she hates being thought of as lazy or ridiculous. She doubts that Lilla will ever be able to understand her grief, but maybe she'll respect it, acknowledge it as something other than weakness.

And so, standing there in the hall, in a quiet voice, she tells Lilla about Ben. His birth, his short life.

Lilla stares, her hand moving up to cover her mouth as Anna speaks.

"He died when he was eight weeks old," Anna finishes.

"I can't believe it. I can't believe you actually had a baby." She looks Anna up and down, as if there should be some evidence of motherhood on her clothes, her person.

"I keep his things up there," Anna explains. "That's all. I go up there to think about him."

"Will you show me?"

Anna nods.

Lilla takes the lead. She holds Anna's arm, walks her to the attic door. "Here," she says, holding out her hand. "Give me the key." She unlocks the door and steps inside. She closes the door behind them and together they climb the stairs.

Lilla doesn't say anything when she first sees the crib. She glances at Anna, then walks slowly towards it, puts her hands on the side rails, stares down at the bed linen.

"This is Ben's?"

"Yes."

Lilla turns away from the crib and lifts one of the framed pictures of Ben. She looks surprised by the image of his face, shocked even, as if she didn't really believe Anna until then. She even blinks several times as if she might actually cry and Anna feels a small rush of warmth for her. Lilla shudders and puts the photo down. She wraps her arms around herself as if she's cold. "He was quite cute. You must miss him a lot."

"Of course. Yes. Horribly."

"What happened? I mean, how did he . . ."

"Die? It was an accident," Anna says. "He drowned."

"Oh, my God. Anna, that's so . . . My God. But how?"

"It doesn't matter."

"You must feel so terrible. You must want to . . ."

"Kill myself?" Anna says. "Yes. Sometimes I do."

"I wasn't going to say that, but, well, yes, I guess you must feel a bit . . ." Lilla shrugs, tilts her head to the side sympathetically. "You poor, poor thing. So. You come up here and, well, do what exactly?"

"I just sit here," she says. "That's all. I come up here and sit in that chair."

"But you come up here for hours at a time." Lilla looks baffled.

Anna shrugs. "It helps."

"It helps? How?"

"I don't know. It just does."

She's not going to go into detail. She doesn't owe Lilla an explanation. And she can tell now that bringing Lilla up here with the hope of garnering any genuine empathy was futile. Lilla would never understand the comfort she gets from being around Ben's things, the transitory moments of pure happiness she gets when she successfully manages to forget that he's gone. A second or two of that feeling is enough reward. Worth sitting there for hours and hours and hours.

"I can't really imagine it. The way you must feel, I mean. I don't understand why you'd want to sit up here. With all this stuff. I don't actually understand how that could help."

"I don't understand it either. I only know it soothes me."

"I guess." Lilla shrugs. "If you say so."

"What?" Anna laughs. "You don't believe me?"

"Oh, I believe you. I just don't think it's healthy. I mean, personally I think it's a bit, well, maybe a bit morbid or something? But then I wouldn't really know because I . . ." She stops, smiles, puts her hand on Anna's arm. "But I have no right to say anything, really. I'm not you, am I? I'm not depressed. Suicidal. And really the whole thing is beyond my comprehension. I've never even wanted children. I don't even particularly like them. So I really can't imagine what you're going through."

"Of course you can't," Anna says. "Nobody can."

67

On Saturday afternoon Patrick turns up at the house.

There were no bookings at the restaurant and Dad was anticipating a dead night, so he gave me the night off. It's been a wet day, and Anna and I have spent most of it in the living room watching movies, eating popcorn, fooling around. Lilla emerged sometime midmorning, nursing a massive hangover. She took some painkillers, made coffee, and took it straight back upstairs.

We're in the middle of our third movie when there's a sharp knock on the door. Anna and I look at each other like a pair of guilty kids.

"Shit." Anna giggles, sits up, straightens her clothes. "Who's that?"

"Dunno. My psychic powers don't work on weekends."

There's another loud rap on the door. Anna raises her eyebrows.

"Go and answer it." She elbows me.

I sigh melodramatically and stand up, tossing the blanket over Anna's head as I leave the room.

I open the door and find Patrick standing there. He's scowling and angry-looking, his arms folded over his chest.

"Where's Lilla?" he demands, and I can smell booze on his breath. He sways.

"What do you want, Patrick?" I say. "Did Lilla invite you here?"

"Invite me?" He laughs. "I need an invitation to see my own girl-friend? Since when?"

Anna comes to the door, stands behind me. I urge her away with my hand.

"Listen, mate," I say. "You're drunk and that's probably not the best way to try and see Lilla. You're only going to piss her off. Why don't you come back some other day, when you're sober, and give her a call first?"

For all I know I'm talking out of my arse. Lilla could be sitting upstairs waiting for him, she might have called him, asked him over, but somehow I don't think so. Patrick has the defensive air of a bloke who knows he's not wanted. He looks down for a moment, staring at his feet, and I can see that this could go either way. He could be cooperative and leave, or try something stupid. When he looks up, his face red and his lips curled in a snarl, I know he's taking the second option.

"Listen, you dumb prick," he spits. "Don't fucking tell me what to do, and don't bother giving me your bullshit advice. Just go and tell Lilla I'm here."

He steps closer, pushing his face aggressively towards mine. My heart rate picks up; my fingertips tingle with adrenaline. And even though he's more than twice my size, puffed up with all that muscle, I would have loved to fight Patrick a few weeks ago, back when I thought he was the major cause of all my troubles. I would have hurt him, too. Desperation can make you stupidly fearless. I used to imagine the satisfaction I'd get from hitting him: my clenched fist smacking into his ugly face. But right now, I'd have no chance. I just want to go back inside and watch TV. I don't care. I don't hate Patrick anymore—if anything, I feel a bit sorry for him. And my lack of passion would definitely be a disadvantage in a fight.

"Patrick. Stop with the insults, okay?" I sound more confident than I feel. "And step back a bit. You're starting to come across as aggressive. Lilla wouldn't like it. You know that."

I'm bluffing a bit, but it seems to work. He steps back, puts his hands up in an appeasing gesture.

"Just go and get her for me. I need to speak to her. Just tell her I'm here." He looks at me then. His eyes are bloodshot, desperate, and I feel even sorrier for him. I can see how unappealing this kind

of desperation is, and I know that Lilla won't respond to it, or respect him. He's only wasting his time, making things worse for
himself.

"Wait," I say. "I'll go and tell her you're here."

I leave Patrick on the porch and close the door. I lock it, not caring that he'll hear the dead bolt click through. Anna's standing in the
living-room doorway and I explain to her quietly what's going on,
then I go upstairs to Lilla's room.

She doesn't exactly look thrilled to hear that Patrick has come to
visit.

"Fuck," she says, rolling her eyes. "You didn't tell him I was home,
did you?"

"I didn't tell him you weren't, and he's not going to believe me if
I say you're not here now."

"Goddamn it to hell and back," she says, and gets out of bed,
clomps noisily over to the full-length mirror. She runs her fingers
through her hair and sighs. "I look like total shit." She's wearing a
big, loose T-shirt and her hair is messy. She starts trying to fix it with
a brush and clips.

"Lilla, why the hell do you care what you look like? I thought you
didn't even like the guy anymore."

"It's a matter of pride," she says, and she takes her loose top off,
puts a tiny black T-shirt on.

I watch her rummage through her clothes. I'm curious, puzzled.
"What's the point? What do you care what he thinks? Don't you
want to get rid of him?"

"What?" She turns to me, exasperated. "What are you on about?"

"If you go down there looking hot you're only going to make
things worse."

"God, Tim, just shut up, would you? This has nothing to do with
you."

"You're right," I say. "I will shut up. Mainly because I don't actually care."

Lilla stops what she's doing and comes closer until she's standing directly in front of me. She puts her hand on my shoulder. "Don't say that," she says, pouting. "You do care. I know you do."

I don't hurry down after her, and I fully intend to return to the living room and Anna, but when I get back downstairs the front door is open and I see Patrick standing drunkenly over Lilla, his hand gripping her arm.

I watch, make sure Lilla's okay.

"That's enough," Lilla says, pulling away from him. "You should go now. We'll talk some other time, when you're sober."

"What the fuck is wrong with you?" he says. "Too good for me now, huh, now that you live in Fairlight? Too good to talk to your own boyfriend?"

"Don't be ridiculous, Patrick. And you're not my boyfriend. We broke up, remember? I know you're thick, but I'm sure you can work out what that means all by yourself."

Lilla flinches as he pulls her roughly towards him, his grip on her arm tightening.

"Hey," I say, stepping towards them.

"Getting too big for your boots, eh, Lils? Think you're something special now, do ya, living here? Big house given you a big head or something, eh? Well, I wouldn't get too smart. Do your new housemates know you haven't even got a job anymore? Do they know you got fired? Bet you haven't told them that little detail."

"Oh, piss off, Patrick. Just go away." Her words are brave but I can hear the embarrassment in her voice, the trace of alarm.

"Mate. Come on, let her go." I put my hand on his shoulder, try to make my voice sound reasonable, nonconfrontational. "Don't do anything you'll regret."

He ignores me. He holds tight to Lilla's arm and drags her down the porch steps and on to the front lawn.

"Fuck, Patrick," she cries out. "What the hell—"

"I just want to talk to you," he says, his voice cracking with emotion. "I just want to talk and you're being a stuck-up bitch."

I follow them onto the grass and push myself between them so that he's forced to let go of Lilla's arm.

"Fuck *off,*" Patrick screams at me. "Just fuck off and leave us alone, you dumb fucking loser."

He lurches towards Lilla again and I grab his shoulder, trying to hold him back, but he's stronger and angrier than me and I don't have much chance. He reaches for Lilla with one hand and takes a swing at me with the other, hitting me straight in the gut. It's not a full-blown punch, more a distracted backhander, but it still hurts like hell, knocks the air out of me, and I double over, trying to catch my breath.

And then a shout comes from the front porch that makes us all stop. It's Anna, her voice strong and furious.

"Let go of her right now and get the hell off my property!" It's the first time I've seen her so angry, and I'm so startled I forget the pain in my gut, stare up at her. Her eyes are flashing, her cheeks are flushed. She's magnificent with rage. "How dare you come here and act like such an arsehole! Get out of here! Now! Or I'll call the police."

Patrick looks startled, too, as if he can't quite believe the small blond girl on the porch could have such authority. He lets go of Lilla and looks from me to Anna, then back at me. I can almost see his brain ticking over, weighing up his options. Should he stay and fight, or go before he makes things worse? Anna has her phone in her hand and is holding it up for Patrick to see. Lilla has her arms folded across her chest and is staring at him with dagger eyes.

"Okay, okay," he calls. "You don't need to call anyone. I'm going."

He takes a step away, but suddenly stops, lurches towards me and grabs my shirtfront. He pulls me so close I can feel his breath against my skin, smell the fumes of whatever it is he's been drinking. "You watch your back, arsehole. Stay the fuck out of my way."

"I have no intention of getting in your way, Patrick," I say. "I'd rather not go anywhere near you." He shoves me and I stumble backwards, only just managing to stay on my feet.

He staggers to the gate, looking drunker than he did when he first got here. It's a pathetic sight, and with the safety of distance, he starts looking more ridiculous than threatening.

He stops and points at me before he crosses the road. "I'm watching you, Ellison," he says. "Ya fucking dog. I'm watching you."

After he's gone, Anna, Lilla and I sit around the kitchen table and have coffee.

"Well, that was an unexpected adventure," I say. "You certainly picked him from the bottom of the barrel, Lilla."

"But he's not like that," she says. "Not really."

"But he *is* like that," I say, exasperated. I'm no longer jealous of Patrick, but it still annoys me that she's sticking up for him. "Obviously. He was just here *being* like that. And what was that he said about your job? You didn't tell me you got fired."

Lilla glares at me. "It's a complicated story. I was treated unfairly. And I didn't tell you because you would only say it was my own fault. Anyway." She turns to Anna. "I'm sorry. I've never seen Patrick act like that before."

"It was probably just an aberration," Anna puts in diplomatically.

"Exactly." Lilla nods. "I'm sure he'll be devastated tomorrow. He'll probably ring and apologize."

"I bloody hope not." I think of the night I saw him at the pub, the footsteps I heard later, the feeling that I was being followed. "I just wonder how well you really know the guy, Lilla."

68

The next morning, for the first time in weeks, I get up early for a surf. The air is cool but the water's warm, and once I'm actually out there, I forget about everything but the water and my body and the sky and the sea. I exist as I only ever do when I'm surfing or having sex—purely in the rush of the moment. And as I walk back up the beach I have my usual post-excellent-surf thoughts: I kick myself for forgetting how awesome and perfect it is, for forgetting how an early-morning surf can set a good tone for the rest of the day. And I swear to myself that I'll make the effort to come out more often—every day, if possible.

When I get back to the house I run upstairs to Anna. It's dark in our room, the curtains drawn, and I take off my clothes quietly. I get beneath the sheet and wrap my arms around her back. Pressing my skin against hers is like lowering myself into a fragrant bath.

"Oh," she says in a soft murmur. "You're cold."

"Make me warm, then."

And she turns to face me, opens her arms, and does just that.

Later, I go to the kitchen and make enough bacon and eggs and fried mushrooms for the three of us. When it's done I go upstairs and tell the girls to come down. Lilla enters the kitchen in her dressing gown, looking a lot healthier than she did yesterday. Anna appears a moment later. She's dressed, her hair wet from the shower. We smile at each other.

"Oh, stop it, you two," Lilla says. "Those looks you're giving each other. You're making me sick."

We each have a huge plate of food and we all go back for seconds. Lilla makes coffee when we've finished and we sit around the table, content, bellies full.

"Why don't we have a dinner party?" Lilla says.

"We just had a party," I say.

"No. I meant a small thing. A *dinner* party, Tim. It's quite different." She smiles sheepishly, looks at Anna. "Actually, I was thinking we should invite your friends over for dinner, Anna. That bloke I met at your party last week. Marcus? And his sister?"

"Fiona?"

"Yes. Them. They seemed pretty nice."

"They are nice," Anna says, looking puzzled. "I'm just not sure—"

"But wait," Lilla interrupts. "I just have one really important question I need to ask first." She grins. "Is Marcus single?"

"You can't be serious," I say. "You haven't even got rid of Patrick yet."

"I have so got rid of Patrick. It's not my fault he's having problems understanding that fact."

"Shouldn't you try being single for a week or two?" I say. "So you can find yourself or something?"

"Nah. That's all bullshit. Why am I more likely to find myself by being alone? All I'll discover that way is that I'm lonely," she says. "And horny."

"God, Lilla."

"Don't be so uptight, Tim. Why shouldn't I pursue love if I want to? I don't like being alone and I'm happy to admit it. It's boring." She shrugs. "And I just thought Marcus seemed nice. Mature. It can't hurt to get to know him, can it? I'm not going to ask him to marry me or anything. I just thought it might be fun to get to know some new people. You know, plant some new trees in my social garden."

I look at Anna but it's hard to know if she's upset or not. I know she wouldn't like the idea, though. She makes an uncertain gesture, lifts her shoulders.

"What is it?" Lilla asks, looking at Anna. "Have I put my foot in it? Did you two have a thing or something?"

"No," Anna says. "Not that. And yes, he is single, but he's also very shy."

"That's okay," Lilla says. "I like shy. I can handle shy. In fact, I'm so *not* shy, I think I'm better off with a shy person. You know, yin and yang? A bit of karmic balance or something?"

"I don't know," Anna says. "He's not really the type to enjoy being . . . I don't know . . . what is this? A setup? A blind date?"

"No," Lilla says. "It's nothing like that. Not at all. It would just be a normal dinner party. I won't make it obvious or anything. If we hit it off, we hit it off. If we don't, we don't. No harm done."

"I suppose I could call him," Anna says. "I suppose it couldn't hurt."

"Of course it won't hurt! It'll be fun!" Lilla stands up and grabs Anna's phone off the kitchen bench, slides it across the table. "Call him now."

"Not now," Anna says. "It's too early. Later."

"Today?"

"Maybe."

"Please?"

"Okay. Later."

"Promise?"

"Promise."

69

She does as Lilla has asked, and calls Marcus. He agrees to come to dinner the following weekend. When she tells him that Lilla will be there, that she's staying with them at the moment, Anna is sure she hears a change in his voice, a slight sharpening in his interest.

She's not sure why she feels bad about it, or quite where this feeling of possessiveness comes from. Surely she wouldn't begrudge him love? Especially not now that she has Tim. All the same, she feels out of sorts and irritable for the rest of the morning.

Later that day, Lilla suggests that they all go down to Manly.

"There's a band playing down at the Corso. And it's such a beautiful day. We can have a beer or ten."

Tim looks keen for a second, then he glances over at Anna, as if only just remembering that she can't leave the house. He shakes his head. "Nah. We might just stay here."

"What?" Lilla says. "You're joking, right? Since when have you been such a homebody? Come on, the weather's perfect. It'll be awesome."

"I won't," Anna says. "But you go, Tim. Really, I don't mind," she says, as cheerfully as she can. "I've got some things I need to do here."

"Oh, come on, Anna," Lilla says, taking Anna's hand, bouncing around her. "Let's go and have some fun."

And though Lilla's words and actions seem friendly enough there's something cold in her face, something sharp in her eyes that bothers Anna, makes her wonder what Lilla is playing at. She gets the strange feeling that Lilla is performing—she just can't work out what or why.

"No. Really." She pulls her hand away. "I can't."

"I'll stay here, too," Tim says, "and help you out."

Anna shakes her head and plasters a big smile on her face. "Don't be stupid. Go on. Leave me alone for a while."

"If you're sure?" Tim can't help but show his pleasure, and though she doesn't show it—it would be like trying to keep him trapped, just as she is trapped—she can't help feeling disappointed.

"Of course," she says. "Go. Have a beer for me."

She watches them from the living-room window.

They walk together, Lilla's shapely brown legs going fast to keep pace with Tim's much longer ones. The two of them are laughing, Lilla leaning into him when she talks, looking up at him, her face so pretty and animated. Both of them are oblivious, taking everything for granted: the world and the fact that they can be a part of it, their own easy confidence.

When she can no longer see them, Anna pulls the curtain closed, turns back to the empty room.

She lies belly-down on the sofa and buries her face in a cushion. She screams as loudly as she can. Nobody can hear her and she screams until her throat is hoarse, screams until the fabric is wet with her spit and tears. She screams until the image of Tim and Lilla walking down the road, away from her, is replaced by a head full of black.

70

"I like Anna," Lilla says, as we walk. "I really do. But she's definitely pretty messed up. You should be careful. I mean, I know her baby died and everything, but that shrine she's got up in the attic? Why the hell—"

"I don't want to hear it, Lilla," I interrupt. "Stop now before you start pissing me off."

"But come on, Tim," she says, glancing at me sideways. "It's creepy. It totally gave me the shivers. You should be worried about her. I mean, I certainly am. She's totally depressed. Like, why didn't she want to come out with us? She never does anything. It's *weird*. She hangs around that house like an old lady."

I watch her face but can't properly read her expression. Is the smile on her face a smug and knowing one, or is she just being mischievous, her normal tactless self?

"Maybe she just likes doing her own thing," I say neutrally. "She's independent. Self-contained. You'd probably benefit from being more like that yourself."

She shrugs and the strange smile is replaced with a more natural one. "Yeah." She laughs. "Maybe you're right. Maybe I would."

When we get to Manly we stand and watch the band for a while but it's hot in the sun and my throat is dry and I long for the beer Lilla mentioned back at the house. We go to one of the restaurants with outdoor seating and order beers and hot chips. And as we eat and drink, and finish our first beer and order a second, Lilla talks, telling me about the recent workplace drama that ended in her being sacked. Lilla's outrage seems misplaced but I don't bother saying anything, instead I nod, only half listening, enjoying the atmosphere, the noises, the people.

I'm sitting there half listening to Lilla, relaxed with the sun and the music and my gently inebriated state, when Lilla's phone rings. She lifts her bag to the table and rummages through it, tossing scraps of paper and tissues on the table as she searches.

By the time she's found the phone it's stopped.

"Damn it," she says, standing up. "Sorry, Tim. I just need to return that call. Won't be a sec."

She walks away, phone pressed against her ear. I start cleaning up the mess she made, putting tissues and papers back into her bag.

Among the mess I find a photo. A photo that has been ripped in half and defaced. It was clearly a picture of Anna and somebody else—the blond hair and thin body are unmistakable—but the second person has been torn away, and Anna's face has been scratched off with something sharp. Jagged marks zigzag aggressively through her head, leaving her face an eerie-looking blank.

I shove everything else back into Lilla's bag and by the time she returns I'm pretty sure I've managed to erase the expression of shock from my face.

She puts her phone back in her bag, pushes it to the other side of the table.

"Sorry 'bout that," she says, taking a chip.

I drink my beer and don't say a word.

71

When she's calmer and can breathe normally again she stands up. Brushes her clothes down. Pulls her shoulders back.

She always feels drained when she loses control like that, lets herself give in to her grief. She feels slightly embarrassed, too, as though she has humiliated herself before the universe, succumbed to something weak and shameful within herself. She considers going to the attic for a while to make herself feel better, to find her equilibrium again, and heads upstairs. But when she walks past Lilla's bedroom she notices something from the corner of her eye that makes her stop.

On the shelf, next to the photo of Lilla, is the ceramic flower. The one her father gave her. Seeing it there makes her heart pound, her fists clench with sudden anger.

Marching into Lilla's room, she is full of outrage, a sense of having been violated. How dare Lilla take such liberties! She picks up the sculpture, runs her hands over its familiar glossy surface. She will take it downstairs, put it back in the living room where it belongs. She will confront Lilla when she gets back—tell her to keep her hands off her stuff.

But then an idea starts forming in her mind. She won't take the flower. Not yet. She returns to the bookshelves and puts it back where she found it.

She leaves Lilla's room and heads back down the hall towards Tim's. She pushes his door open and goes to his desk. His laptop starts up when she lifts the lid, the pages Tim was last looking at appearing on the screen. The surf report. Facebook. She sits down. Leans forward. Starts searching for some answers.

72

I insist on going back to Fairview as soon as I finish my beer. Lilla complains and calls me a piker, but as we're leaving she bumps into a group of friends and decides to stay with them. I head home alone.

I find Anna sitting in the kitchen. My laptop is open on the table in front of her. She has an intense, thoughtful look on her face.

I sit next to her.

"What are you doing?"

"Look at this." She turns the computer so that I can see the screen. She's on Lilla's Facebook page. There's a picture of Lilla standing in the street, holding her clenched fist in the air.

"Lilla being Lilla." I shrug. "What about it?"

She points to the building behind Lilla, then flicks to another website, another image of the same building.

"But that's—"

"Yes. And the interesting thing is that this image was uploaded over a year ago."

I feel my mouth drop open in shock. I can't believe it. It can't be coincidence—it would be far too unlikely—but I can't figure out what it means.

"I don't get it," I say.

"Neither do I. But I think I'm starting to."

"There's something else," I say. I take the photo from my wallet and hand it to Anna.

"This fell out of Lilla's bag earlier. I wasn't sure whether I should show you."

"My God." Anna's eyes go wide. "Does she know you have this?"

"No."

"Good. Let's not say anything. Not yet. We need to think first. We need a plan."

Later, as we're lying side by side in bed, both of us quiet, still partly in shock from what we discovered earlier in the day, I turn towards Anna and put my hand on her stomach, trace a small circle on her soft white skin. "You okay?"

"I'm fine. You?"

"Don't know. Confused."

She grabs my hand and turns away from me, pulling my arm around her. She shifts backwards, nestling close.

"Maybe we should cancel that dinner thing next week?" I say. "With Marcus and Fiona?"

"No." She shakes her head. I can't see her face but her voice is determined. "Let's have it. It's the perfect chance, Tim. They'll all be here. We can finally get to the bottom of this. Find out what she's playing at, what's really going on."

73

I spend the following Sunday afternoon in the kitchen, doing most of the food preparation before Marcus and Fiona arrive. Lilla heads out for a while and comes back to the house with booze.

"Cocktails!" she announces, loading bottles of tequila and Cointreau and a bag of limes onto the counter.

She starts making a batch immediately. She collects ice in a jug, pours the spirits generously, squeezes lime over the top, stirs it all together.

"Want one?" she asks.

"Nah," I say. "Not yet. I'll wait."

"God, Tim, don't be such a drag," she says. "Where's Anna? We should all have a pre-party cocktail."

"Still upstairs. Having a bath, I think."

She ignores the fact that I declined and edges three wineglasses with salt. She pours the cloudy concoction in, filling them right to the brim. She hands me one.

"Bottoms up!" she says, pressing her glass against mine.

I take a small sip, grimace with the salty, bitter heat of it.

"You don't like it?"

"It's okay." I put the glass down. Turn back to what I was doing. "But I told you I didn't want one."

"Maybe I know you better than you know yourself."

"Maybe you just don't know how to take no for an answer," I say irritably.

"I think you might be right about that." She laughs as she picks up the other two glasses and leaves the room. "In fact I think you're absolutely spot-on."

74

Lilla walks into the bathroom without knocking and Anna's so startled to see her, so unused to being naked around other women, that she brings her knees up and plunges down beneath the water, putting her hands between her legs.

"It's okay." Lilla rolls her eyes at Anna's modesty. "I've seen it all before. I was just bringing you a drink." She puts the glass on the vanity near the bath and turns to go, stopping in the doorway. "Come to my room when you've finished. We can get ready together."

Anna must look either blank or baffled or both because Lilla laughs. "We can do each other's hair. You can help me choose what to wear. And if you bring some clothes I'll help you."

"Oh, I'm just wearing jeans," Anna says. "I don't need any help."

"No, you're not. No way. You're going to have some fun tonight, Anna London. You're going to dress up. We both are. We're going to make an occasion of it. And you may not need any help, but I do." She stops to think for a moment, tapping a finger on the rim of her glass. "In fact, I've got the perfect dress I can lend you. It's gorgeous. It's a bit too small for me these days, tight around my back, but you're so thin, it'll definitely fit. Come straight to my room. I'll be waiting."

Anna can't be bothered arguing and she doesn't particularly care what she wears—jeans, a dress, it's all the same to her—so she nods her agreement. She'll save her energy for the fights that matter.

When Lilla has gone Anna reaches up for the glass and, holding it carefully, slips back down into the bath, so that she is almost lying flat on her back, only her hands and head above the water. She holds the glass in two hands and swirls the liquid around so that some of it spills over the rim. And then she lowers the glass into the water, slowly, until bathwater spills into the liquor and turns it soapy, until the entire glass is completely submerged.

"It's perfect!" Lilla says.

The dress is black and short and tight. It's very low cut in the front, showing a lot of cleavage, and dips low at the back. It fits perfectly, snug without being too tight, and ends well above Anna's knees.

It's an effort to hide her discomfort when Lilla stands too close. Lilla's hands go everywhere—touching Anna's arms and back and hips—fixing the dress, straightening the shoulders, pulling the skirt taut over Anna's behind. She wants to pull away when Lilla's hand touches her skin, but she closes her eyes, breathes through it and pretends not to mind. When Lilla's happy with the fit of the dress she persuades Anna to sit on a stool so she can fix Anna's hair and makeup.

Lilla works for ages on Anna's hair, blow-drying and straightening, putting some kind of gel in it to give it body. And when that's done she turns her attention to Anna's face, using three different kinds of foundation, blush, a gallon of eyeliner. Lilla bites her lip with concentration as she leans close to Anna, and for a moment Anna is filled with a sharp sense of regret.

"Okay. Finished. Come and have a look." Lilla guides Anna to the full-length mirror, stands behind her. "See, look at you!"

The dress is sexy and revealing, so different from the kind of thing Anna normally wears that she can't help but gape stupidly at her own reflection. Lilla has teased Anna's hair and brushed it back from her face, making her look much edgier, tougher. And her makeup is startling and dramatic. If Anna wears makeup at all it's usually just a swipe of gloss on her lips and not much else, but Lilla has neglected

Anna's lips, concentrating instead on her eyes, outlining them with so much black they look deep-set and dark. She looks sexy, wild, slightly mad.

"Thank you." Anna smiles uncertainly. "A bit tarty, maybe. Very different. Nice. I think?"

"Tarty? You look hot, not tarty, Anna, hot," Lilla says. She stares at Anna with one eyebrow raised. "You are a strange person, Anna London. You're so repressed and old-fashioned, like someone out of a book. But that's okay. I like you anyway. And as my nan would say, it takes all sorts to make the world go round."

"I'm so glad you like me, Lilla," Anna says with cold sarcasm. "Thank God you approve."

"Oooh." Lilla laughs. "And there go your manners and out comes your nasty side. And that's exactly what I like about you. You're surprising. Complex. I never know what to expect."

Lilla persuades Anna to stay while she decides what to wear. She tries several outfits before eventually choosing a short black miniskirt, black boots and a red gypsy-style top. She layers beads around her neck and bracelets on her wrists so that they clatter together musically whenever she moves. She styles her hair with a handful of gel and finishes up with a long pair of earrings. Anna watches in genuine admiration. Lilla certainly knows how to put herself together.

"You look gorgeous," Anna says, when Lilla stands before her and spins on the spot. "Absolutely beautiful."

"Not too wild for your conservative friend?"

Anna shrugs. "I wouldn't know."

Lilla puts her glass to her lips and takes a deep sip. She looks around the room. "Where's your drink?"

"I finished it," Anna says. "Ages ago. In the bath."

"See? You are surprising!" Lilla says. "So meek and mild and yet you drink like a trouper. How about we go downstairs and get another one?"

"Won't we be drunk?" Anna says. "Before they even get here?"

"I bloody hope so," Lilla says. "That is the point, after all." And then she reaches out and takes Anna's hand. "Come on. Let's go downstairs and see what Tim's doing. We can put some music on and wait for your sexy friend Marcus to get here."

When Tim sees Anna his eyes go wide and he gives a low whistle.

"Doesn't she look hot?" Lilla asks, but Tim doesn't answer, he grabs Anna around the waist, pulls her towards him, kisses her.

"Oh, for God's sake. I'm going to go and put some music on," Lilla says, flouncing off towards the living room.

"Are you ready for this?" he asks when Lilla has gone. His voice is suddenly a whole lot deeper. "For tonight? Are you feeling okay? And what the hell are you wearing?"

And then he kisses her again, giving her no chance to respond.

By the time Lilla returns, Tim and Anna have separated. Tim is at the fridge, Anna is sitting on a chair. Lilla sits on the table above Anna and swings her legs, drums her fingertips, nervous energy radiating from her like heat from an oven.

"God," she says. "I hate waiting." Her statement comes out like some kind of prophetic demand to the universe, because a moment later the doorbell rings. She lifts a fist in the air triumphantly and slides from the table. "Let the part-ay begin!"

Somehow the five of them get stuck in the hallway, standing around making stiff conversation. Anna can feel the self-consciousness coming off both Marcus and Fiona in waves, and she and Tim aren't much better.

"God, this is painful," Lilla says, pushing off the wall. "We need to get some drinks into you two. We're all ahead of you. And I don't want to be rude, but look at you! You're both so uptight. It's as if you're at a work meeting."

Marcus gives a small, embarrassed laugh. Fiona only frowns.

"I'm driving," Fiona says. "Sorry."

"And I'm working tomorrow," Marcus says. "I can't really—"

"Work schmerk. You're only young once, Marcus," Lilla says, and she takes his hand and attempts to drag him towards the kitchen. But he resists, doesn't move a millimeter.

"Thanks, Lilla, no. Really."

Lilla doesn't give up. Instead she uses her other hand to take his free hand and leans back hard so that he's forced to step forward. "I won't stop until you have one. And I'm not joking. If you think I am, just ask Tim how persistent I can be."

Anna wonders if Marcus will hold his ground, and watches with interest as he gives in. He laughs and lets Lilla drag him down the hall, towards the kitchen.

"I think I'll go and get a drink, too," Tim says. "Anna? You want one? And Fiona—are you sure?"

When Tim has gone, Anna turns, smiling, to face Fiona.

"What on earth are you wearing, Anna?" Fiona says, looking Anna up and down. "You look completely different."

"Of course I look different!" Anna laughs. "Lilla dressed me. And I've got all this eye makeup on. It hasn't smudged down my face or anything, has it?" When Fiona doesn't answer she leans towards her and whispers, "Anyway. None of that matters. The important thing is . . . the thing I really can't wait to tell you is that I actually think I might be happy. Really, genuinely happy. Tim and I—"

Fiona jerks away, looks at Anna as if she has smelt something bad. "Don't tell me you're starting something with Tim. You're hardly in any kind of emotional state for a new relationship."

"But listen," Anna says. "Fiona. I know what Tim's been telling you. He told me. And it's not what you think. The spiders, the paint on the walls, I didn't—"

"Stop it, Anna. Just stop. Now. I refuse to listen to this . . . to this . . ." She stops and turns away, starts following the others towards the kitchen. But Anna hears her last muttered words. "This insanity."

75

Fiona marches into the kitchen, looking like she's prepared for some kind of war. She pulls a seat from the table and sits down, folding her arms across her chest. Anna appears behind her looking flustered. I look at her quizzically, wondering what has happened, but she just mouths the word "Later."

Lilla makes another jug of drinks and forces a big glassful on everyone except Fiona. Anna holds her glass in both hands, and though she lifts it to her mouth, I don't think she actually swallows much. Like me, I know she wants to stay sober, alert. I take the smallest sip I can, barely wetting my lips. Tonight I have to be sharp. Fully present.

We all sit at the kitchen table. Anna sits opposite me and I stretch my legs out, press her feet between mine, a gesture of support, comfort. She flashes me a brief, tense smile.

I'm not sure what the deal is with Fiona, but her face remains dark and angry, and she drinks her water with a sour expression, as if she'd rather be anywhere else. She glares at Marcus every time he takes a drink, and deliberately ignores Lilla.

"To Fairview." Lilla lifts her glass in a toast. "The most beautiful house in Sydney."

We all touch glasses. Drink.

Lilla grins across the table at Marcus. "Drink up. I want you to catch up with me," she says. She takes a large sip of her own drink and sighs contentedly. She looks at Fiona. "Enjoying your water?"

Fiona glares at her, but doesn't respond. She turns to look at Marcus. "You're going to regret this tomorrow," she says. "We're supposed to be meeting Frank Fletcher at eight. You really need to be in top form."

Lilla splutters rudely into her drink. Then she wipes her mouth with the back of her hand, leans forward slightly and looks at Fiona as if she's some kind of fascinating specimen. "So," she says. "I know I don't exactly know you, and feel free to tell me to mind my own business, but I think it's safe to say that you're more than a little uptight. So—what's wrong? Anything you want to share? It might help to talk."

"I'm not uptight," Fiona says coldly. "I simply find certain things tedious."

"Tedious? Really?" Lilla says. "And what exactly are these certain things? If you don't mind me asking."

"Leave it, Lilla," I say, glaring across at her. "Just bloody drop it, okay?" She's incredible. Unbelievable. She insisted on inviting Fiona and Marcus only to start an argument before we've even finished our first drink.

Lilla stares at me for a minute, her eyes flashing in anger, and I can almost see her wondering whether it's worth putting up a fight. She must decide it's not, because eventually she puts on a wide-eyed, innocent expression. "No problem, Tim. I'll drop it. Though I don't know why you're getting so mad at me. I'm not the one being rude."

76

Though Tim has cooked dinner, Lilla insists on helping him take it to the dining room, and when everything's ready she takes charge, clapping her hands together bossily and telling everyone that it's time to eat.

"There's a bit of a surprise in here for you," she says to Anna, as she opens the dining-room door with a flourish.

The dining room looks beautiful, and though Anna hadn't even realized that it needed a clean, it has very obviously been scrubbed from top to bottom. Everything looks fresher and brighter. On the sideboard there's an enormous bunch of white gardenias from the backyard, their fragrance thick in the air. The curtains, which have been closed for as long as Anna can remember, have been tied open so that the garden is visible. The dining table, which normally sits tucked close to the back wall, has been shifted forward so that it sits in the middle of the room, directly beneath the chandelier. The table has been set elaborately: crystal glasses, white linen napkins, a fine bone-china dinner setting that Anna doesn't even recognize. A collection of white candles in a silver candelabra flicker in the center of the table.

"Ta-da!" Lilla beams, glancing only briefly at Anna before speaking directly to Marcus. "Doesn't it look fantastic? I've been spending hours in here over the last few days. The poor room needed quite a bit of TLC. I even had to get up there and polish the chandelier. It was a massive job, absolutely backbreaking because I had to hold my head up like this." She tilts her head backwards to show them what she means, then straightens up, smiling, obviously pleased with herself. "It took hours, there was just so much built-up dust on it. But it was worth it. Such a beautiful old piece, such a pity to see it so . . ." She glances at Anna, then rushes to the table and picks up one of the napkin rings. "And I found these in a box in the junk room a few days ago. Real silver. I knew they'd be perfect. Sorry, Anna, but I knew you couldn't possibly mind. No point having beautiful things hidden away in boxes. So anyway, what do you all think? Amazing what a difference a bit of elbow grease can make, isn't it?" She claps her hands together again and doesn't wait for an answer. "Come on, everybody. Sit down. Enjoy."

It's easy to fake it when the person you're trying to deceive is getting drunk. Anna only pretends to drink the cocktails Lilla makes her. She barely swallows any. Whenever she gets the chance she tips some away—down the sink, into a potted plant, a small splash straight onto the carpet. She also tries her hardest to act as though all the alcohol is going to her head. She talks louder than she normally would, laughs more often. She sits heavily at the table, sighs, smiles at nothing.

"Should you really be drinking so much?" Fiona says, staring at Anna's glass. "Do you think it's a good idea?"

"I'm fine, Fiona," Anna says. "Please. Don't worry so much."

Lilla doesn't say anything, but she sniggers into her own drink, rolls her eyes.

It's obvious that both Lilla and Marcus are getting tipsy. Lilla's cheeks are flushed and her voice is getting louder. Marcus has a permanent small smile on his face, and all his careful control seems to have slipped away, leaving him open and relaxed, vulnerable in a charming way. Anna has only seen him like this once or twice before and it suits him—Lilla suits him—and the thought makes her suddenly sad. In a different situation she's sure they would have made a good couple. What a terrible shame that there have been so many secrets and lies, so much deception.

77

Finally I've had enough. I make a decision.

"How long have you really known Marcus, Lilla?" I ask. "I mean, from the way you act together you'd think you'd known each other for a lot longer than a few weeks. In fact, you'd think you were in some kind of relationship."

Everyone is startled into silence. Anna looks down at her plate, pretends to be preoccupied with eating. But I know that she's listening to every word, every sound and nuance.

"What the hell?" Lilla says. "Where did that come from? God, you can be random, Tim."

"I'm just curious," I say, my voice deliberately light, as if it doesn't really matter. "I was just wondering. You both just seem very . . . close. Anyone would think you'd known each other for years."

"We've known each other for a few weeks," Lilla says quickly. "Since your birthday party. You know that."

She's a good liar. She meets my eyes squarely, without wavering.

"Yeah? You sure?"

"Of course I'm sure!" she says, looking around the table with wide eyes, as if she's outraged that I'd even ask.

"But there's just a few curious things, Lilla. Maybe you can explain them." I put my knife and fork down. "Why don't we get it all out into the open. You know when you and I broke up? That fight we had? Remember how I came over to your flat a couple of weeks later? I'd been surfing. I was still dripping wet. I had my board with me."

"Of course I remember," Lilla says. "What about it?"

"You said you were seeing someone," I say. "And later that person turned out to be Patrick."

"So?"

"So I was surprised. Surprised that you were going out with someone like Patrick. A plumber, a tradesman. I expected you to be going out with someone who wore a suit. The kind of bloke that carries a satchel."

"Why? I went out with you, didn't I?" Lilla sneers. "And you're not exactly the suit type."

"Exactly. So why was I surprised? It doesn't make sense, does it? But just the other day I remembered what it was that gave me that idea in the first place."

Lilla shrugs as if she couldn't care less.

"I didn't see Patrick the day I came to your house, I didn't actually see anyone. But I saw a satchel in your hallway, and a tie draped over it."

"God, Tim," Lilla groans. "So there was a satchel in my house and you thought I was going out with a businessman. What has that got to do with anything? What is your point?"

"The satchel had these fancy red initials in one corner. H&H. I remember thinking it was some kind of royal crest or something." I look at Marcus. "It was yours. You were at Lilla's house that day. And that's why I was surprised when I met Patrick. I was expecting someone like you." I turn back to Lilla. "I think you've known each other since then. I think you've known Marcus all along."

Fiona turns to stare at Marcus.

Marcus doesn't say a word. He keeps his eyes down on the table. I waver between feeling sorry for him and wanting to shout at him to look up, be a man, face up to things.

Lilla laughs, her eyes flash. "Don't be ridiculous. I know a lot of men with satchels, Tim. And that was years ago. I think you might be confused, and probably jealous, knowing you."

"I'm not confused at all. It's a distinctive engraving. I recognized it as soon as I saw it," I say. "Anyway, that's not all, Lilla. Remember that day we went to Manly? On the ferry?"

"What about it?"

"I told you about Anna. I told you a bit about Marcus and Fiona. The weird thing was that you knew they were lawyers even though I never told you what they did. How did you know?"

"Don't be dumb," Lilla scoffs. "You've got a shit memory and now you're trying to blame me for it. Not fair. Of course you told me they were lawyers. You just can't remember. God, Tim. I thought we were supposed to be friends."

"I thought we were, too. But you're bloody well lying to me." I look at Anna. She nods and rushes from the room.

"Where the hell is she going?" Lilla asks.

"Wait a minute. You'll see."

Anna returns a moment later with my laptop and puts it on the table. It's already booted up. I go to the Facebook home page, type in Lilla's name, flick through her photo album to the picture I need.

Then I turn the computer so that it faces the middle of the table, so that everyone can see. I double-click on the image and Lilla's face fills the screen.

"You're standing in front of Harrow and Harrow," I say, pointing to the letters R, O and W that can be seen in the sign above Lilla's head. "Anna recognized it." I click to the next tab. It's the Harrow and Harrow home page. There's a photo of the building from the street, the sign that sits over the front windows. The green lettering is distinctive, unmistakable. "And the photo was uploaded to your Facebook account a long time ago. Way before you even supposedly met Marcus."

Lilla pulls the laptop closer, leans over it. Then she pushes it away, straightens up, glares at Anna and me. "You went through my Facebook photos?"

"We looked at them, yes," Anna says. "But they're public access anyway. Any stranger with an Internet connection could look at them."

"A bit creepy, though, isn't it? You looking at my stuff?"

"Come *on*," I say, almost laughing at Lilla's nerve. "That's a bit bloody rich, isn't it? Considering the lies you've obviously been telling."

Lilla shrugs dismissively. "I have no idea when that photo was taken. Or even what I was doing there. It's as old as the hills. I haven't had my hair like that for ages. Think what you like. I couldn't give a shit."

"Stop it," Marcus says to Lilla, looking up suddenly, his voice sharp with impatience. "Stop lying. What does it matter anyway? Just tell the truth." He sighs, turns to face me. "Yes. We know each other. We've known each other for a while. And I apologize for being less than straight about it, but it was a private relationship. Just between me and Lilla. Nobody else's business as far as I'm concerned."

"God, Marcus," Fiona says, looking at Lilla with undisguised horror. "What on earth . . ."

"Look, Fiona. I'm sorry but it's not a big deal. Lilla and I have had a . . . well, a casual friendship, I suppose you could call it. And when you and I were looking for a tenant for Fairview, Lilla said she knew the perfect person. That was you, Tim. She said that I'd be doing her an enormous favor if I let you get the room because it was too cramped with you in her flat. I was just trying to help her out of an awkward situation. Anna got a housemate, someone trustworthy to help out, and Lilla got her flat back without offending you, without having to kick you out and ruin your friendship."

I stare at Marcus and try to make sense of it. "So the two of you basically set the whole thing up?"

"If you want to put it like that, then yes, more or less. And I'm sorry for that. But there were no bad intentions involved," Marcus says. "I put the ad in the paper, and simply waited until I saw your number come up on my phone. It wasn't hard." He shrugs. "And it hasn't turned out all that badly, has it? There's been no damage done."

Anna smiles sadly. "I don't know, Marcus. I think some damage may have been done, yes. And maybe your intentions were good, but I don't know if the same can be said for Lilla. I don't know what her intentions were."

"I'm not sure what you mean," Marcus says, turning a puzzled face to Lilla. We all turn to watch her. She doesn't squirm or turn away or blush, she looks genuinely amused. "Why should Lilla have any other intentions?"

"I just wanted to get rid of an unwanted houseguest." Lilla lifts her hands. "Sorry, Tim. But that's it. The sad truth. And, okay, yeah, I shouldn't have lied, but you know how awkward it can get in situations like that. Patrick was about to totally lose his mind, and you were just refusing to get off your arse and find somewhere else to live. I had to do something. I had no choice."

78

Anna pushes her chair back.

"Lilla," she asks. "Would you give me a hand?"

In the kitchen Anna scrapes the plates into the bin. Lilla doesn't actually help Anna—no real surprise—instead she gets the jug and the bottle of tequila, busies herself making more drinks. Anna works slowly, pausing frequently to stare at nothing.

"What is it?" Lilla asks. "You're not worried about the whole Marcus thing, are you? Seriously. It was nothing. I just had to get rid of Tim. You know what it's like. And it's all turned out pretty well, hasn't it? For you two."

"God, no." Anna shakes her head. "It's not that. I don't care about that. I was just thinking about Ben. Remembering. Missing him."

"Oh. Right. The baby. Maybe you should try not to think of him so much?" Lilla says. "Focus on happier things."

The suggestion is so ludicrous and insensitive, so stupidly offensive, that something snaps. Anna has to fight an urge to slap Lilla. She clenches her fists by her sides, then forces herself to release them, to smile even.

"You're absolutely right," she says through tight lips. "I should stop feeling sorry for myself. And God, I'm not the only one who misses him, am I? I'm just being selfish."

"What do you mean?"

"Well, you know, I wasn't the only person who loved him. People don't make babies all on their own, you know."

"Oh. Of course. The father," Lilla says, looking down at her finger-nails, as if the topic is all a bit of a drag. "How's he coping with all this? The whole accident thing?"

"How's he coping?" Anna says vaguely, going to wash her hands at the sink. "Well, actually, I think he's okay. I think he's doing quite well."

"So you still see him, then?"

"See him?" Anna turns so that she can face Lilla, watch her reac-tion. "Of course I do. I see him a lot." She smiles. "But you're just teasing me now, aren't you? Playing more games? Pretending not to know?"

"What?" Lilla's eyes snap up. "What do you mean?"

"Marcus," Anna says, her eyes on Lilla's, her voice firm and clear so there can be no misunderstanding. "Marcus was Ben's father."

Lilla takes a step back. "Marcus? No. No way." She shakes her head. "He never . . . I mean, he couldn't have—"

"You didn't know, Lilla? Really? That's so strange . . ." Anna shrugs. "Though I guess that's just Marcus, isn't it? So secretive. So private. Nobody can ever really get close to him."

Lilla nods, but her face is closed tight with fury, her lips drawn together in a thin line.

Anna collects the platter of cheese and fruit that Tim had pre-pared earlier.

"Would you mind just handing me a knife, Lilla?" she asks, indicat-ing a drawer with her chin. But Lilla's obviously distracted, upset, and she reaches vaguely for a kitchen knife from the block on the benchtop and puts it on the platter. It doesn't matter. Cheese knife. Kitchen knife. Nobody is likely to notice or care.

"Thanks." Anna smiles. "I'll just take this out." And as she leaves the room she can feel Lilla's eyes on her back, like two little daggers, pointed and sharp with malice.

79

While Lilla and Anna are in the kitchen, Marcus goes to the toilet.

Fiona crosses her arms over her chest and turns to me.

"You and Anna?" she says. "You're seeing each other?"

"Seeing each other?" I imitate the gruff tone of her voice in an attempt to lighten the mood, but her expression doesn't change. "Yeah. I guess we are."

"Serious, is it?"

"Don't know yet," I say. *And it's none of your bloody business,* I think.

"You know what happened, don't you?"

"Happened?"

"Last winter."

"She told me about her son, Ben, if that's what you mean?"

She gives a curt nod. She's watching my face so closely that I feel like I'm being put through some kind of test, one that I have no chance of passing.

"I think she's pretty amazing," I say. "And incredibly strong."

"Strong? Really? That's what you think?"

"Yeah. Why not? I haven't had a kid, obviously, but I know it's the worst thing in the world to lose one. That's what people say, anyway. And the circumstances with Ben, I mean, they make it even worse. And she's been here dealing with that, pretty much on her own. That makes her strong in my eyes."

"She's not strong at all," she says, now so angry or upset—I can't tell which—that her voice is shaking. "How can you say that? You of all people? You told us what she did, Tim. You know what's been going on. She's vulnerable. She needs help."

"I don't think so. I think she's getting better," I say.

"She forgot to lock the pram," Fiona insists. "Did you know that?"

"Yeah. She told me the full story. And it's crap and I know she must feel like utter hell. But it was an accident, Fiona. And she's dealing with it. She is. I know she is." I'm abrupt, trying to make it clear that I don't want to talk about it.

"I don't think so. In fact I think she's getting worse," she finishes urgently as Marcus reappears. "Imagine what that guilt would do to a person. It would drive you crazy."

80

"Who wants some of this amazing cheese?" Anna asks as she enters the dining room a moment later. She's holding the cheese platter and a pile of plates.

Lilla marches in with a venomous look on her face. She doesn't take a seat; instead she stands behind her chair and glares down at everyone. We all watch her as she takes three big gulps of her drink. She grimaces, gasps. Then she lifts the glass to her mouth and finishes the rest.

"Whoa," Marcus says. "Lilla. Take it easy. What are you trying to do?"

"I'm trying to get drunk, Marcus," Lilla says coldly. "What are you trying to do?"

"Nothing." Marcus looks bewildered at Lilla's tone.

Lilla puts her glass back on the table so roughly that it wobbles. "So, anyway," she says. "In case you're curious. Anna and I were talking about Ben in the kitchen." She stares at Marcus. "Such a horrible tragedy, wasn't it? So terrible. Unimaginable, really."

"Yes." Marcus looks down. "Terrible."

"And it must be hard for the father, too. Hard for him to accept," Lilla says. "To forgive. Move on."

"I suppose so." Marcus goes white. He picks up the knife as if to cut himself some cheese but puts it straight back down again without doing anything. He looks suddenly ill or frightened or both.

"What's wrong with you, Marcus?" Lilla asks.

"What's wrong with *me*?" he asks. "What's wrong with you? Why are you staring at me like that?"

She leans over the table. "What the hell do you think is wrong, Marcus? I don't like being lied to. That's what's wrong. I don't like being tricked."

The hypocrisy of her words would be funny if she wasn't so serious, so genuinely outraged.

"Tricked? I haven't tricked you."

"You didn't tell me about Ben, though, did you? It's a pretty big thing to forget to tell me. I mean, fucking hell, Marcus, if I'd known . . ." She slaps the table with her open palm, making everybody jump. "You're a fucking liar!"

"Ben?" Fiona stares at Marcus. "What about Ben? What's she talking about?"

Marcus puts his head in his hands. "Jesus Christ. I don't believe this. I simply do not believe it." Then he sighs, lifts his head to look at Fiona. "I'm so sorry."

"Sorry? What are you sorry for?"

It's clear that Marcus is rattled: he clears his throat, blinks. "Anna and I didn't tell you . . . or rather I didn't tell you, because I couldn't. I didn't know how to. I didn't want you to find out like this. Not tonight. And all I can say is sorry. I'm sorry I was such a coward. I'm sorry for all of it."

"I don't . . ." Fiona says. "What are you saying?"

"I'm saying Ben was my son. I was Ben's father." Marcus's voice cracks, and he looks down.

"Ben's father? What? Is this really . . . I don't . . ." Fiona stands up. She's completely still for a moment, a look of stunned confusion on her face, as if she's forgotten where she is, what she's doing. Eventually she collapses back into her chair, puts her face in her hands. "Oh, no. Oh, God, no. *No.*"

"I'm sorry, Fiona." Marcus pats Fiona's back awkwardly. She flinches, her shoulders shaking. "I'm sorry you had to find out like this."

He turns to Anna, his eyes full of despair. "Are you satisfied now? Are you happy?"

"Not at all," Anna says. "Don't think I'm getting any joy out of this."

"Then why? I thought we had an agreement. Why tonight? Like this?"

"Well, and why not?" Lilla spits out. "What do you expect, Marcus? She's mad. Obviously. You must be mad yourself, getting involved with someone like her. What exactly do you expect? You can't expect normal behavior from a lunatic."

"That's right, Lilla. I'm mad," Anna says. "Or is that just what you want everyone to think?"

"Why would I give a shit what people think? All I know is you need a lot of help. And so does everyone else here." Lilla looks around the table as if for confirmation. "You're all sick in the head. Face it. And you, Anna—that whole crib scenario up in the attic? You sitting up there every day pretending your baby's alive? It pretty much confirms that you're seriously screwed. Not to mention all the weird stuff you've been—"

"Shut up, Lilla," I interrupt. I'm suddenly so angry I can't control myself. My voice comes out in a rough growl, my hands shake. Lilla stares back at me with shock at first, but her expression quickly shifts to one of hostility. It's hard to remember what I ever saw in her, how I ever thought I loved her. "Don't you dare bloody stand there insulting Anna in her own house. Why don't you just shut up for once in your life?"

"I'm only stating the truth, Tim. Your girlfriend's sick."

I want to smash her, wipe the self-satisfied look from her face. It's the first time in my life I've had an urge to hit a woman. Anna puts a restraining hand on my arm.

"Maybe I am mad," she says quietly. "I don't know. I can see that it probably isn't all that good spending so much time in the attic. Living in my head like that. And obviously being agoraphobic isn't . . . well, it's not exactly healthy." She lifts her chin. "But I'm not an aggressive or malicious person, Lilla. I don't destroy things. I don't paint horrible phrases on walls or put spiders on people's beds."

"Come on," Lilla scoffs, "you don't really expect any of us to believe that."

"I do expect you to believe it. And, just so you know, for a while there at least, I really did think I was going mad. I thought it must have been me doing all those things even though I had no memory of it. I thought I was as crazy as you say. But when I discovered that you and Marcus have known each other all along, I started thinking about it. You've been lying, Lilla. To me and Tim. And we don't get it."

"And you know what else we don't get?" I interject. "This!" I pull out the torn and defaced photo and put it on the table where everyone can see. The raw violence of it is stark, shocking.

Lilla's mouth drops open, but she recovers quickly.

"Going through my bag now?" she spits. "First you perve through on my Facebook photos, then you raid my bag. I don't believe this!"

"I wasn't going through your bag. You threw the picture on the table yourself the day we were in Manly. I was just putting it back, cleaning up your bloody mess as usual, just like we had to clean up the spiders. And the paint on the wall."

"My mess?" Lilla says viciously. "My bloody mess? I don't think so, Tim. It wasn't me who started this. The truth is you and Anna have been invading my—"

"Oh, for Christ's sake," Marcus interrupts, standing up. "This is all getting out of hand. You're all getting worked up and hysterical and if you want my opinion all three of you are sounding quite mad right now. I think you'd be a lot better off having this conversation tomorrow. When you haven't been drinking."

"Marcus, stop. Wait," Fiona suddenly interrupts. She has been sitting there in silence, staring at the laptop. She turns to Lilla. "It says here that your last name's Buchanan?"

"Yeah? So?"

"What's your mother's name?"

Lilla is completely taken aback. "What?"

"Hazel," I answer for her. "Hazel Buchanan."

"Hazel Buchanan." Fiona turns to Marcus. She straightens up, her voice is crisp and full of urgency. "I knew Lilla's name was familiar. My God, Marcus. We set the payment up, for Anna's father, for Stephen London. Remember? He asked us to keep it strictly confidential. You must remember? Two hundred dollars a month to Hazel Buchanan. And then in his will, to be paid from the estate, in perpetuity . . ."

Marcus puts his head in his hands. "What?"

"Where did you meet her?" Fiona asks, taking his arm. "Marcus? Listen to me. Where did you and Lilla meet?"

"Don't answer that," Lilla says to Marcus, grabbing his other arm. Marcus looks from Lilla to Fiona and back again. Lilla's voice is as brash and as arrogant as ever, but there's a change in her eyes, a distinct flicker of fear. "It's none of their damn business."

Marcus brushes her away. "That's easy," he says to Fiona. "We met at Stephen London's funeral."

"Right," Fiona says. "The funeral. Of course. So—"

"*Daddy's* funeral?" Anna interrupts. Marcus nods.

"But . . ."Anna looks over at Lilla. "Why were you there? You didn't know my father. Why would you go to his funeral?"

Lilla doesn't respond. She toys with the knife in the center of the table, pressing it down on one end so the blade lifts in the air.

"Lilla," Anna says. "Answer me."

"You're right," Lilla says. "I didn't know him at all. I never met the man. Not once."

"So why were you at his funeral?"

An odd-looking smile appears on Lilla's face. "I had every right to go to that funeral. Every right in the world."

"Every right? What?" Anna's voice is low and full of loathing.

"What are you, Lilla? Some kind of gold digger? Is that it? Money? Is that what you're after? Or . . . *what*? Do you just like to prey on vulnerable people? Grieving people? What is it? What's your game?"

"Vulnerable people?" Lilla says, still giving all her attention to the knife. Her voice is mild enough, but I can see the tremor in her fingers, the tension in her jaw. "What would you know about being vulnerable?"

"Oh, for God's sake, I'm not going to get into another one of these ridiculous conversations." Anna stands up and slaps both hands on the table so that Lilla is forced to look at her. She leans forward, speaks furiously. "I just want to know, Lilla. *What the fuck were you doing at Daddy's funeral?*"

The response from Lilla is dramatic, shocking. The two of them glare at each other over the table. Then Lilla lets out a low howl, raises her glass above her head and throws it with full force at the wall behind Anna.

Anna jumps, visibly startled. Then she shakes her head, gives a small, shaken laugh. "You're a fool, Lilla. A trashy fool. And I can't be bothered with you. I'm not interested in what you've been doing here or why you hate me. I just want you to get the hell out of my house."

Lilla moans softly and shakes her head from side to side as Anna talks. She puts her hands over her ears as if she can't stand to hear the sound of Anna's voice.

"Lilla?" I say. Seeing her like this is disturbing, chilling. For all her talk of Anna's mental health it's Lilla who looks crazy right now. "Lilla?"

She opens her eyes and suddenly, her movements as quick and agile as a cat chasing a mouse, she snatches up the knife and dashes around the table towards Anna. She presses her forearm against Anna's chest and shoves her backwards, so that Anna's back slams hard against the wall.

"I hate you, Anna London," she screams. "I fucking hate you. I wish you were dead!"

"Lilla!"

"Stop!"

"No!"

But before anyone has had the chance to react she thrusts the knife at Anna. We all move to stop her, but Fiona's there first.

"I hate you! I fucking hate you," Lilla screams, raising her arm again and again, but her rage has made her oblivious and it isn't Anna who takes the brunt of her attack, but Fiona.

81

"Anna, Anna, are you okay?" Tim shouts, as he and Marcus pull Lilla away, dragging her to the other side of the room.

"I'm fine," Anna says. "But Fiona's hurt. She needs help."

"I'll call an ambulance," says Marcus. "And the police."

Anna doesn't watch them, she's too intent on Fiona, but Lilla's animal sounds and Tim's raised and angry voice echo loudly around the room, making her pulse race, her mind unclear.

There's blood everywhere. All down Anna's front and on her hands. Fiona's blood.

"Oh, God," Fiona says, collapsing to the ground. "I'm bleeding. Oh, God."

Anna grabs a handful of napkins from the table, crouches down and presses them against Fiona's wounds. There's so much blood it's hard to know where it's coming from or how to staunch it.

"I'm scared," Fiona says. "I'm really scared."

"You're going to be fine," Anna says, trying to hide the fear in her voice. "It's not as bad as it looks."

When Marcus comes back, Tim is sitting on the opposite side of the room with Lilla, their backs pressed against the wall. Tim's hands are wrapped firmly around one of Lilla's arms. Marcus goes to sit on the other side of her, pressing his elbow against her arm to restrain her. It's a particularly hostile gesture, as if he finds her repellent, as if he can't bear to touch her with his hands.

Anna slides closer to Fiona. She would like to lift Fiona's head, let it rest more comfortably in her lap, but she's afraid of making her bleed more. She settles for brushing her hand over Fiona's hair. Fiona grabs Anna's hand and pulls it close to her face, presses her lips against the skin of Anna's palm. It's the first time Fiona has ever touched her voluntarily. The only act of physical intimacy Fiona has ever initiated. The realization brings tears to Anna's eyes.

"I'm sorry, Anna," Fiona says. "So sorry."

"Shhhh. Don't be silly. You've got nothing to be sorry for."

"All of this wouldn't have happened if not for me."

"No. Be quiet. Please. Just rest."

"I abandoned you," she says. "When Ben died. I left you here all alone."

"It's okay. It's understandable. I would have left, too."

"No, you wouldn't," Fiona says, closing her eyes for such a long while that Anna grows afraid, leans over her, whispers her name.

Fiona grimaces, opens her eyes, and Anna squeezes her hand gratefully, wills the ambulance to hurry.

"I've been a coward," Fiona says. "I couldn't handle your sadness. It was so messy and I couldn't help you. I couldn't do anything. So I ran away."

"It's okay, Fiona," Anna says, crying openly now. "It's okay. It's not your fault."

"I only wanted to help," Fiona says, closing her eyes again, her voice growing weaker. "From the moment I first met you I just wanted to help. Be a good friend. But then I did the worst thing possible. I left you. Just when you needed me. I abandoned you."

82

There's a long silence in the room as we all wait for the ambulance and the police to arrive. Lilla eventually stops resisting us and slumps against the wall, her head down.

Marcus sits there wide-eyed and pale. His face is covered by a thin sheet of sweat. He stares at Fiona, as if he can will her to be okay with the power of his eyes, as if he's afraid she'll die if he doesn't watch her for a second.

Suddenly Lilla lifts her head, stares at Anna. I squeeze her arm tighter in warning, but she ignores me, takes a deep breath.

"I had every right to go to that funeral," she says.

Anna and Marcus both seem to sigh and grow tense at the same time. Nobody wants to listen to any more of Lilla's shit. Anna lifts a blank face and gazes at Lilla with cold eyes.

"Every right," Lilla repeats.

"Okay," Anna says. "Whatever you say."

"But don't you want to know why?" Lilla says. "Don't you want to know why I had the right?"

"I'm not particularly interested in what you have to say anymore," Anna says. "You can tell the police."

Lilla smiles at this, shakes her head as though Anna is an amusing child. "Oh, but you would be interested. If you knew. You'd be very interested indeed."

Anna turns away, gives her attention to Fiona.

I can feel Lilla's mounting irritation. She's always hated being ignored. She sits up straighter, and I hold her arm more firmly. She feels poised and tight, ready for battle, like a gun cocked and ready to fire.

"He was *my* father, too," she says.

Anna looks up sharply. "What?"

"Stephen London was my father," Lilla says, her voice triumphant, spiteful.

Anna gasps as if she's been hit. The color drains from her face.

"There. See? You know it's true. I can tell by the look on your face. That's why he was paying off my mother." Lilla laughs. Her tone of voice becomes conversational, friendly even. "And if you think it's a shock for you, imagine what it's been like for me. My whole life. Not knowing who my father was until my mum saw his picture in the paper after he died and lost her shit. But it was too late to do anything about it by then. Nineteen years too late."

I wait for Anna to deny it, to tell Lilla she's a liar, but she doesn't say a word.

"Mum told me everything," Lilla continues. "And what a surprise. After all that time, all those years of living in a shitty neighborhood, I find out that my father was rich. But not just rich, not just comfortably rich, *mega* rich, *filthy* rich. And then to make things worse I find out that he has another daughter. A daughter he actually loves."

Anna shakes her head.

"So," Lilla continues, and she lifts her head to look around the room deliberately. "You got the big house. The private schools. The nice clothes. I got a lousy two hundred bucks a month. Shut-up money, basically. Hardly fair was it? And if you think I was neglected on a material level, on an emotional level things were even worse. I have to say, Anna, that your dear *daddy* was slightly negligent in his duties. I never spoke to the man, never met him. Not once in nineteen years. I didn't receive a single phone call or a letter. Nothing. Zilch. Nada. You got everything, Anna. As far as *Daddy* was concerned it would have been better if I didn't even exist."

It's impossible to fathom. Insane. And yet Anna's making no attempt to argue, no attempt to defend her father.

"But I wonder," Lilla continues. "I wonder what he would think now. If he could see you. He wouldn't be all that proud, would he? Pregnant at eighteen. Letting your baby drown. Living here like some kind of hermit. Too scared to go out."

"Lilla, please."

"He'd probably think he'd wasted all his attention on the wrong one. All that money and time and effort and look at you. A useless waste of space. A noncontributing member of society. A freak."

Anna starts to cry.

"You couldn't even look after your own son. Couldn't even keep him safe."

"Lilla," I say, low and angry. I pull her arm back tight against the wall, resisting a second urge to really hurt her, to smash her arm, break her bones. "Stop it. Now. I'm warning you."

"But it's true, though, Tim," she says. "Anna is so useless she can't even manage to lock the wheels of a pram, stop her baby rolling into Manly Dam."

Anna's head snaps up. "What did you say?"

"You heard me. I said your—"

"No," Anna says, and there's a fury and determination in her voice that makes us all pay attention. "Not that. About Ben. The pram. What did you say?"

"What? I can't remember what I said," Lilla says dismissively, but I can hear the fear in her voice. "And anyway that's not the point."

"She said you didn't lock the wheels of the pram and that it rolled into Manly Dam," Marcus says, turning to stare at Lilla with an expression of intense hatred. "That's exactly what she said."

Lilla's eyes remain fixed on Anna's.

We hear the sirens then, screeching up the street towards us. But neither Lilla nor Anna move or react. They watch each other; the air between them thick with hostility and something even bigger, some emotion more fundamental than hatred, something so ugly it makes my skin crawl.

83

They spend hours with the police. Explaining things over and over. Making official statements. Going over the long, involved story. Anna tells them everything. Marcus leaves for the hospital just after midnight to see Fiona, and Anna receives a text an hour later.

Fiona has lost a lot of blood. She is in intensive care, but the wounds will heal.

84

We head straight upstairs when we're finally through with the police. Dawn is near. We don't talk and we move slowly, like old people. I hold Anna's hand, stay close to her, but she feels distant and removed. She holds my hand limply and stares straight ahead, her expression blank. I just want to take her to bed and hold her, get her to see me again. Bring her back from whatever internal hell she has retreated to.

But Anna doesn't go to my room or hers. Instead she heads to Lilla's room. When she gets there she goes to Lilla's bed, lifts the pillows and blankets as if searching for something.

"What are you doing?"

"Looking."

"For what?"

"I don't really know," she says.

She goes to the desk and rummages through the drawers. Then she goes to the wardrobe and opens one of the wide timber doors. Something makes her cry out and take a step back. I step up closer to take a look. On the inside of the door is an elaborate photo collage, and at first I don't see anything shocking about it. But when I get close enough I see that they are Anna's photos. Anna's family. Pictures of what must be her parents. Fairview. Snapshots of the three of them on holiday, at the beach. The bizarre thing is that Anna has been cut out of each picture. Wholly in some cases, just her face in others. The effect is surreal. Chilling.

"Come on," I say. "Let's get out of here." And I reach out to take her hand, but she ignores me, and turns around as if to take in the entire room. She pauses, then walks quickly to the bookshelves on the far side of the room. There's something broken on the top shelf. Shattered pieces of red ceramic stand out starkly against the white surface. Anna collects the broken pieces and holds the shards in both hands as if trying to put them back together.

"Anna," I say, approaching. "Careful. You'll cut yourself."

But she shakes her head and moves away from me. A sob escapes her lips as slowly, deliberately, she opens her hands and lets the pieces clatter to the floor.

85

They go to Tim's room and climb fully clothed onto his bed. They lie spooned together, Tim behind her, his arm wrapped around her.

"Anna?" Tim starts. "Do you think—"

"Shhh," she cuts him off, takes his hand. "Please, Tim, let's not talk. Not now. I can't. I just can't. Go to sleep. We can talk later."

"Okay. Sure." He kisses the back of her head, squeezes her tighter. Soon she can hear the slow in and out of his breath, the regular rhythm that indicates sleep.

She moves carefully out from beneath his arm and tiptoes from the room.

86

When I wake up the other side of the bed is empty. I have a good idea where Anna is but I go downstairs first and put the kettle on for coffee. I make two mugs and take them back upstairs to the attic.

Anna's sitting cross-legged on the timber floor. Ben's blanket is on her lap. She looks up and sees me, smiles tiredly.

"Hey." I stop in the doorway, hold up a mug. "You need some coffee?"

She nods and I go and sit beside her, hand her a cup.

Her eyes are red-rimmed and bloodshot as if she's been crying. Her hair is loose and messy around her face. I push a strand of hair from her eyes, tuck it behind her ear.

"You okay?"

She shakes her head.

"Did you get any sleep?"

"Nope." She sips her coffee, sighs. "I think it's time I put Ben's things away," she says quietly. "In fact I think it's time I left Fairview altogether."

I nod as if I think it's a smart idea but the truth is I don't know if this is a good or a bad thing. I don't know whether it means she's feeling better or worse. I don't know what it means for me. For us. I don't even know if she still wants there to be an us.

"We need to talk," she says.

"Sure," I say. "Okay."

"Can we go for a walk?"

"A walk?"

"You know that bench seat above Fairlight Pool? The one that looks out over the Harbor? I used to love going there when I was sad or if I just wanted to think. We could go there now."

"Sure," I say. "But how . . . what about—"

"I don't care. I've had enough of this," she says, her voice full of weary determination. "I don't care if I panic. I just need to get out of here."

I take her hand and squeeze. "Let's go, then."

We don't do much talking on our way there. Anna starts having a full-on panic attack almost as soon as we cross the road. She starts breathing too fast, almost hyperventilating. Her skin goes pale and sweat breaks out on her forehead. Her whole body trembles. If I didn't know it was panic I'd assume she was having some kind of seizure.

"I'm okay," she insists, tightening her grip on my hand. "Just keep walking."

But we don't make it far before she has to sit down on the grass. She pulls her legs up and rests her head on her knees. I sit beside her and put my arm around her. I have no idea what to do or how to help and when I talk—thinking the sound of my voice might be soothing— she tells me to shut up. So I just sit there and wait and hope that my presence is at least some comfort. Eventually her breathing slows down. She unclenches her fists, lifts her head.

"You okay?"

"I've been better."

"Want to go back?"

"No."

I help her up and we make our way to the bench seat. We walk slowly, Anna taking small careful steps and breathing heavily, as though the effort is physical rather than mental. It's still early but there are a few people out: joggers, people in work clothes making their way down to the ferry, to their jobs in the city. People smile as they pass, and I know that we must make a curious-looking couple. Both of us scruffy and unkempt, Anna struggling and breathless, leaning against me as though she can barely walk without my help.

We reach the bench seat and sit side by side, our thighs pressed close.

"You made it."

She flashes a wobbly smile. "Only just."

"Still. I think it's awesome, Anna. You did it."

She nods and stares out towards the Harbor. Her face is preoccupied and despite the beauty of what she's looking at I know she isn't really seeing any of it. She's thinking about last night. About Lilla. Her father. The whole miserable story.

"So you think it's definitely true?" I say. As much as I'd like to avoid the whole topic—talk about the weather, or the color of the water, anything but what happened last night—I know there's no hope of that. "What Lilla said?"

She takes a deep, shaky breath. "The payment Fiona mentioned, the one my father paid in secret, that pretty much confirmed it for me. And in a way it makes a lot of sense. The way my parents were together. Mum's anger . . ."

"So she's really your father's child, your sister?"

"Half sister," she says. "I guess so . . . probably."

We're both silent for a minute, both caught up in our own thoughts.

"So why? Why didn't she just come and talk to you? Why did she have to do all that crazy stuff?"

"You're asking me?" she says. "I might be biologically related to her but you know her best."

"I thought I knew her," I say. "But I was wrong. I mean, she's always been obsessed with material stuff. With having a better life. I knew that about her. But I didn't know she could be so malicious. When she saw how much you had, the big house and all that money, it must have made her mad with envy. It's sad when you think about it." I shake my head. "Sad and unbelievable."

"But it's not only that, Tim." Anna hesitates, falters, rubs her eyes. She looks suddenly exhausted and overwhelmed. She takes a breath. "That's not the only thing I wanted to talk about. There's something else. Something worse."

The look on her face and the tone of her voice—the idea that there could even be something worse—fills me with a sick sense of dread.

"What?" I ask reluctantly.

"Do you remember what Lilla said about Ben? She was very specific. She mentioned Manly Dam. She mentioned the lock on the pram. Remember?"

"Yeah." I frown.

"And remember how I told you I was always sure I'd locked the pram? How I wondered if someone else, one of those kids maybe, had accidentally unlocked it or knocked it down the ramp?"

I feel a rush of blood to my head—it's a feeling I've become far too familiar with lately—and somehow I know that what Anna's about to say is going to be something I don't want to hear or face.

"Yeah."

"I didn't tell Lilla that he drowned at Manly Dam. And I didn't tell her that I left the pram unlocked. I didn't even mention a pram. I told her Ben drowned. That's all she knew."

"Marcus?"

She shakes her head. "There's no way. When Ben died Marcus made me this promise. And he was deadly serious—you know what he's like. He swore that he'd never tell anyone what happened. He didn't want me to worry about it, about what people thought or said behind my back." She shrugs. "I didn't ask him to do that, I didn't even particularly care what anyone thought at that stage. But I know he didn't tell her. He didn't even tell her that he was Ben's father. Marcus is the most private, secretive person I know. He would never have told a soul."

"The newspapers?" I say. "Maybe she read about it?"

"It wasn't in the papers. And there was an inquest but it was closed. She couldn't have known."

"So? I'm not sure I . . . ?" I stop. Suddenly I know what she's saying. I get the whole thing. And it's as if the ground has suddenly opened in a massive chasm beneath me. I can't bear to look down—the fear of falling is too great, and I'm dizzy and terrified with shock—but I know I have to. I have to step up to the precipice and gaze straight down into the black below. "Fuck. Anna. You think she—"

She nods urgently, as if to stop me talking, as if she can't bear the words to be said aloud. She bites her lip, stares straight ahead. I watch the tears run down her face while she tries to gather herself. Eventually she closes her eyes, takes a deep shaky breath. "I would say I can't be one hundred percent sure, that it's just a possibility, but I am and it's not," she says. "She was there. She did it. I saw the truth in her face. She knew I knew."

"Jesus, Anna." I breathe out heavily. "*Jesus*. Did you tell the police?"

"Yes," she says quietly. "Last night. I don't know what they can do, but they know the truth, they know everything. It's up to them now."

I have to remind myself not to apologize. I have this persistent but illogical feeling of guilt as if the whole thing is my fault. I let Lilla into Fairview. I asked Anna if she could move in. Lilla was my friend.

I keep forgetting the truth: that it was Lilla who started the whole thing in the first place.

"I wish—shit—I just wish I'd known," I say.

"I wish, too. So many things." She sighs. "I wish my parents were still here. I wish Marcus had been more honest. I wish I'd been paying a bit more attention."

I push my hands through my hair and kick at a loose stone so that it bounces over the grass and rolls away. I can't work out what I'm feeling, I'm overwhelmed by such a range of violent emotions. I'm so sad I could cry, so frustrated I could run for hours, so angry I could punch something. "She fucked everything, didn't she?" I say. "She's wrecked your whole bloody life."

Anna's quiet for a long time, and I feel a horrible ache in my chest, a painful fear that she's going to agree with me. She's going to tell me there's no point. No point in anything. No point in us. In me and her.

"I don't think so, no. I really hope not. I'd hate to give her that satisfaction," she says, turning to me. There's so much sadness in her face. I notice it all the time now. And there's a definite stillness and wisdom in her eyes that's unusual for someone her age. I reckon it'll always be there—that sadness—like the scar on a tree where a big branch has broken off. It'll heal over a bit, and change shape with time, but it'll never disappear completely.

"She took a lot," she says. "She took my baby . . ." Her voice breaks. "But she didn't take everything. She gave me something, too."

And just now I notice something in her face that's temporarily bigger than the sadness.

"She gave you something? What?"

She turns to look out over the Harbor. We're both silent as we take in the view; the impossible blue of the water and the sky, the Manly ferry approaching in a smooth glide from the city. She takes my hand and links her fingers between mine.

"I'll let you figure that one out," she says.

Our new flat is small and poky, just about as different from Fairview as you could possibly get. It only consists of three rooms: one living space which functions as both bedroom and lounge, a kitchen that has definitely seen better days and what must be the smallest bathroom ever.

Anna could afford something much bigger and flashier, of course, but I want to be able to pay my way, and Anna doesn't scoff, or tell me I'm being stupid. She seems to understand. And for now, at least, this place will do.

Lilla is in a lot of trouble, the court case is coming up, and the charges are all pretty serious. I worry about Anna, how she's going to feel when she has to rake through everything again, but she seems surprisingly calm about it. And the truth is that ever since that night she has seemed a whole lot lighter, easier in her skin, as if at least one burden has been lifted.

Sometimes I think about what Anna said about Lilla that day. How not everything she did was bad. And sometimes I watch Anna when she's in the kitchen, cooking us a meal from scratch. She's getting pretty good at cooking these days and she never gets pissed off about the inconvenience or lack of space—our entire preparation area must be less than half a meter long—and I marvel at her determination, at her ability to adapt. And I feel lucky for the way things have turned out. Lucky to be with Anna, living here.

The best thing about our flat is the big east-facing window. There's no fancy view, but sometimes, at night, if I'm very, very quiet, I can hear the ocean. And in the morning when we wake up and pull the curtains open, the light pours in, a perfect rectangle over the surface of our bed, our own personal blanket of sunshine.

ACKNOWLEDGMENTS

I'm enormously grateful to my former agent, Jo Unwin, not only for the help she gave me with this book, but also for the tireless encouragement, faith, friendship and enthusiasm she offered during the years we worked together.

I cannot thank either Erica Wagner or Sarah Brenan enough for their support throughout the writing of this novel. From the very early stages right until the end they made what can be a tricky process much easier. Their enthusiasm and persistence—particularly during some eleventh-hour changes to the plot—gave me the confidence to keep going until I got it right. Our numerous phone calls also kept me smiling.

Huge thanks to Leah Thaxton and Kate Miciak, whose combined input and advice made this novel infinitely better.

Thanks also to Sonja Heijn—whose brilliant last-minute insights made an enormous difference.

Thank you to Vanessa Lanaway, Susila Baybars, Jen Castles, Gillian Stern, Kirsty Eagar, Hilary Reynolds, Sue Armstrong and Aline Le Guen.

To my first readers for their advice and encouragement—Wendy James, Emma James, Jenny James, Tony James, Prue Macfarlane and Haidee Hudson—thank you!

And to the precious people I live with—Hilary, Charlie, Oscar, Jack and Jimmy—thank you for everything.

ABOUT THE AUTHOR

REBECCA JAMES was born in Sydney, Australia, in 1970. She has worked as a waitress, a kitchen designer, an English teacher in both Indonesia and Japan, a barmaid and (most memorably) a minicab telephone-operator in London. Rebecca lives in Australia with her partner and their four sons. Her first novel, *Beautiful Malice,* was published to critical acclaim across the world. *Sweet Damage* is Rebecca's second book.

Rebeccajameslollygag.blogspot.com
@Rebecca_James_

ABOUT THE TYPE

This book was set in Sabon, a typeface designed by the well-known German typographer Jan Tschichold (1902–74). Sabon's design is based upon the original letter forms of sixteenth-century French type designer Claude Garamond and was created specifically to be used for three sources: foundry type for hand composition, Linotype, and Monotype. Tschichold named his typeface for the famous Frankfurt typefounder Jacques Sabon (c. 1520–80).